Battling Demons

Battling Demons, Volume 1

Kris Morris

Published by Kris Morris, 2016.

This is a work of fiction. Similarities to real people, places, or events are entirely coincidental.

BATTLING DEMONS

First edition. August 29, 2016.

Copyright © 2016 Kris Morris.

Thank you to my dear husband for believing in me, my sons for inspiration, and my friends Carole, Abby, Janet, and Anneke for ceaseless encouragement and for tolerating my insecurities.

Special thanks to my dear friend, Abby Bukofzer and my son, Karl for countless hours spent assisting me with editing. And to my talented husband, Tim, for designing my book covers.

I love you all!

Prologue

When Dr. Martin Ellingham arrived in the little Cornish fishing village of Portwenn a little more than four years ago, he was still reeling from his devastating fall from grace. Once a renowned London vascular surgeon, he had been blindsided by haemophobia. The resultant panic attacks, accompanied by nausea and vomiting, sweating, chest pain, and blackouts, had forced him from the surgical theatre.

Whether it was a subconscious desire to rekindle his relationship with his aunt Joan, with whom he had spent his boyhood summers, or to seclude himself to lick his wounds, Martin came to Cornwall in hopes of securing the position of Portwenn's general practitioner. He was expecting a hospitable and perhaps even welcoming environment, but then he met Louisa Glasson.

The spiky but beautiful young school teacher, who served as the lay-member on his interview panel, immediately dismissed his impressive credentials and challenged his suitability as the village's standard-bearer for health.

Though his skills as a surgeon were unsurpassed, dealing with people had never been Martin's strong suit. And as Miss Glasson made clear to him immediately, "If you want to be a GP in our village, then social skills and a good bedside manner *are* really essential."

The ways of the quirky inhabitants of the village frustrated and, at times, infuriated Martin. Their stubborn refusal to follow medical advice, as well as their go-with-the-flow approach to life, would have made life in Portwenn unbearable if it weren't for Louisa Glasson's presence there.

Despite their frequent rows and the constant interruptions that come with being the sole physician in a village full of eccentrics, a romantic relationship developed between the new doctor and the school teacher. The path their tumultuous relationship took was a convoluted one, leading them from an aborted wedding, to parenthood, back to the altar, and finally to a marriage in crisis.

For four decades, Martin had kept the demons spawned by an abusive childhood buried. But the stresses of fatherhood and married life had exhumed them, and the hour of reckoning had come.

Chapter 1

The procedure had been textbook—Ellingham textbook. Martin recited his own written words in his head as he conducted the operation step by step. The flood of adrenaline in his system honed his focus on the sterile surgical field in front of him. Only when he had finished tying off the last meticulous knot in the incision in her neck did he allow his gaze to be drawn to the face of the patient on the operating table—his beloved wife.

He quickly dispensed with the requisite postoperative details before exiting the theatre, fighting to keep his composure. The halls were empty as he made his way towards the surgery changing rooms, their tiled walls seeming to echo the loneliness that he felt.

Loneliness. It had been his almost constant companion for the last four decades. Only Auntie Joan and Louisa had been able to shine a light on that shadow that had pursued him through life. He had already lost one of them, and now he was on the verge of losing the other.

He slipped into a lavatory stall and quietly closed the door behind him before allowing the tears to fall. The guilt he felt over the public row that they'd had the day before was all-consuming. He was to blame for upsetting her to the point of running after him and into the path of an oncoming car. Her fractured clavicle would heal in time, but could she ever forgive him?

The mad dash to the airport to prevent her from getting on the plane to Spain that afternoon had provided a temporary distraction from his guilt. As had his need to focus on the just completed emergency procedure to seal the vascular malformation in her brain, a congenital anomaly discovered on scans performed after the accident that resulted in her fractured collarbone.

His legs trembled as the emotions of the last days and the fatigue from sleepless nights swept over him.

With Louisa resting comfortably, and having assured himself of the adequacy of the hospital staff, Martin made his way back home to Portwenn. His thoughts turned to his small son. James would probably be sleeping peacefully by the time he arrived home.

Peace. Martin had yearned for a sense of peace for as long as he could remember. He had always lived with an inner chaos, something he couldn't explain brewing just under the surface, often erupting in hurled insults, cantankerous behaviour, and a general intolerance for the foibles of others.

Something was wrong with him. Louisa had said she needed a break from him, that she wasn't happy, that she wasn't making him happy. Why couldn't he allow himself the pleasure that other people seemed to find in life?

Although emotion had always been an enigmatic concept to Martin, he was sure he could identify with happiness. He had experienced the feeling when Louisa accepted his first proposal and then leapt into his arms. The feeling that had warmed his inner core with an intensity that caused him to squeeze his eyes shut tightly to keep it from escaping as he held her close to him. The same feeling flooded over him the day that James was born, filling him with a sense that his life now had purpose. James and Louisa were the source of his happiness, yet something in him had resurfaced to deny him any sense of it.

Negative emotions were less ambiguous: anger, hatred, fear. Many of them help to keep the hostile world out. Positive emotions, however, what purpose do they serve? Don't they make a person more vulnerable?

The sense of security, love, and belonging that the stays at Joan and Phil's brought to him were all too soon replaced by the loathing stares of his parents when he returned home, or the fear and sense of abandonment when he was sent back to boarding school. The happiness that he felt when he proposed to Louisa was soon replaced by an overwhelming sense of loss and rejection when she fled from Portwenn ... and him ... to go to London. And when James was taken from them by the psychotic Mrs. Tishell, the joy he felt in being a father was overshadowed by the guilt he felt for putting his son in danger and the fear that he may have lost him forever.

Allowing himself to succumb to a positive emotion only seemed to exacerbate the distress of the negative experiences that were sure to follow. The way a rare warm and sunny day in January seems to whet the sting of the inevitable cold, dank, and grey days more typical of a Cornish winter that were sure to lie ahead.

Martin's thoughts drifted to a memory from his childhood, the day he first became aware of just how severe the consequences of a misstep could be. He was with his parents, visiting at his Grandfather Ellingham's home. The adults were involved in a discussion in the kitchen, and Martin had been shooed away to entertain himself elsewhere.

He roamed the house looking for some sort of amusement with which to pass the time. He found himself in his grandfather's bedroom. Dappled sunshine coming through the lace curtains drew his attention to the pocket watch lying on the bedside table, its ornately etched gold case casting rays of reflected light to his eager eyes. His grandfather had shown it to him once. The workings inside ticked away a perfectly steady rhythm, similar to the even *lub-dub* that Martin could hear when he put his ear to the chest of the friendly mongrel that frequented the bins in his parents' backyard. The watch was off limits, but Martin wanted so badly to hold it. He had often watched as his grandfather held it in his hand, fingering it absentmindedly.

He had been warned that the watch was not to be touched, but he was alone in the room, and its ticking seemed to beckon to him as it resonated off the hollow drawer of the table. He glanced quickly towards the door and out to the empty hallway. He would be very careful. It couldn't hurt anything to take a quick look, he reasoned.

He reached out slowly until he could touch the watch case, tracing the etched lines lightly with his fingertips. The constant movement of the gears emitted a steady pulse of waves that travelled through the air, setting in motion a cascade of events, culminating in nerve impulses which his brain interpreted as sound. His heart was pounding with the knowledge that his misdeed could be discovered. But oh, how he wanted to see the inner workings of this wonderful little machine.

He hesitantly pressed the small button on the side of the watch as he had seen his grandfather do so many times. The cover popped open to reveal an amazing array of miniature gears. Each moved perfectly in sync with the others, like dancers in an elaborately choreographed routine. Each performing their own job flawlessly so that their miniature cogs were kept in perfect alignment. How dependent these little gears were on one another. One small misstep and the entire system would fall out of balance.

Martin could resist no longer and picked up the watch, holding it in his hand. Is this how his father felt when in the surgical theatre, cutting through the dermal layers, fascia, and muscle to reveal all those gears in the human body, working together to keep the system in balance?

Martin was so lost in thought that he missed the sound of approaching footsteps. The soft, quiet ticking of the watch was interrupted by the thunderous bellow of his father's voice. "Martin! Put that down!" Startled, he let the precious object slip from his fingers on to the wood floor below. He looked down to see the cover lying several feet from the rest of the watch, the gears now inert in their case. Lifeless.

A sickening feeling came over him. The guilt he felt for his misdeed and the sadness for the damage that he had caused was soon followed by a paralysing fear of the punishment that awaited him. He could see in his father's cold glare, and the crimson shade his face had taken on, that he was more than irate, and Martin fought the urge to flee.

There was a rustling in the hall, and his grandfather appeared in the doorway. A disheartening sense of shame came over him. Henry Ellingham could never be described as a warm man, but he had always had a soft spot for Martin, and he seemed to appreciate the boy's curiosity and thirst for knowledge. But he had been clear about what he expected from his grandson, and Martin knew that he had fallen short of the elderly man's expectations.

Martin avoided eye contact, keeping his head down and his eyes on the floor, the broken watch staring back at him. "I'm sorry, Grandfather."

The elderly man walked over and quietly stooped to pick up the pieces of the watch. He glanced up at his grandson and gave him a small smile and then straightened himself before putting his hand on the boy's head. "I know you are," he said as he turned and walked back down the hall.

For a fleeting moment, Martin felt understood. Then his father's hand connected sharply with the side of his head. He fell to the floor before being yanked upward by his collar. He was dragged down the hallway, through the front door, and across the lawn to the storage shed.

Martin couldn't see well in the murky dimness of the small building, but he could make out the rapid movements of his father's silhouette as his belt buckle clinked. "There are consequences when we lose control, Martin. People get hurt and things get broken." Then he felt the sting of the leather as it raised welts on his body.

Neither Martin's mother nor his father spoke a word during the entire trip home. There was just painful silence. He was almost grateful for the persistent pain left from his punishment in the shed. He felt somewhat absolved of his sin.

He watched as his parents got out of the car and went into the house, wishing some greater power would make him disappear. It wasn't his parents' anger and harsh punishments that hurt the most; it was their indifference. The fact that, aside from his grandfather and Auntie Joan, who lived so far away in Cornwall that it could just as well have been the other side of the Earth, no one would notice if he just vanished one day.

The mongrel stray was lolling in the sun on the side lawn. Martin wondered if he had a home, a family who noticed he was gone. He got out of the car and walked over to the dog. The tip of the animal's tail bobbed up and down as he got close. He lay down on the ground next to it and put his ear to its chest. *Lub-dub.* Martin could picture the intricate workings of the watch.

Chapter 2

As Martin approached Portwenn, he pulled the car to the side of the road and shifted it into park. Night had fallen over the little village, and the front lights illuminated the houses spilling down the hillside, the moon casting a silvery lace on the tops of the waves as they pushed into the harbour.

The village had been here for more than six hundred years. Many of its old stone cottages had given safe haven to generations of fishermen and their families.

Martin's own small cottage served as both his home as well as the village surgery. Positioned atop a cliff, it was safe from the flooding ocean surges that came with the inevitable winter storms. It also allowed Martin to enjoy his morning cup of coffee while gazing across the harbour to the school where Louisa was head teacher.

The cottage was quaint, immaculately kept, and built in a time when very few men attained Martin's six-foot three-inch stature. Therefore, the low doorways, as well as the hallway which ran under the staircase between the consulting room and the kitchen, were ever-present obstacles which he needed to heed lest he acquire yet another knot on his head. It was cramped but it was home.

Portwenn was the place he had longed to be during those difficult childhood years. This had been his safe place, the place he felt wanted. However fleeting his time here may have been, he had considered Auntie Joan's home, this maddeningly backward little village, his home as well. In the end, though, it was always taken away from him when the summer holidays drew to a close and he was packed off to boarding school.

Martin swallowed hard as he imagined his son having to endure what he had for so many years.

The surgery was quiet and dark when he arrived. His aunt Ruth and James were asleep in the nursery. He peered into the baby cot, the pure innocence on his boy's face causing a sense of calm to wash over him.

But it was hard not to worry about what the future might bring. Baby James was easy to get along with—quite calm, perhaps a bit on the quiet side like his father, but a generally happy little boy.

Martin was plagued by doubts, however, about his ability to parent James, especially once the boy was old enough to identify his many shortcomings. It delighted him to see his son's face light up when he entered a room, and he was filled with pride when James struggled to get to his arms from another's. If someone should happen to take notice and comment on the child's fondness for his father, Martin tried to feign nonchalance. But it always touched him. James's affection was an all new experience for him. His son was the only person who had ever loved him *because* of who he was, not despite who he was.

Would this all change once the boy was old enough to know better? Martin grew up with a painful awareness that he was an embarrassment to his parents, and he had spent a lifetime trying to redeem himself but to no avail. He couldn't bear it if James should grow to look at him with the same disdain that he saw in his mother and father's eyes. He dearly wanted to make both James and Louisa proud—to have their respect. But could he ever be the man they wanted him to be?

Martin woke the next morning from yet another restless night, his sleep again punctuated by the nightmares that haunted him from childhood. But the sun was shining brightly, and he could hear the sweet gurgles and babbles of infant conversation coming from the nursery. He wrapped himself in his dressing gown and moved quietly across the hall so as to not disturb Ruth.

James squealed when he saw his father appear in the doorway, and Martin quickly hushed the boy. "Shh, shh, shh, shh, shh. You'll wake Aunt Ruth," Martin said as he lifted the wriggling baby from the cot.

The child grabbed at his father's ears, pulling him forward in order to complete their morning greeting, a moment of silence with their foreheads touching.

"Best get a nappy and clothes, then change you downstairs, hadn't we? We don't want to disturb your aunt."

There really wasn't much chance of that. Aunt Ruth slept like the dead. In fact, Martin had been known to check her wrist for signs of life a time or two.

Before Joan died, leaving Haven Farm and her house to Ruth, Martin had little contact with his psychiatrist aunt. She was a Londoner at heart, a career woman who had devoted her life to her work with the criminally insane, and she had little time for family. But after Joan's death, she moved to Cornwall, sequestering herself to work on her book about recidivism in psychopathic criminals.

James was dressed for the day and in his high chair, picking at the chopped banana in his bowl when Ruth came through the hallway a short time later. Martin was putting breakfast on the table—boiled eggs, toast soldiers, and tea.

"You know, you'd be a dab hand at our B&B, Martin. We'll need someone in the kitchen," she said as she slipped into a chair across the table from him.

Martin cocked his head. "I'm sorry, I don't follow."

"Well, it seems that while you were off playing surgeon with your wife, Al propositioned me."

Martin peered up at her from his plate. "You two spend far too much time together, you know."

Al Large, the twenty-eight-year-old son of Martin's portly oft-times nemesis Bert Large, had been working as Ruth's farm manager.

"No, really," Ruth said, jabbing at the air with her spoon. "He pitched some very interesting ideas to me, well worked out on paper, mind you, for turning the farm into a fishing holiday retreat. I was quite impressed, actually. It could just possibly work."

"Oh, don't you think you're a bit ..." Martin shifted uncomfortably in his chair. "You're just rather busy with your book, aren't you?"

Ruth narrowed her eyes at him. "*A*, I'm *not* too old, and *B*, Al would be in charge of running the operation. There's a lot to plan yet, of course; it's still in the beginning stages."

He gave her his trademark grunt. "Mm." The mannerism had served him well over the years, allowing him to avoid needless or uncomfortable conversation.

"Thank you for the phone call last night," the elderly woman said as she dipped a bit of toast into her warm egg yolk. "I took the liberty of relaying your synopsis of Louisa's surgery on to Morwenna. She said she'd cancel your appointments for the remainder of the week."

They sat quietly for a few moments. Then Ruth peered at Martin over her teacup. "Will Louisa be coming home today?"

Martin picked up the remnants of the banana lying on the table and sliced a bit more into his son's bowl. "Ah, yes. Unless I see something this morning that causes me concern. In fact, I should get upstairs to wash and dress. I hope to be back at the hospital by eight-thirty. I may be able to spare her the indignity of being poked and prodded by the registrars who will no doubt be making the rounds through her ward."

Ruth scrutinized her nephew's face for a few moments. "You know Martin, it makes me very happy that you came to me for help yesterday. I've suspected that Joan left me the farm in hopes that I might make a move down here."

"Quite possibly. She was concerned about your growing old in London. All alone and no one to look out for you."

The elderly woman narrowed her eyes and jabbed a bony finger at him. "I *mean*, I think she didn't want for *you* to be alone ... to have no one to talk things through with."

"I highly doubt that, but what you said yesterday did give me a lot to think about. I want to change. I *will* change ... whatever Louisa needs from me. I can't lose her, Ruth."

"Well, Martin, just remember that I'm here if you need me, and I have willing ears. In fact, it's rather nice for an old—a *busy* lady like me to know that I can still contribute something to this world."

After dabbing at her mouth with her napkin, she stared pointedly at her nephew. "You really are an extraordinary individual, Martin, and in more ways than I think you realise. Don't sell yourself short. *You—deserve—Louisa.*"

Martin swallowed back the lump in his throat and pulled in his chin before diverting the subject. "Might you be able to watch James for me again today? Things would go much more smoothly in Truro if you could."

Ruth gave him a crooked grin. "I'd be happy to. Though I do think I should be getting hazard pay. Your son nearly took me out when he hurled a purple dinosaur in my direction yesterday."

Chapter 3

A nurse was attending to Louisa when Martin arrived at her ward. His stomach churned with the uncertainty of what was to come next, but the small smile she gave him provided some reassurance that their marriage might still be salvageable.

"How are you feeling?" he asked as he conducted a quick visual inspection of his patient.

"Well, my head hurts. I'm a bit tired, but better than I expected."

"Mm, you could probably go home later on today."

She hesitated, cocking her head at him. "Right."

His fingers twitched at his sides as he gave himself a silent upbraiding for making an assumption. "I mean, you won't be flying anywhere for a while. But I'm not saying you have to come home."

"Martin, you know this doesn't ... doesn't change anything."

"I know."

"I don't want us just to go back and pretend everything's fine."

"I know." His fingernails dug into his palms as he struggled to contain the stew of emotions brewing in him.

"Or to fall back into the way things were."

"Mm. I agree. I don't want that either," he said, his curled fingers tightening.

"Okay?" Louisa sat a bit taller. Was her husband finally acknowledging that something was wrong? That he needed help?

"I'll let you get some sleep," he said as he turned to go.

"Martin ..."

He turned to face her. "Yes?"

"Thank you. For comin' after me."

His heart fell as he walked towards his wife's bedside. He grasped for words. Did she understand him at all? Had he so failed her as a husband that she wasn't aware of how deeply he loved her? That he would have chased her not just halfway across Cornwall, but across the universe if necessary? Of course he came after her.

He had been teetering on an emotional precipice and was now in danger of going over the edge. Fighting to keep his composure, he went to his safe place. He shifted into a professional, medical mode and choked out the words, "You're my patient ... and you're my wife," before turning quickly to leave.

Retreating to the solitude of his Lexus, he released a heavy sigh, contemplating where he and Louisa were to go next. At least they were finally agreeing on something; they couldn't continue to function the way they had up to now. Reclining the seat, he closed his eyes and allowed himself to drift off to sleep.

He was awakened an hour later by the vibrating of his mobile against his chest. He reached for the device, and a female voice informed him that his wife could be discharged at anytime.

Well, Ellingham, what's it going to be? Are you going to put things right or are you going to bugger it up again?

Louisa was sitting up in the bed, her knees bent, chewing on the end of a pencil when he arrived back at her room. She gave him a hesitant smile, and his tightly curled fingers relaxed a bit.

"Hello," she said as she swung her legs over the side of the mattress. "A nurse stopped by ... said I can leave ... if you're ready to take me home that is."

Martin blinked back the moisture gathering in his eyes. "Yes, erm ... yes. I'll get your things." He pulled open the door of the cupboard and removed the clothes she had been wearing when she arrived the day before. "Is there anything else I need to get together?"

She stared at him, tight lipped. "I don't have much with me, Martin. Just the bag you brought this morning."

"Right." He walked across the room and helped her to her feet.

"Louisa, I know that this hasn't been one of our simple rows. I'm sorry, I've bollocksed things up terribly. But I *did* mean what I said; I want to learn to be a better husband."

She reached a tentative hand up to touch his cheek, but instead brushed it across his shoulder. "Well, s'pose it wasn't right for me to run off. I'm sorry, too."

He pulled in his chin and then helped her to dress. "Is ... is there anything else I can help you with?"

Louisa's ponytail swung back and forth as she shook her head. "No. Just ... take me home. We can start to sort things out tomorrow."

Neither of them spoke a word for the first ten minutes of the drive home. Louisa gazed out the window at a deserted, ramshackle farm as it passed them by. It looked so lonely and forsaken, much like the man in the seat next to her. "Martin, I haven't given up on us just yet."

The sudden breaking of the silence caused Martin to jump. He felt like a tightly wound mainspring in one of his old clocks. He pulled in a slow, deep breath before releasing it, trying to relieve the tightness in his chest.

"We have a lot to get figured out," she continued. "And you need to find someone you can talk to. I think you have some inner demons that need to be dealt with."

Martin cringed at the thought of baring his soul to anyone, but he nodded his head in agreement.

"It doesn't have to be me. I'd love to be the one that you feel you can talk to, but ... I think you need more help than I can give you."

She batted at a stray wisp of hair. "You said Ruth gave you the name of someone in London who might be able to help ... or maybe recommend someone. I think you should call them."

"Mm."

They rode in silence for several more miles before Martin pulled the car to the side of the road and shifted the gear box into park. He sat, his eyes focused in front of him.

"Louisa, why did you ... why did you marry me?"

She cocked her head. "Well, because you asked me to for one thing."

He turned to face her, his eyes red-rimmed. "When you thanked me at the hospital for coming after you ... Louisa, I don't think you understand me."

He swallowed and hissed air from his nose. "And that's my fault. I realise that. I *do* love you, Louisa. I love you more than you can possibly know. But it overwhelms me. I get confused and ..."

Martin looked at her with downcast eyes. "Louisa, I want to be able to talk to you, to say all the things you'd like to hear. I want to make you happy, but I don't know what you need me to do ... to say. I want to learn, but until I get better at this ..." He stopped to clear the catch in his throat. "Please ... remember that I love you. And that will never change."

Louisa's eyes grew moist as she stared in surprise at her normally dispassionate husband. Resting her hand on his thigh, she gave him a small nod of her head.

Chapter 4

When Martin and Louisa walked in the door of the surgery, Ruth was sitting on the sofa with her feet up and a glass of wine in her hand.

"Oh, Ruth, thank you for watching James," Louisa said as she dropped her purse on to the kitchen table. She walked over and kissed the elderly woman on the cheek, taking note of the dark circles under her eyes. "Did he give you any trouble?"

"Well, he hasn't done me in quite yet. He went down for a nap a few minutes ago. How are you?"

"A bit of a headache. But I understand the surgeon who performed my procedure is a top vascular specialist and does quality work, so I feel quite confident that the problem's been taken care of. I just need some time to heal now."

Martin stepped down into the lounge, and Louisa gave him a feeble smile. "I think I'll go up and look in on James before I have a bit of a lie down."

"Yes." He watched as she moved slowly towards the stairs before picking up her bag. "I'll be up in a minute to help you get settled."

Ruth got up from the sofa and put her hand on her nephew's shoulder. "Martin, are you all right?" she asked. "You look positively shattered."

He stared back at her for a moment before answering. "I'm ... fine," he said, taking in a deep breath. "You don't have to go. You could stay for dinner."

"Thank you, Martin, but I think you and your wife need some time to yourselves right now." She turned as she reached for the doorknob and looked pointedly back at him. "Do let me know if I can be of any help."

"Yes. Thank you." Martin headed up the stairs. Louisa was in bed and had already drifted off to sleep. He stood watching her for several minutes, his fingers twitching at his sides as he tried to shake the awful memories of their Sports Day row, his confusion over her unclear expectations of him and the sound of the car impacting her body. Leaning over, he brushed his lips across the bruise on her cheek and tucked the blankets in around her.

Soft baby gurgles could be heard coming from James's room, and he hurried off quietly to get the boy.

When Louisa came downstairs a short time later, she found her husband and son in the kitchen. James was seated in his push chair near the sink. She looked on surreptitiously as her husband went about washing dishes, and James gnawed on a teething biscuit. Martin explained the importance of proper kitchen hygiene to the boy, filling his cupped hands with soap bubbles and lowering them down so that his son could investigate. James grabbed on to a fistful and brought it to his mouth.

"No, no, no, no, no. You don't want to eat that. It would likely cause some stomach upset and diarrhoea," Martin explained. "You best stick with the biscuit for your snack." He brushed over the top of the child's head with the backs of his fingers, giving a soft grunt before returning to the task at hand.

Louisa smiled, watching the interplay between this big man and his small son. She released a resigned sigh. *Why is it so bloody hard for you to let that gentle side show, Martin?*

She knew it was there. So did Ruth. And certainly Joan had been aware of it. But her husband had built an impenetrable wall that very few people in his life had been allowed to breach.

Louisa stepped into the kitchen, and James caught sight of her, babbling and waving his arms excitedly.

"Hello, James. I missed you. Did you have fun with Aunt Ruth?"

"I very much doubt that," Martin said, raising an eyebrow. "She's spent most of her adult life in the company of axe murderers and serial killers."

"Well, yes. But, nevertheless, we're lucky to have her help."

Martin pulled the tea towel from its hook and dried his hands. "I fed James before you came down. Are you getting hungry? I could make you an omelette ... or whatever you like. I'm not ... I'm not saying you have to have an omelette."

Louisa hid a smile as her husband attempted to avoid a repeat of an argument some time ago which had precipitated her leaving him.

"No, an omelette sounds good," she said, trying to stifle a yawn.

They ate dinner in relative silence, neither of them having the physical or emotional energy for conversation. The rest of the evening passed quickly, and Martin took James upstairs to get him ready for bed. Louisa stayed downstairs reading a book on the sofa.

Her mind drifted as she tried to focus on the tale in front of her. Martin had asked her why she had married him. *Because you asked me to*, she had said. *That was a pretty rubbish answer. Because he asked me to? I should have told the poor man that I love him! I complain because he never says those words to me, but how often do I say those words to him?*

Martin had become sullen and withdrawn after they married. It was frighteningly obvious that he was struggling with something. She tried to excuse her recent behaviour as understandable defensiveness, but her thoughts kept returning to their wedding day and the vows they had exchanged.

Marriage is about promising yourself to someone else. Promising to be there for them in sickness and in health, til death do you part. To be there for one another in good times and bad so that neither person has to face life alone.

Martin's been so bloody difficult—distant, irritable, even more so than usual. I couldn't just stay in this house. Being ignored ... shut out ... For God's sake, even my attempts at some sort of normal sexual activity were rebuffed!

Her book landed with a thud on the coffee table. After turning out the lights she headed upstairs.

The baby was in his pyjamas, and Martin was rocking him while reading a bedtime story. Louisa listened to her husband's smooth velvety voice. It was really very soothing. She slipped in quietly behind them as he read the last few pages. He glanced back and gave her a pained smile.

James had fallen asleep. A bedtime story read by his father was sure to have that effect. Martin laid the boy in his cot before he and Louisa crossed the landing to their bedroom. Louisa finished with her night-time preparations, and then Martin helped her get situated in bed before using the lavatory himself.

He re-emerged a short time later and stood by the bed, hesitating. Not knowing if he should crawl in with his wife or sleep in the nursery.

"Problem?" Louisa asked.

"I'm not sure if you want me ... erm, perhaps it's not wise for us to be in the same bed. I could bump you in the night. Maybe I should sleep in James's room for a few nights."

"I don't think you'll bump me, Martin."

He hesitated. "You'll wake me if you find I'm jostling you too much?"

"Yes, Martin. Now climb in here, I'm totally knackered."

Martin slipped carefully under the covers, trying to not shake the bed while getting in. Then he positioned himself along the far edge of the mattress.

They lay silent for several minutes before Louisa said softly, "Martin ... could you please come closer."

Rolling towards her, he inched his way over until he made body contact.

"That's better." Sighing, she reached over and took his hand. "We'll work it out, Martin. We'll work it out."

Chapter 5

Martin woke shortly after 1:00 a.m. to the sound of his mobile ringing. He muffled the phone under his arm, hurrying out of the bedroom to answer the call where he wouldn't wake his sleeping wife. A male voice on the other end of the line informed him that there had been a fight at the pub, and one of the men involved had sustained a laceration to his arm.

"Well, have someone bring him to the surgery, and I'll ..." He cast a glance towards their bedroom. "Never mind. I'll come there. Give me a few minutes to get dressed." Boisterous, inebriated fishermen were sure to rouse his family.

He rummaged in the dark and found the clothes that he had taken off a few hours earlier. Then he went downstairs to dress.

Martin could hear whoops and hollers as he approached the Platt, the lowest and oldest area of the village where the fishing boats came in to unload their catch. He slowed his pace, now doubting the wisdom of his decision to come to the patient.

Pushing on the door to the historic old establishment, he stepped into the dimly lit room. The smell of raw fish and stale cigarette smoke emanated from the men, clad in their yellow, rubberised brace trousers, there to relax and blow off steam after a long shift out on the Atlantic waters. The old floorboards, worn by a century of foot traffic, felt uneven and sticky under his feet as he made his way towards the fellow serving up drinks behind the counter.

"Where's the injured man you called about?" Martin grumbled.

"That'd be Harry over there," the bartender said, wagging a finger towards a darkened corner of the room.

The doctor grunted and began to pick his way through the crowd. "Careful!" he snapped as he dodged a reeling reveller. *Idiot.*

He found his patient slouched in a chair nursing a drink. "'Bout time you showed up, Doc," he slurred. "Thought I was gonna bleed ta death before you got 'ere." Harry's head listed to the side as he thrust an arm out.

Martin set his bag down on a table, and then he leaned down and yanked at the young man's sleeve. "Oh, for goodness' sake. You're not bleeding to death," he said, rolling his eyes. "It's a superficial wound. A plaster would have done the job."

Harry pulled his arm up and peered closely at the injury. "It don't look so bad now, Doc."

"Of course not. The mere act of my dragging myself out of bed in the middle of the night always has that effect. Gawd!"

Martin opened his bag and pulled out a drawer, removing a bottle of antiseptic and a gauze pad. He cleaned and bandaged the fisherman's wound before straightening himself. "In future, I would sugges—" Something clipped his ear before shattering against the wall behind Harry.

The young man sprang to his feet, his eyes flashing. "Why you bloody pillock!"

Martin whirled around as another fisherman lunged towards Harry. He pushed his hands against the aggressor's chest, attempting to protect his patient. "Hey, hey, hey, hey, hey! Just back off!"

Harry took a swing at his opponent, landing a blow to the man's cheek and drawing half the room full of imbibers into the skirmish. Martin suddenly found himself on the floor in the middle of a pugilistic feeding frenzy.

Chippy Miller, Eddie Rix, and several other locals hurried over, pulling the fray apart before helping the doctor to his feet.

Martin felt himself being propelled towards the door and out into the cool night air.

"You okay, Doc?" Chippy asked, bending over and peering up into his face.

Martin cleared his throat and straightened his tie. "Fine! I'm ... fine!" He shook Eddie from his arm. "Bloody Hell!"

The fisherman gave him a reassuring pat on the back. "Hey, Doc. Don't you worry 'bout those blokes in there. The other boys will 'ave told 'em ta bugger off back ta Padstow by now."

"Wonderful." He touched his cheekbone gingerly.

"You'll probably wanna get some ice on that," Chippy suggested.

"Thanks." Martin began to move unsteadily towards Roscarrock Hill.

"I think we better help ya get back 'ome." Eddie tried to take hold of the doctor's arm but it was yanked away.

"I said I'm fine!" "Just ... back off. Just ..." He shifted his bag and put a hand to his side. "Thank you, but I'll be fine."

The men watched as Martin walked back up the hill towards home.

Oh, God, he groaned internally. *Louisa will blow this all out of proportion. She doesn't need anymore stress right now.*

When he reached the surgery, he went into the lavatory off the reception room to assess the damage. He could see he would have a shiner, but he could cover for that. Any other possible bruises could be a different matter, however. He'd have to be careful around his wife for a while.

He went to the kitchen and pulled several cold packs from the freezer before lying back on the sofa to ice his injuries.

He woke shortly before sunrise and crept upstairs to their bedroom before putting on his pyjamas and slipping quietly back under the covers. Guilt niggled at him, but he knew that not sharing all the details about this incident was in his wife's best interests.

He had just dropped back off to sleep when he was awakened by a wail from James. He breathed out a long sigh and began to pull himself from his cosy nest, stifling a groan as his stiffened muscles resisted his efforts.

James woke irritable and uncooperative, forcing his father to wrestle him into a clean nappy and his clothes. Martin braced himself for the pain and then hoisted his ever-growing son into his arms.

Like his father, James was an early riser. So, when they came into the kitchen the sun's rays were just beginning to peek in over the windowsill.

Martin usually enjoyed this time alone with the baby, but this morning his head was throbbing, his muscles ached, and all he wanted was to go back to bed and close his eyes to the world.

But he had things he wanted to do before Louisa came down for the day. First, he had to get breakfast down a less than agreeable child.

He pressed two fingers to the baby's forehead. "You're not febrile, James. Are you cutting another tooth?" He added a few bits of dry cereal to the selections already on the high chair tray. "I hope you won't be this cranky for your mother. I want you to be on your best behaviour today, understood?"

James gurgled back at him and reached out with a chubby fistful of partially macerated banana, perhaps meant as a peace offering.

Martin wiped the excess fruit and cereal from the boy's face and with a soft groan he hoisted him from his high chair. After busying his son in the playpen with several toys, he hurried into his consulting room to get the business card for the psychiatrist Ruth had recommended.

Picking up a pad of paper and a pencil, he began to make two lists. One a list of what he saw as strengths in their marriage, the other a list of deficiencies.

Chapter 6

The sound of running water that could be heard coming from the upstairs bathroom was Martin's cue to make breakfast for Louisa and himself. On a chilly morning, oatmeal and fruit seemed a good choice. He was emptying the dishwasher and the tea was steeping on the table when Louisa came downstairs.

"Good morning, James! How are you today?" she asked in the singsong voice that she used with their son.

The baby gave Louisa an unhappy scowl and began to fuss.

"Oh, dear. Is he sick?"

"I think he's teething. He's been like this since he got up," Martin informed her.

"Oh, poor little pup." She tipped down and nuzzled her nose into his neck.

"And how are you?" she asked as she walked over to put bread into the toaster.

"Fine," he answered, reaching in front of her and setting several plates in the cupboard.

"Martin!" she gasped. "What have you done to yourself?"

He pulled a hand up self-consciously and turned away. "I didn't do *anything* to myself, Louisa. I was just trying to do my job," he replied defensively. "I was called out last night to treat some drunken dolt injured in a fight at the pub, and I got in the way of someone's fist."

"Oh, Martin," she sighed. "How's the patient?"

"Perfectly fine. If he hadn't been so inebriated, he would have known he didn't need a doctor." Martin silently cursed the man as he carried several cups to the cabinet and began to arrange them on a shelf. "The idiot ... getting me up in the middle of the night ... complete waste of my time," he grumbled.

"Hmm, I think you should put some ice on that."

"I did when I got back last night."

Louisa cocked her head at him and, lest she ask any more questions, Martin thought it best to change the subject. "How are you feeling this morning ... any improvement?"

She took a cup from his hand and walked towards the table. "I think so. I certainly feel more rested."

"Good, it's important that you're getting an adequate amount of sleep." He shelved a stack of bowls and then turned to her. "Would you like fruit and porridge for breakfast ... or dry cereal? Whatever you like."

"The porridge sounds lovely."

"How about raisins ... or maybe dried cranberries ... nuts? Whatever you like."

"Just the porridge, Martin," Louisa said, a crispness now in her voice.

He filled a bowl and set it in front of her before moving the bottle of milk to her side of the table. Then he filled her cup with tea. "Can I get you anything else?"

"I'm fine, Martin. Why don't you come and sit down? Please."

They sat quietly, each uncertain of what to say to the other.

Martin looked across the table, gazing at her as he often did, before pulling in a deep breath. "Erm ... I made a call this morning to the psychiatrist that Ruth recommended I speak with. He gave me the name of someone in Truro who he feels is quite competent. I was wondering if you would consider ... maybe ... erm, possibly we could arrange for some sessions to go to together?"

Louisa stabbed her spoon into her porridge and huffed out a breath. "Why don't you get *your* problems sorted first, then we'll see about couples therapy."

He pulled in his chin. "I see."

She got up and carried her dirty dishes to the sink before turning to lean back against the counter. "Are you sure that's all right?" she asked, wagging a finger at him. "It's a very nasty bruise."

"It's fine." It was time to divert the conversation again. "We need a few groceries and some nappies. I could run down to the market, or I was thinking ... if you'd like to get out a bit, we could drive to Wadebridge, or even Truro. It's a nice day and the sunshine would be good for you."

"That would be nice, Martin."

"Right. I'll go get dressed, then make my appointment."

Martin's head was pounding, and the stiffness in his body had been increasing as the morning wore on. He scaled the steps, his feet feeling unusually heavy, and then gathered his clothes together so that he could dress in the bathroom.

His muscles began to relax a bit as he sat in the warm bath, and he closed his eyes, allowing himself to shut his mind to his many worries.

They headed out shortly after eleven o'clock. Concerned that a trip to Truro might be tiring for Louisa, Martin decided that perhaps it would be best to stay closer to home. So, they did their shopping in Wadebridge, picking up some items for a picnic lunch before driving out to Ruth's farm.

Martin had always found the gazebo, built by his Uncle Phil, to be a relaxing and comforting place— aside from one regrettable morning spent there with his parents and Auntie Joan.

He looked out over the sea, thinking back to his and Louisa's wedding. They did have a few brief moments to enjoy each other that night. He reminded himself to add "not enough moments alone together" to his list of marital deficiencies.

"Martin? Did you hear me?"

He turned quickly. "I'm sorry. What did you say?"

"I was wondering if you'd made your phone call."

"To the psychiatrist?"

Louisa gave her head a shake. "Yes, Martin."

"Ah. Yes, Barrett Newell. I have a standing appointment with him on Wednesdays at four o'clock."

"Sounds perfect. Thank you for doing that."

Louisa slid closer to him. "Did you sit here looking at the ocean when you were a boy?"

"Mm. Joan and Phil and I would eat our evening meals here ... if the weather allowed."

Louisa could see the sadness in her husband's eyes whenever he spoke about Joan. She knew there were a lot of emotions associated with her life and death that he kept bottled up in him.

She was trying not to get her hopes up that this psychiatrist could get him to talk about the many issues he kept locked away. She had watched as the emotional baggage continued to pile up on his shoulders day after day, slowly dragging him down, and she was becoming increasingly concerned for his mental *and* physical well-being. He had been experiencing persistent headaches, sleeplessness, and, most concerning to her, an obvious weight loss.

James began to stir in his baby seat. Considering how irritable he had been when he first got up, he had tolerated their activities very well. But his patience now seemed to be wearing thin, so they decided to make a move for home.

Martin allowed Louisa to carry the empty baby seat to the car, but he insisted on carrying James and the picnic supplies. He had leaned over to set several items on the ground by the car and was standing back up when the boy let out a squeal before arching his back and kicking out in frustration, hitting his father's bruised ribs in the process.

Caught off guard, Martin let a short yelp slip from his mouth.

Louisa furrowed her brow at him. "You okay?"

"Yes. Let me get him situated, and we'll be on our way. I think he's had enough of being strapped down today."

He could feel his wife's eyes on him as he ducked his head inside the car, and he took his time getting his son buckled into his seat. She glanced over at him periodically as they drove back to the village, but as far as he could tell she didn't suspect anything. However, he was beginning to doubt the wisdom of his ruse. He knew she wouldn't be happy with him if she discovered his deception. And hell hath no fury ...

Chapter 7

Louisa was startled out of a deep sleep that night by her husband's thrashing in the bed, trapped in one of his frequent nightmares. She rubbed his shoulder in an attempt to rouse him. "Martin, wake up; you're dreaming."

He sat up abruptly, yanking his arm away from her and crying out, "The red one!" The sound of his own voice woke him, and he looked wildly about the room, grasping on to his wife.

The sling on her left arm prevented her from embracing him, but she slid in close so that their bodies touched. "Martin, it's all right." She peered at him in the dimly lit room. "Are you awake now?"

His breathing began to slow, and his muscles relaxed as he clung to her. She brushed her fingers against his damp cheek. "A nightmare?" she asked.

He pulled away quickly as he began to shake the torpid fog. Nodding his head, he rubbed a large palm across his face and cleared his throat. "It's fine. Did I hurt you?"

"No, not at all. But are you sure you're all right?" She could feel fine tremors running through his hand as it rested against hers.

"It was nothing, Louisa. I'm fine," he said, trying to deflect her attention as tears began to sting his eyes.

"It might help to talk about it. I'm a pretty good listener," she said softly.

"Are you sure your shoulder's okay? Maybe I should take a look at it."

"I'm just fine, Martin. Now, *please*, can we talk about the dream? If things are going to change between us, this might be a good place to start." She looked at him with the same supplicatory expression he'd seen on her face when she'd tried to get him to talk about his father's death.

He hesitated for a few moments. This was exactly the kind of thing he found so difficult to discuss. He had never really talked about his past with anyone, not even Auntie Joan. But he remembered Ruth's words to him just days before, and he decided it would be unwise to push Louisa away again.

He blew out a long breath of air. "It was about boarding school ... something that happened shortly after I arrived. It had to do with an initiation the first-year boys were subjected to."

Louisa gave him an encouraging nod, and he cleared his throat again before continuing on. "I had to choose between a red or a green envelope, then one of the older boys would open it up to reveal what I had to do—typical idiotic hazing rituals. I'd already had my head held down in a bucket of ice water and had to run out to the school gate and back—naked." He pressed his fingers to his eyes.

Louisa cringed as she could imagine the other boys taunting and egging each other on ... the certain whoops of laughter.

"And ...?" She gave him an encouraging nod.

"I realized pretty quickly that it didn't matter which envelope I chose, the outcome would be the same. I refused to pick a colour."

Louisa nestled her hand more tightly against his.

"They were angry when I wouldn't play along with their moronic game, and a couple of the oldest boys grabbed me and held me out the second story window, threatening to drop me if I didn't say which colour I wanted." Martin shook his head. "I doubt now that they really would have done it, but at the time I thought ..." He gave a shrug. "So, I gave in ... yelled out, *the red one, the red one!* I just wanted to have the floor back under my feet."

Louisa let out a small sigh, and then went into the bathroom, returning with a wet face cloth. She pushed her husband back on to his pillow and began to wipe the sweat from his face.

He reached up and pulled the cloth away from her. "I can get it," he mumbled.

"I'm sorry, Martin ... for what happened." She pulled the covers back up and kissed his forehead. "Do you want to talk any more?"

"God no."

The corners of her mouth tugged up as she brushed a hand across his head. "Do you think you can get back to sleep now?"

"Mm. I'm sorry to have disturbed you." He rolled on to his side, facing away from her as he tried to reinter the painful memories he had kept buried for so many years.

Louisa woke before Martin the following morning. She lay thinking about the story he had shared with her the night before. She'd had an inkling that boarding school had been difficult for her husband, but she now wondered how much damage had been done by his experiences there.

Her thoughts turned to his upcoming appointment with the therapist. Martin needed to face his inner demons if they were to stay together, but she worried about what may lie ahead for him.

She inspected the unusual but striking features which had ignited a physical attraction to him the day they met. The nicely shaped ears which protruded from the sides of his head, the full sensuous lips, and the thick head of greying blonde hair, closely cropped, no doubt, to reinforce the stern expression he wore to hide the caring and sensitive man he was underneath the facade.

The soft sounds emanating from James's room caused Martin to stir. When he opened his eyes, Louisa was leaning over him with a smile on her face.

He cleared his throat. "What are you looking at?"

"You. I like to watch you when you're sleeping."

He tipped his head back, giving her a quick visual examination before placing his fingers against her forehead. "Are you feeling ill? Any headache ... stiffness?"

"Oh, Martin, stop it. I'm fine. It's just ... well, your face is relaxed when you're sleeping. All the grumpy, frowny lines go away. You look especially handsome."

He stared at her, blinking slowly.

She rested her hand on his arm. "Thank you for last night ... for telling me about your dream."

Martin averted his gaze and began to roll away, but Louisa grabbed hold of him.

"I mean it, Martin. I need you to talk to me ... not shut me out."

"I ... don't really talk. You know that."

"Yes. But you *can* talk if you try. Like last night. And I *need* that."

"I see."

A smile slipped across her face. "That baring of your soul to me kind'a makes me want to climb up and have my way with you."

"Louisa! You better not try anything of the sort."

"Mm, now you're *really* tempting me."

He wagged a finger at her. "No! Your shoulder."

"Oh, Martin." Her ponytail whipped to the side.

James's complaints grew louder and Martin jumped out of bed to go tend to him. His battered body resisted, and a small groan slipped from his mouth.

"All right, Martin, what's going on?" She asked, tipping her head down and peering up at him.

"It's James ... I need to take care of James." He glanced down at her, recognising the look on her face. She was not going to let it go. He hurried out of the room before she could ask any more questions.

Plucking his son from his cot, the boy gave him a nearly toothless smile.

"Good morning, James. Did you sleep well?"

"Martin, you didn't answer my question! Is something the matter?" Louisa called out.

He groaned softly at the sound of her approaching footsteps.

"I think I've been found out, James. This could get a bit ugly." He held the boy up, looking him in the eye. "Sorry about that."

Louisa stood in the doorway with one hip swung out, her free arm resting on it. Her lips were tight as she narrowed her eyes at him. "Well?"

Martin waggled his head and put his nose in the air, a mannerism she had come to know as defensive posturing. "I didn't tell you about it because I didn't think it was worth mentioning, Louisa," he said as he busied himself changing the baby's nappy and getting him dressed for the day.

"Well, I want to know. So now it *is* worth mentioning, Martin."

"All right, but I don't want you to worry about this. You don't need the added stress."

"Don't decide for me what I do or don't need to know!" Her ponytail flicked to the side, a warning that he knew he should heed.

"Yes, I'm just saying that—"

"Martin Ellingham, I know you're hiding something. And the longer you dance around the issue the more stressed I get. So, if you're concerned about my stress level ... out with it!"

"Yes, fine. But please try to be calm about this."

He inhaled deeply and hissed a long breath from his nose.

"I ended up in the middle of a free-for-all at the pub the other night ... a group of inebriated morons. I got roughed up a bit, but I'm fine. That's all there is to it."

"Roughed up a bit! What do you mean, roughed up a bit? Are you all right?"

"Yes, Louisa. Just a bit sore. You really needn't worry; I experienced much worse at boarding school."

"Oh, *that's* reassuring. Especially after what I heard last night." She let out a sigh. "Did you tell Joe Penhale about this?"

"No, I didn't see any need to involve the law in this. The men involved weren't even from the village ... according to Chippy Miller. He and a couple of the other fishermen came to my rescue, and the idiots went on their way."

"You should *not* have kept this from me, Martin. That was dishonest."

"I said *nothing* that was untrue, Louisa. Try to calm down. It really isn't good for you to be stressed right now. It raises your blood pressure which could potentially affect the—"

"Martin, hush. I understand you were concerned for my physical well-being. But the next time you get ... roughed up, please just come out with it straight away. I'll do my best to stay calm."

"I should *hope* there won't be a next time," he said, raising an eyebrow at her. He held his son up in front of him, checking that he was presentable before nestling him in the crook of his arm.

"James is sanitary now. Are you ready for breakfast?"

Louisa huffed out an exasperated breath as she turned and headed for the stairs.

"Louisa? Louisa!" Martin shook his head.

Chapter 8

Aside from a new tooth for James, the weekend came and went uneventfully. Monday morning brought a reception room full of patients. The summer tourist season was in full swing, and that meant more than the usual number of mundane maladies presenting—sunburned skin, jellyfish and weever stings, allergic reactions, and Martin's personal favourite—hangovers. He was beginning to long for an outbreak of dysentery. Whenever he passed through to get a new file from Morwenna he would cast a quick glance down the hallway, hoping to catch a glimpse of James and Louisa. He tried to dismiss his concern that Louisa could take James and leave again.

She hadn't said anything to him about the dream he'd had the other night. Was she having second thoughts about trying to make a marriage work with a man so traumatised by something as trivial as a childhood prank as to be plagued by nightmares? To have their son raised by someone with such a constitution?

One more thing to add to his crap list. When would that list get so long that his "stick of rock" quality couldn't make up for it anymore ... that she would decide he had more emotional baggage than she cared to deal with?

The morning dragged, but lunchtime brought welcome relief from the constant yammering and whinging of patients. He closed his eyes and took in a deep breath as he sat down to eat with James and Louisa. They were his oasis.

"I didn't see you at all this morning. Did you and James go out?" he asked.

Louisa's eyes shifted away from his. She didn't know how he would react if he knew she'd been to see Ruth. She had really needed to talk to someone about the nightmare that Martin had experienced, and she knew Ruth could be trusted to keep the information to herself.

She had also hoped that Ruth might have some knowledge, perhaps passed on by Joan, that could be useful in helping her husband to deal with the dreams that seemed to be occurring with an ever-increasing frequency.

"I'm sorry, I can't be of much help, Louisa," the elderly woman had told her. "Joan spoke about Martin quite often, but I don't think even she was aware that boarding school was going so badly for him. It's very easy for adults to dismiss children's problems as trivial." Ruth had quickly added, "I'm not saying that we weren't concerned for our nephew, just that when Martin would share a bit of information, which wasn't often, mind you, I'm afraid we probably downplayed the significance of it."

"Louisa? I asked if you and James went out this morning," Martin said.

Louisa refocused her attention on her husband's question. "Erm, yes. We did get out for a walk, didn't we, James." She dropped a few more peas on to the boy's high chair tray. "And we stopped in to say hello to Ruth. She sends her love, by the way." She took a bite of her sandwich, and then brushed the crumbs from her fingers.

Martin jutted out his chin. "Mm, I see."

Dabbing at her mouth with her napkin, Louisa asked, "How are you feeling about your appointment on Wednesday? Apprehensive?"

Martin shrugged his shoulders. "I don't really know what to expect. The usual psychoanalytical claptrap, I would assume."

"Martin, nothing will come of this therapy if you go into it with a negative attitude," she said, slapping her napkin down on her lap. She sighed. *"Please* ... try to keep an open mind and respect the fact that this man has a fine reputation. I expect you to give this a fair chance. Understood?"

Martin sat shaking his head. "I'm really not comfortable discussing my feelings."

"Yes, and that is a good part of the problem! Both yours and ours! You'll only get out of this what you're willing to put into it, Martin. And I expect you to give it your all!"

She sat with pursed lips for a moment, and then her voice softened. *"I'm* a bit nervous about this even if you aren't. What you do with your chance ... our chance ... to improve things between us ... it'll tell me a great deal about how important this is to you. How important James and I are to you."

Martin returned to his patients feeling chastised but strangely uplifted. Louisa wanted him to try for them. She still wanted him.

He slipped a set of patient notes into its sleeve and slapped it down on the corner of his desk. "Morwenna!" he yelled. He heard the approaching flap-flap of his receptionist's overly casual footwear.

"Yeah, Doc?"

"Morwenna, I need you to reschedule any appointments after half two on Wednesday. And don't schedule any more appointments during that time in future weeks until I tell you otherwise."

"Why? What's goin' on?"

"Just ... do it!" Martin said as he slammed a drawer shut. "And take these patient notes ... file them away."

Morwenna gave her boss one last quizzical look before picking up the stack from the desk and hurrying out the door.

"And send Mrs. Poustie in!"

There was a rustling and jingling in the hall before Martin looked up to see Joe Penhale, the village's conscientious and amiable, but marginally competent police constable, standing in the doorway, thumbs hooked over his tool belt. "We need to have a little chat, Do-*c*," he said with great gravitas and his tendency to emphasise the end of a word. "Word on the street is you had a run-in with some toughs down at the pub the other night."

He puffed out his chest and walked towards the desk, peering imperiously down at Martin. "I'm here to take your statement. Can you describe your assailants?" he asked, reaching into his shirt pocket before brandishing his biro, clicking it with a flourish.

"Oh, it's over, Penhale. It was a one-off. Just leave it alone."

"No can do, Doc. The perps could escalate to murder next time."

"When was the last time we had a murder in Portwenn?"

Joe tipped his head and shrugged his shoulders. "I'd have to check the homicide file; can't say right off."

"Do you even *have* a homicide file?"

"Well, not a homicide file, as such." He moved over and dropped into the chair across from the doctor. "Did you get a look at the perps? Height, weight, any identifying characteris-*tics*?"

Martin grimaced. "What sort of identifying characteristics?"

"Scars, tattoos, obvious deformities ..."

"Penhale," Martin groaned, rubbing at the throbbing that had set in behind his eyes.

"Sorry for the third degree, Doc. But as an officer of the law, I am duty bound to head off any potential murderous malfeasance in the community."

"I thought malfeasance usually pertained to those in positions of authority. Is a fisherman in a position of authority?"

Joe gave him an oafish grin. "I suppose he is to a sardine."

Martin glared at him. "I have patients waiting."

"I noticed that. You'll have to step things up a bit, eh? The natives are getting restless. Perhaps we better move this process along." He flipped a small notebook open.

"Penhale, I'm *not* giving you a statement! Now *please* ... leave!"

"Well, Doc, that's your decision. Just don't want to be scrapin' you up off the pavement next time. Remember, I'm just a phone call away, twenty-four/seven." He held his thumb and little finger to the side of his head as he left the room.

Martin shook his head as he watched the constable swagger away. He called out to his next patient. "Mrs. Poustie!"

As they were preparing for bed that evening Louisa again addressed the subject of her husband's upcoming appointment. "Martin, I was wondering ... I mean, I haven't asked you if you'd like me to join you when you see Dr. Newell on Wednesday."

"I'm not sure that would be the most efficient use of the time at this point. I would imagine there'll be a lot of questions about my haemophobia and my past, but I doubt we'd get much beyond that in the first session. Perhaps there might be a time in the future where it could be useful."

"Would you mind if James and I rode along? You could drop us at the children's shop before you head to Dr. Newell's. I need to pick up some clothes for him; he's been growing so fast lately. I think he's going to be big like his daddy."

"Mm, I was a rather small child until I hit my teen years," Martin said as he kicked his slippers from his feet and sat down on the bed.

"Well, still ..." she said, eyeing him up and down. "So, would it be okay if we rode along?"

"That would be fine ... it would be good," he said, nodding his head.

Martin had enjoyed two relatively peaceful nights in a row, but tonight sleep would prove to be more elusive.

His mobile rang at around half twelve. He needed to make a trip out to the Hanley farm to see Jim Hanley. The man was known to hit the bottle quite hard, and his imbibing had resulted in a fall into the corner of a coffee table, opening a nasty gash in his forehead.

Martin fought nausea as he checked Jim's pupillary reflexes, but lost the battle when he went to clean the wound prior to stitching it up. He vomited a second time after he inadvertently jabbed the curved suturing needle into his own thumb.

Once finished with his patient, he tended to his own wound, washing it with a liberal amount of disinfectant before applying a plaster.

Mr. Hanley was a mean drunk, and Martin was uncomfortable leaving him alone with his wife and children, so he stayed until the man had sobered up a bit and fallen asleep on the sofa. It was going on 3:00 a.m. before he was able to get away from the Hanley farm.

He arrived back at the surgery and had just made it to the top of the stairs when he heard James begin to cry. The baby didn't wake in the night very often, but if he was going through a growth spurt he would occasionally need an extra bottle to get him through until morning.

He sat with his son, scrutinising the features which betrayed the source of his genetic material. His finger traced its way around the rim of the tiny, pliable ear which protruded slightly more than usual.

A scratching could be heard on the roof over the nursery as a bird sought out a roost for the remainder of the night. The soft, airy hooting that followed distinguished the bird from the ubiquitous herring gulls that made Portwenn their home. James looked up at his father, his eyes widening as he recognised the sound as something new.

"That's an owl, James," Martin said softly. His son's large blue eyes stared back at him. The child's blonde hair fluttered in the breeze created by the rocking of the chair, tempting Martin's fingers to return the wisps to their proper place.

James patted his hand against his father's as it held the bottle. They were almost amusing in their similarity to Martin's. Large, broad-palmed, with straight, sturdy fingers but in miniature.

The baby's eyes drifted shut, and his body grew heavy against his father's arm as a mouthful of unconsumed formula dribbled down his chin.

Martin dabbed the small face dry with a face cloth and then laid the child back down in his cot. Then, half asleep, he walked back to their bedroom, pulling off his shoes, suit coat, and tie before crawling in under the covers. Two hours later his alarm went off.

Chapter 9

Martin pulled the Lexus up to the kerb in front of the children's shop on Wednesday afternoon and shifted it into park. "You're sure you'll be all right? I'm not really comfortable just dropping you here like this."

"Oh, for goodness' sake, Martin, stop making a fuss of this. We'll be fine," Louisa said as she leaned across the gear shift to place a kiss on his cheek. "I've been looking forward to this ... James and me on our own in the big city."

"Well, relatively speaking, Truro really isn't a big city, Louisa. The population of London is nearly three-hundred and fifty times tha—"

"Martin, it was a joke. Sort of."

He tugged at his ear. "I see."

She huffed out a breath, zipped her purse shut, and picked the nappy bag up from the floor in front of her. "If we get done with our shopping before you get back, we'll go to the park down the block. I'll text you if we do, though."

Her gaze met his, and she gave him a weak smile, stroking her fingers lightly across his arm. "Please ... give this therapy a chance. *Try.*"

"Mm."

Martin pulled in his chin and then got out of the car, opening up the push chair before lifting his son from his car seat. "Be good for your mum, James," he said, settling the boy and fastening the safety harness.

He turned back to his wife. "Be careful. And call me if you run into any trouble," he said before giving her an awkward kiss on the side of her head.

A feeling of dread had begun to descend on him the night before, and Martin had slept restlessly. He woke several times, filled with trepidation. He didn't want to admit it to Louisa, but he worried that this Dr. Newell would resurrect long forgotten hurts and painful memories.

But maybe there was nothing to be remembered. He knew he had been blessed with unloving, vile parents, and he knew his years shut away in boarding school had been miserable. It could very well be that there was nothing more to be dredged from his painful childhood.

However, the brief flashes of memories that had permeated his sleep of late caused him to feel a great deal of anxiety as he walked up the pavement to the therapist's building, and his pace slowed almost uncontrollably as he neared the door.

The office was quite unremarkable—a contemporary, nondescript exterior with a white walled interior. The air smelled not of antiseptic, like his surgery, but of new carpet and fresh paint. The receptionist greeted him without a needless amount of chatter, and, after only a few minutes of time spent waiting in the reception area, the psychiatrist emerged from his inner sanctum at the end of the hall.

"Hello, Dr. Ellingham ... Barrett Newell," he said, extending his hand. "Come on back."

Dr. Newell had a very professional air about him which immediately put Martin at ease. The taut muscles in his neck and shoulders began to relax as he looked around the office. It was very neat and well organised, much like the man himself.

Martin had done his research beforehand, so he knew the man was well-qualified. The doctor's credentials, which were quite impressive, were displayed on the wall. After the formal introductions, the psychiatrist sat down behind his desk and gestured to the chair on the opposite side. "Please ... have a seat."

He flipped a file folder open in front of him, scratched a note into it, and looked up. "Well, Martin, I won't insult your intelligence by asking what you hope to get out of these sessions. That's a bit like asking you to predict the future, isn't it?"

The man had a penetrating gaze that made Martin shift in his seat. "Mm, I suppose it is."

"I *will* ask you to begin by telling me a bit about your life as it is today, and then we'll look at your past history a bit. You're free to refuse to answer questions that you're uncomfortable with, but I want to remind you that approaching these sessions in that manner will not provide you with the results that could be achieved otherwise. In general, the most painful areas of discussion often yield the greatest benefits."

He pushed himself back from his desk and pulled his foot up over his knee. "Do you have any questions for me before we get started?"

Martin cleared his throat. "My wife did ask whether it would be helpful for her to come to any of my sessions. I'm not sure I'm comfortable with that, but if you think it would be of some use ..."

The therapist nodded his head. "I'm happy to hear that you're willing to leave your comfort zone and do whatever might be necessary to make progress. And yes, your wife's presence may indeed be helpful at some point, but for now I think it best if the focus is on you." He leaned back in his chair and folded his hands in front of him. "All right then, how long have you and your wife been married ...?"

The standard format continued for the next half hour before Dr. Newell shifted gears rather abruptly. "Tell me about the last visit you had with your parents, Martin. I'm making an assumption that they're both living?"

"Erm, my father died recently. My mother showed up on our doorstep about two weeks ago to deliver the news. Do you want to know about my mother's visit or the visit from my parents four years ago?" Martin wiped his moist palms on his trousers.

"Why don't we discuss the most recent visit first. You mentioned earlier that you have an aunt who currently lives in Portwenn and that a deceased aunt had lived in the village for many years before her death less than a year ago. Was your father's funeral in Portwenn as was your aunt's?"

Martin sighed. "No, the funeral had been held two weeks prior to my mother's arrival."

"I'm not sure I follow. Why didn't your mother *call* you to tell you about your father's death? I would imagine you would have liked to have been there."

The psychiatrist waited as his patient sat, silent. "Your mother must have felt it was more important to tell you in person than for you to be notified in time to attend the funeral?" he prodded.

Martin's head was beginning to pound, and he wanted nothing more than to get up and dash out the door. He pressed his fingertips to his forehead and then looked up at the man. "Her objective with the visit wasn't to tell me about my father's death. It was to ask for money. My father had made a number of bad investments and left her with no capital. She wanted money."

"I would imagine that was a painful realisation for you."

"Mm."

Rocking back and forth in his chair, Dr. Newell steepled his fingers and tapped them against his lips. "What did your wife ..." He glanced at his notes. "What did Louisa think about not being told in advance about the funeral? I would imagine she might have liked to have been there as well."

"Louisa had never met my parents. She would have accompanied me if I had attended, but she didn't know the man, so I assume it would make no difference to her one way or the other."

"I'm guessing you're not close to your parents, Martin," the psychiatrist said.

"No. We had a falling out when they came four years ago. I was actually quite surprised to see my mother when she showed up. I didn't think I would see either of them again."

"I see. The parent-child relationship can be complicated."

Martin scowled and looked at the floor. "I don't know that it could be called a relationship."

The therapist nodded his head. "I think you've just raised an important issue ... one I'd like to explore further." Glancing down at his watch, he hissed a breath from his nose. "Unfortunately, we're out of time for today, but we can pick this up at your next session."

He stood up and reached to shake Martin's hand before moving towards the door. "This can be a stressful process, Martin. But the time and effort that you put into it will yield positive results."

"I hope so."

"It was very nice to meet you. I'll plan to see you next week."

"Yes." Martin breathed a sigh of relief as the door closed behind him.

He pulled his mobile from his breast pocket and glanced down at the message from his wife. *Pick us up at the park.*

Filling his lungs with fresh air, he shot his sleeves and slipped behind the wheel of his car.

Louisa tried not to press her husband for answers, but she was curious about how his first session had gone, and he wasn't being terribly forthcoming. "What's Dr. Newell like?" she asked hesitantly.

Martin sighed softly as he glanced out his side window. "He's about the same age as myself, I would guess. Well organised, professional ..."

"Did you like him?"

"I'm not sure that it matters whether I like him."

"Well, no. I suppose not. I'm just wondering about his personality ... does he seem nice?"

Martin rolled his eyes before snapping, "I don't see that any of that is relevant, Louisa!"

She huffed out a breath and turned away to look out the window.

All the warning signs were on her face; the crinkles around her eyes, the taut lips, and the flick of her ponytail. Martin knew he now had to defuse the situation he had created.

"Erm, did you and James enjoy your walk in the park?"

Louisa folded her arms across her chest before delivering her frosty reply. "It was fine, Martin."

They drove along for several minutes before he spoke again. "I'm sorry, Louisa. I'm feeling rather tense, and I'd rather not discuss my appointment right now. I didn't mean to snap at you."

Louisa turned to him. "I'm sorry, too. In future, I'll try to let you initiate the conversations about your visits with Dr. Newell." She stroked his arm, and he glanced her way. They exchanged strained smiles before she added, "I'm just very nervous for you, and I think I need the reassurance that you're all right."

"I'm ... fine. But I do have a headache, so can we please discuss this later?"

"Yes, Martin."

Neither of them broached the subject of the session with Dr. Newell again until that night after they had gone to bed. Martin lay on his back, his arms folded across his chest as he stared at the ceiling. He closed his eyes and inhaled her sweet scent, finally feeling the tightness in his chest give way to relaxation.

"Erm, you were wanting to know about my appointment. He was just gathering information today. Mostly about my life now ... my job, family, where I live, what brought me to Portwenn."

Louisa rolled towards him and settled her hand on his.

"Then he asked me to tell him about the visit from my mother," he continued. "I told him she claimed to have come to give us the news about my father, when in reality she wanted money. I think he was trying to get some idea of what my relationship with them is ... was like. He didn't ask very many questions today. I think it was more of a fact-finding mission this time around."

Louisa pulled down her brow. "What do you mean she came to ask for money?"

Martin pulled a hand up, resting it on his forehead. "After you left in the taxi for the airport, I confronted her about why she was here. I knew she hadn't come to, as she put it, tell me about my father in person ... that she was so concerned about my feelings that she didn't want to tell me over the phone. She told me he loved me ... he just hadn't been able to say it. That in his last moments of life he asked her to ... relay the message. I knew it was a lie."

Louisa pushed herself up, sitting back against the headboard. "Maybe you shouldn't be so quick to reject the idea that your father loves you ... or loved you. I actually find you pretty lovable ... most of the time," she said as she lightly brushed her fingers through his hair.

"Louisa, I spent a lifetime trying to win their love. I realised four years ago that they would never feel that way about me, and I gave up trying."

"Oh, Martin. I can't say that I like your mother, and I never met your father, but don't you think you're being a little unfair?"

Martin blinked his eyes and then stared up at her. "You think I'm being unfair?"

"Well, it's just ... I mean, you may not have seen eye to eye with your parents, but I'm sure they love you. They *are* Ellinghams. Maybe it's just been hard for them to show it."

Louisa could feel her husband's body tense, and he sat up abruptly. When he turned to face her, the intensity of the hurt and disbelief in his eyes took her aback. His breathing became rapid as his eyes drifted shut. "I, er - I - I'm not sure I remembered to lock the doors. I'll just go and double check."

He got up quickly and hurried off. Louisa heard his footsteps on the stairs and then the sound of the front door opening and closing.

She waited, and when he didn't return, she grew concerned. Wrapping her dressing gown around her shoulders, she made her way downstairs to look for him.

"Martin?" she called softly. When there was no response, she went to the front door and peeked out. Her husband was sitting on the top step of the terrace, staring off at the harbour.

"Mind if I join you?" she asked as her feet hit the cold slate.

He slid over to make room for her but turned his gaze away as she sat down.

"Martin, is something the matter?"

"It's not important, Louisa."

She put her hand on his back. "Martin, we both agreed that we can't fall back into the way things were, but that's right where we're headed if you won't talk to me."

She took in a deep breath as he remained unresponsive, and she tried to push her frustration aside. "Please ... tell me. Is something wrong?"

She could hear his breathing becoming ragged and more rapid again. "Louisa, I don't think I can possibly explain to you why ... God, I feel like a complete *idiot* to have thought someone would— I have no clue as to how to explain this!"

Martin got to his feet. "I don't know!" Storming back inside, he left his wife mystified as to what was troubling him.

When she came into their room, he was in bed. She slid in next to him before leaning over to kiss his cheek. "Love you."

"Mm, yes."

Each for different reasons, they fell asleep with heavy hearts.

Chapter 10

The atmosphere was tense in the Ellingham household. Louisa felt Martin pulling ever further into himself, and it only served to strengthen her insecurities. Martin, on the other hand, was feeling like a stranger in his own home.

He had tried many times as a child to tell someone about the pain of being Christopher and Margaret Ellingham's son, about how he craved their love and attention. But he was told repeatedly that he just didn't understand his parents. No one wanted to hear him. How could he have been so naive as to think things would be any different with Louisa?

There was no comfort for him when he joined his wife and son for lunch on Thursday. He now felt hurt and humiliation when he was in the same room with her.

They sat on opposite sides of the kitchen table, facing each other, but Martin's gaze refused to meet hers.

Louisa laid her sandwich on her plate and slowly brushed the crumbs from her fingertips. "Martin," she said softly. "Would you mind calling Dr. Newell ... ask him about scheduling some sessions for the two of us?"

Martin brought his head up and stared at her for a moment. "Really?"

"I just wonder if it might be helpful." She got up from the table and pulled the tea kettle from its base, filling it with water. "You know ... for me to know how to deal with you when your issues come up."

"Ah. I see." His gaze returned to his plate. "Yes. I'll call him first thing after lunch."

When Martin reached his psychiatrist a short time later, the man had just had a cancellation for the following day.

Louisa seemed resigned when he informed her of their four o'clock appointment, saying only, "That's fine. I'll line someone up to watch James."

Ruth came over at three o'clock on Friday to babysit while her nephew and his wife attended their session with Dr. Newell. Martin was still with patients when the elderly woman arrived, so Louisa took the opportunity to discuss the ill-fated conversation on Wednesday night.

"I just don't know what went wrong, Ruth. All seemed to be going fine, and then he got this horribly hurt look on his face, made an excuse about needing to double check the locks on the doors and ran off. I found him later sitting on the terrace steps. I tried to talk to him about it, but he said he didn't think he could begin to explain it to me ... that he felt like an idiot."

Ruth tapped her fingers against the table. "Well, if the conversation did truly transpire in the manner you're remembering, then I suspect Martin may have felt rather betrayed. And he was probably feeling like he had let his guard down, resulting in him being hurt."

"How did I betray him ... or hurt him? I was just trying to reassure him that his parents love him."

"But are you sure that's the case?"

Louisa laughed uncomfortably. "What, you don't think Martin's parents love him? Ruth, this *is* your brother we're talking about."

"I think this is something you really need to be hearing from Martin, but I'm afraid he may be wary of discussing it with you now, Louisa. I know you meant well, but I think if you could see this from his perspective you might understand where things went awry. You should definitely bring it up during your session with Dr. Newell."

Louisa left her son in Ruth's competent hands and went to check on her husband.

He was just finishing with the last of the patient notes when she stuck her head in the doorway to the consulting room.

"Ready to go?"

"Erm, yes. Let me just file these." The same pained expression was still in his eyes when he glanced up at her.

They drove the forty-five-minute trip to Truro in uncomfortable silence, punctuated by brief, stilted exchanges about pedestrian household matters.

Relief from the tension came when they arrived at Dr. Newell's office. After introductions had been made, they settled into chairs in front of his desk.

"I thought we could start our session today by asking each of you to tell me what you see as strengths and weaknesses in your marriage," the therapist said as he leaned back, rolling his biro in his fingertips. "I'm a chivalrous man, so let's begin with you, Mrs. Ellingham."

There was a gentleness in the psychiatrist's face that instantly put Louisa at ease. "Well, I would say our greatest strength is our love for one another ... and, of course, our love for our son." She glanced over at Martin. "And we're certainly patient. It took us quite a while to finally get together. And persistence ... we *are* persistent. We keep trying to get this right. Although, we obviously haven't been very successful."

"And what do you see as weaknesses ... things you need to work on?" he asked.

Louisa lowered her eyes and shifted uncomfortably. "We don't communicate well. We're constantly having misunderstandings ... mini-rows. We're very different people, and that often causes disagreements."

Louisa sat stiffly, picking at her fingernails. "Our personalities are quite opposite. Martin's taciturn ... doesn't really like most people that much, and I—"

"I like people!" Martin interjected.

"Well, maybe I shouldn't have put it that way. I like to get out ... you know ... socialise. Martin would prefer to stay at home." She crossed her legs and smoothed out her skirt. "I'd also say that I'm a people pleaser. Martin pretty much says what's on his mind. People often find him rude ... insulting."

"I would imagine those differences could create problems on occasion."

Louisa's ponytail whipped to the side. "It can be a *real* problem. When he's rude, then I'm compelled to apologise for his behaviour. Martin takes offense to that."

Dr. Newell swivelled his chair. "And what about you, Dr. Ellingham?"

Martin reached inside his coat pocket, pulling out the list he had been compiling before sliding it across the desk.

The psychiatrist scanned over it before handing it back to him. "Could you read that out loud, please."

Martin screwed up his face and squirmed in his chair. "I agree with Louisa that our greatest strength is that we love one another. I also think that we're both intelligent people and, with some guidance, should be able to figure out how to function better as a couple."

He glanced down at the list again. "We, erm ... share similar values. Despite what Louisa may think, we *both* care about people but may act on it in different ways. And we both want what's best for our son. But there again, we may not show it in the same way." Martin folded the list in half, running his fingers over the crease. "There's more here, but ... well, can't she just read the rest?"

The annoyance in Martin's voice was not missed by the psychiatrist. "Sure, that would be fine. Why don't you move on to what you have titled, *marital deficiencies*."

Martin sighed, unfolded the sheet of paper again, and continued on. "I agree that our lack of communication causes us the greatest problems, by far. I can be somewhat taciturn, so Louisa tends to fill in the blanks with her own assumptions." His eyes shifted to his lap. "I assume that people say what they mean ... mean what they say, and Louisa ... doesn't. I think that quite often gets me into trouble. Again, there's more, but you can read the rest. Mm." Martin looked away as he handed Louisa the sheet of paper.

Dr. Newell pulled in a breath and pressed his fingertips together. "Okay, I think that gives us a good foundation to work from."

He pushed back from his desk, straightened his legs out in front of him and crossed his ankles. "Since the communication issue and frequent misunderstandings seem to be of greatest concern, why don't you tell me about your most recent row."

Louisa glanced over at her husband, and after giving a recap of their exchange on Wednesday night, she continued, "So I just really don't know where the conversation broke down ... what I said to upset him."

The doctor pulled himself forward and rested his elbows on his desk, steepling his fingers. "Martin, you've had some time to think this through a bit ... would you be able to answer Louisa's question now?"

Martin brushed at his trousers, roughly. "It's really not necessary to rehash this. It doesn't matter at this point."

Dr. Newell got up and came around, perching himself on the corner of the desktop. "I disagree with you, Martin. You and Louisa seem to be in agreement that your frequent misunderstandings are a source of friction in your marriage. Discussing this recent row is an opportunity to learn to communicate more effectively."

Martin grimaced. "I'm just not very good at it."

"Communication is a two-way street, Martin. This is an opportunity for Louisa to learn as well."

Martin rubbed his hand across the back of his neck and blew out a hiss of air. "I was trying to share something and it was dismissed."

Louisa stared at him. "I was just trying to reassure you that your parents do love you, Martin."

Martin gazed at the floor and shook his head. "No. They don't. They never have and never will."

"And see, I think you're the one making assumptions this time, Martin." She turned towards him and put her hand on his arm. "You don't know what's in their hearts. Unless you've given them some reason to not love you, I think you should assume they do."

Martin's jaws clenched as his wife spoke, the hurt that he had left unexpressed for the last two days threatening to bubble to the surface.

Louisa turned to the psychiatrist. "The Ellingham family has a very difficult time expressing emotion. Well, the loving, caring sort, anyway. It's just difficult for—"

Unable to contain himself any longer, Martin jumped up from his chair. "This has nothing to do with whether the Ellingham's are incapable of expressing themselves or what is or isn't in my parents' ... *hearts!*" he spat.

"Louisa, you know nothing about this! You never even met my ghastly father, and you spent the sum total of three days with my mother, during most of which I should remind you, you were at the bloody school!

"My father never had a good word to say about me. My school performance—*You're capable of more than this, Martin. You're never going to get anywhere if you don't start applying yourself,*" he said mockingly.

"He made no effort to conceal his embarrassment when I presented him with my Youth Chess Championship trophy. I found it in the bin in his study the next morning. 'Chess won't pay the bills, boy. You're wasting your time with that ridiculous game. You should have that nose of yours in the books if you intend to amount to anything'.

"He belittled everything about me. My position as a GP, my lack of financial nous, even the implausibility of my ever finding someone who would consider marrying me."

Martin cocked his head at his wife. "And why the hell should I assume my mother loves me when she told me in no uncertain terms four years ago, that my mere existence ruined her life? That she did everything she could to get rid of me— boarding school, Joan's in the summer. And I still managed to be in the way. Being bullied and teased ... wetting the bed. Her exact words were, 'forty years of my life wasted ... because of you'. And I'm supposed to assume the woman loves me?" Martin looked at Louisa with disbelief before dropping heavily into his chair.

Sitting stiffly, he continued on, his voice barely audible. "I thought you'd listen ... that maybe you'd understand. I tried to talk about this with Auntie Joan ... a teacher once, but it was dismissed as just being *the Ellingham way*. So, I quit talking. When you dismissed it the other night ... I felt like the room was closing in on me, and I had to get out of the house.

"I was embarrassed. I felt like an idiot for having let myself walk right into it again. I felt like a child again. I had to get away from you ... from the room."

After several moments of silence, Martin raised his head. "I didn't mean to lose control like that. Louisa, I'm very sorry that I yelled at you."

Dr. Newell cleared his throat. "That's quite all right, Martin. I would have to say that you were communicating very effectively. Questions have been answered ... information and feelings were shared. Well done."

The therapist got up and took a step towards the door. "I'd like to give the two of you some time to talk, so I'm going to step out for a bit ... make a quick phone call. I'll be back in a few minutes."

Louisa pulled a chair over in front of her husband. "Martin, I'm so sorry. I can't believe your mother said ... I mean, I *do* believe she said it, but I can't imagine how that must have hurt you. And I should have let you talk the other night instead of trying to jump in and fix something I didn't know anything about. I didn't intend it, Martin, but I can see now that I *was* dismissive."

She tipped her head to the side to try to see his downward facing eyes. "I hope you can forgive me ... give me another chance. I'll do my very best to not violate your trust the next time."

She stood up, took his chin in her hand and tipped his head back before kissing him. "I love you, Martin."

"I love you, too."

Chapter 11

"You sure you're okay?" Louisa asked, eyeing her husband as he steered the car down Church Hill and into the village.

He gave a shrug of his shoulders and shook his head. "I'm tired. If you don't mind I think I'll head up to bed when we get home."

"That's fine. You sure you're okay, though?"

"Mm."

Her brows drew together as she reached over to caress his thigh. He had been all but silent the entire drive back to Portwenn. She wondered what was on his mind. But after what, for Martin, had been an effusive soliloquy, she didn't want to push him any further.

The light outside the little cottage glowed warmly as they climbed the steps to the terrace, and Martin stopped for a moment to look out over the tranquil harbour. "There must have been a hundred mornings that I stepped out here to drink my coffee and watch you," he said absently.

"You watched me?"

"Mm. Usually just imagined." He kissed her forehead, and then turned, reaching towards the lock on the old door.

"Here, let me help." Louisa took the keys from his trembling hands and turned the deadbolt. "There we go." They jingled softly as she slipped them back into his pocket before turning the knob and entering the house.

Martin gave her a wave of his hand and then turned the corner to climb the stairs, his legs aching and every step seeming to reverberate in his head.

Ruth had just finished feeding James his dinner when Louisa entered the kitchen.

"Were you a good boy for your aunt Ruth, James? Did you have fun?"

"I'm not sure that this old lady is a good source of entertainment for your son. He is very tolerant of me, however. How was the appointment?" She peered down the empty hallway. "I don't see my nephew. You didn't get fed up and decide to leave him in Truro, did you?" She eyed Louisa soberly.

"No, Ruth, it was actually very productive," Louisa replied, squirming under the woman's gaze. "But it was a long session ... a tough session. Martin was quite tired." She jerked her head. "He went up to bed."

Picking James up, she excused herself to change the baby's nappy. While she was upstairs, Ruth made each of them a cup of tea and a sandwich as well as a small salad for Louisa.

"Oh, thank you, Ruth," Louisa said when she returned to see her dinner laid out for her on the table. She settled her son into his high chair before dumping some bits of dry cereal on his tray. "Martin's out like a light. Between late night calls and the nightmares, he hasn't been getting much sleep recently."

Ruth shot her one of the deadpan looks that Louisa suspected she used to great effect when counselling the criminally insane. "I'm assuming you discussed what happened the other night with Barrett Newell?"

Louisa let out a long sigh. "Yes. Oh, Ruth, I feel terrible about how I trampled on Martin's feelings. I've always felt quite sorry for myself because I thought my parents had messed *me* around. But I never doubted their love for me. I just can't fathom that Margaret and Christopher really didn't love their son."

She stared pensively towards the window before shifting her gaze back towards the elderly woman. "I grew up in a home where money was always a concern." She gave Ruth a small smile. "We ate a lot of beans and toast."

Her fingernails tapped against the table top. "Martin grew up privileged. I just assumed *I* was the one who'd gotten the short end of the stick. But it turns out money *doesn't* buy happiness."

"No dear. Money buys *comfort,* not happiness. There isn't enough money on this earth to buy love or compassion from the likes of my dear brother or his wretched wife, I'm afraid."

"Ruth, did you know that Margaret had told Martin that he had ruined her life by being born?"

"No, I wasn't aware of that, but I'm afraid it doesn't surprise me. Margaret and I had a conversation while she was here. I was concerned for Martin. She's been an abysmal mother, barely tolerating her son. I knew her presence here could only harm him further."

"Ruth, I need to know what to prepare myself for. I mean, after hearing about the incident at boarding school and now finding out about Martin's unloving parents ... Well, it's rather frightening to think about how much other stuff there is that I don't know about. Do you think this will be terribly hard for him?"

"You're referring to the therapy, I assume."

"Yeah. Martin's made some comments here and there, but they've always been made in such an offhand manner that I never gave them a lot of consideration. But now when I think back on things he's said ... think about it in a different context, it's disturbing."

Ruth's fingers traced a path around the rim of her teacup. "Well, it won't be easy for sure. I don't know what Martin's said to you before, but I do know that Christopher was firmly in the 'spare the rod and spoil the child' camp when it came to discipline. And he was *very* determined that his son not be spoiled." She pushed away from the table and got up to get the tea kettle. "Joan told me that Martin was always very fearful and upset about having to go back home after the summers with her and Phil."

She filled her cup with water and dropped a teabag into it. "Another cup?" she asked Louisa.

"No ... thank you, Ruth."

The old woman returned the kettle to its base before taking a seat again. "Aside from that, I'm probably as in the dark as you are."

They sat in silence as the old woman sipped at her tea. She finally looked up at her nephew's wife. "I'm sorry that I can't be of more help."

Louisa reached across the table to take her hand. "You have helped immeasurably, Ruth. Both with James and with lending a kind ear whenever I've needed it. I'm glad you decided to stay in Portwenn. Joan's death was harder on Martin than he wants to admit, but I think it softened the blow a bit to have you here."

Ruth pushed herself up from the table. "Well, I should be moving on. I'll leave you two to enjoy your evening. Perhaps it would be best to get the baby off to sleep early ... join your husband in bed. Don't forget, you're still healing."

"Yes, Ruth. Your nephew keeps reminding me of that as well."

Louisa read as James played on the floor at her feet that evening. After putting the boy to bed, she slipped under the covers as quietly as she could so as to not wake her husband. She lay thinking about their session with Dr. Newell and how skilfully the man had gotten Martin to open up about his feelings. She was cautiously optimistic about how fruitful the investment of their time and effort in therapy might be. She was also reminding herself to be realistic in her expectations about how much Dr. Newell could do.

Martin was awakened halfway through the night by disturbing dreams. He sat bolt upright in bed, his heart racing. His jostling disturbed Louisa's slumber as well, and she pulled herself upright next to him.

"Another nightmare?" she asked sleepily.

Martin tried to slow his breathing. "No, not really. Just ... I'm not sure." His head was spinning.

Louisa reached over to rub his back. "Martin, you feel hot. Are you ill?"

"Mm, possibly," he said as he leaned forward, holding his head in his hands.

Louisa got out of bed, pulling on her dressing gown and slippers. "I'm going down to get a thermometer ... be right back."

She returned carrying a glass of water. Grabbing hold of her husband's head, she stuck the thermometer in his ear. "One hundred and two point four. It's official; you're sick. Here, I brought you some paracetamol and a glass of water. Is there anything else I should get you, Doctor?"

Martin fidgeted uncomfortably. "I think that's fine, thank you. I'm sorry I disturbed your sleep." He swung his legs over the side of the bed and stood up, putting a hand out against the wall as the room began to spin again.

Louisa reached out to steady him. "What in the world are you doing, Martin?"

"You need your rest. I'm going to get a blanket ... go sleep on the sofa. I don't want either you or James getting this."

"That sounds like kind of a silly idea to me. I think we already shared plenty of germs when we kissed at the therapist's office, don't you?"

"Mm, no. Possibly not. I wasn't febrile yet, so I may not have been contagious at that time. It really would be safest for me to sleep downstairs."

Louisa pushed on his chest and he toppled back on to the mattress. "Let's live dangerously," she said, pressing her lips to his.

"Louisa! That was *incredibly* reckless of you!" he said, trying to pull away.

"Oh, well. What's done is done. Can't do anything about it now." Leaning over, she kissed him again, allowing her lips to linger on his. "Goodnight, Martin."

He watched her moonlit form as she moved around the bed and crawled in the other side. "Mm, goodnight."

Louisa was awakened several more times as Martin tossed in his sleep. She caressed his back until his febrile mumblings had quieted and he had drifted off again.

Morning brought with it a heavy mist, the grey sky matching the colour of Martin's mood. The unpleasant images and fearfulness that woke him the first time had accompanied him throughout the rest of the night. He felt an intense edginess, and he found himself snapping at his wife as she attempted to care for him.

"I'm sorry, Louisa. I appreciate your help, but ... it's just that I'm a bit tense, and I'm not used to having someone take care of me. It feels ... awkward."

"Well, I'm sorry about that, Martin. But you're sick and I *am* going to take care of you whether you like it or not." Louisa plumped the pillows behind him and plopped a stack of medical journals on to the bedside table before pushing her face up to his. "It's not like I'm asking you to let me operate on your brain, now is it?"

Martin grumbled unintelligibly before adding softly, "Could you ask Morwenna to reschedule my appointments? And could you ... bring me some toast?"

"I'd be more than happy to," she said, cupping a hand against his cheek. "I'll be back in a tick."

He picked up the latest issue of the *BMJ*, flipping haphazardly through the pages before settling on an article about the worldwide incidence of wild poliovirus. He slapped the magazine down on the bed a few minutes later.

His stomach was churning, whether due to his illness or the vulnerability that he felt after yesterday's spewing of emotion, he didn't know. Either way, trying to focus his eyes on the fine print in the periodical was exacerbating his symptoms.

He heard his wife's footsteps on the stairs and watched for her to appear in the doorway.

"Got your toast," she announced as she set the plate on his lap. "Morwenna's shifted your appointments to next week. She said to tell you there were a couple of patients who called in with symptoms similar to yours. She sent them over to Wadebridge."

"Mm, good."

Louisa sat down on the bed next to him and watched as he nibbled half-heartedly at the pieces of bread.

"Who, er ... who's watching James?" he asked, trying to divert his wife's attention.

"Ruth. She wanted to come up and say hello, but I didn't think you'd want her up here."

"You're right about that. Someone of her advanced age could succumb easily to this type of a virus. The immune system is weakened, giving the bacteria that occur naturally in the lungs a chance to proliferate, leading to pneumonia."

"Is she okay being in the house?"

"Yes. It's highly unlikely that she'd be exposed as long as she stays downstairs." Martin picked up the glass of water from his bedside table and washed down a mouthful of the moisture-wicking toast.

Louisa took her husband's hot hand in hers and brought it to her lips. "I'm sorry you're not feeling well, but I must say, this is nice for me."

"Watching me eat toast?"

Her eyes sparkled as a smile broke out on her face. "No, Martin," she giggled. "Taking care of you!"

"Ah, I see."

"You're not used to that are you ... having someone care for you."

Martin picked up his *BMJ* and focused his gaze back on the polio article.

Louisa pulled the magazine from his hands and laid it behind her. "You're not feeling well, so I'm not asking you to have a heart-to-heart with me. I'm just curious ... besides Joan, did anyone ever care for you?"

Martin screwed up his face and released a heavy sigh. "I *did* have nannies, Louisa."

"Yeah, but do you remember them? Do you remember being cared for?"

"It's a long time ago," he said, rubbing a hand over the back of his neck. "But no, I don't remember. It feels very uncomfortable now ... to have you doing things for me. I'm not used to it."

Louisa got up from the bed and leaned over, kissing him on the cheek. "Well, it may take some time, but I'm afraid it's an adjustment you're just going to have to make."

He watched her as she breezed out of the room, and then he laid his head back and closed his eyes.

Chapter 12

The virus that had taken Martin down had run its course by Monday morning, so he was back to seeing patients as usual, many of them afflicted with the same illness. Therefore, his words, "Drink a lot of fluids, get plenty of rest and call me if you're not better in forty-eight hours," seemed to echo in his head all day.

He never thought he would be happy to see Malcolm Raynor, but when the hypochondriac came through the consulting room door he breathed a sigh of relief. Malcolm walked towards the chair in front of his desk and began to lower himself into the seat.

"Not there ... over there," Martin barked as he snapped his fingers and pointed to his examination couch. He eyed the man briefly, put the earpieces of his stethoscope into his ears, and yanked Malcolm's shirt up, placing the diaphragm on his chest.

"Cough."

The patient managed a feeble hack as the doctor listened to his breath sounds. "Have you seen any improvement in your breathing?"

"No, 'fraid not, Doc. Just the opposite. Last night I thought I was dyin'. Literally saw my life flash before my eyes."

"Don't be ridiculous," Martin grumbled, rolling his eyes.

"I'm serious, Doc. You're gonna have to hit me with the heavy drugs, I'm afraid. In fact, it may already be too la—"

"Be quiet. Your lungs are perfectly clear today." He wagged a finger at the man. "Tuck your shirt back in, then come over and sit down.

"Have you been using the inhaler as I directed?" the doctor asked as he dropped into his chair.

"Just like you said to."

"Good." Martin's biro scratched and tapped away as he added new notes to the patient's file. "And you got rid of your pigeons?"

Malcolm took a seat and studied his hands, folded in his lap. He peered up warily. "I'm gettin' to it."

"What do you mean, you're getting to it? Have you listened to a word I've said? You have a serious illness, Mr. Raynor. Hypersensitivity pneumonitis could very easily result in your death! Is that what you want?"

"Course not, Doc. It's just that ... well, they listen to me. I'm one'a them people that kind'a gets under other people's skin, if you know what I mean."

Martin glanced up, fighting the urge to agree with the man's assessment of himself. He finished writing on the patient card and slipped it back into its sleeve.

"You cannot keep those birds, Mr. Raynor. You're going to have to find another ... listening ear. Get rid of the birds and keep up with the regular use of the inhaler for another month. Come back and see me then. Otherwise, call if you develop any *genuine* breathing difficulties."

He pulled the next patient notes from the pile on his desk and began to pore over them before looking back up. "Why are you still here?"

Malcolm screwed up his face before plodding out to the reception room.

Martin was restocking his medication cupboard when there was a knock on the door. "Come!" he shouted over his shoulder.

Chris Parsons, Martin's boss and mate from medical school, entered the consulting room.

"Looks like you're busy. Do you have time to talk?"

Martin turned quickly at the sound of his friend's voice. "Chris! What brings you here?"

"I had to meet with someone in Wadebridge ... thought I'd kill two birds with one stone."

Looking up from the syringes he was sorting, Martin's brow furrowed. "Should I be worried?"

"No, quite the opposite," Chris said as he dropped into the chair left warm by the hypochondriac. "Thought you'd like to know that the governing board met last night."

"Oh?" Martin shoved the box of syringes on to a cupboard shelf and took a seat behind his desk.

"The subject of your rather unconventional approach with Mr. Westmore two weeks ago was discussed. I have to say Mart, there were a couple of board members who thought we should bring the hammer down on you.

"Fortunately for you, Mr. Westmore—for a reason I can't fathom—seems to idolize you. He dropped by my office yesterday morning with a letter addressed to the board. Let's just say you owe him a bottle of that fancy single malt you like. His letter helped to swing the decision in your favour."

Martin sank back into his chair and breathed out a heavy sigh. This was an issue that he had been trying not to think about, but it had been weighing on him nonetheless.

"I'm happy for you, mate," Chris said, pulling an ankle up on his knee. "I can't say that I wouldn't have done the same thing if I'd been in your position. How *is* Louisa?"

"Her recovery from the embolization seems to be progressing satisfactorily. The fractured clavicle will need a few more weeks to heal, but the AVM repair looks good. I'm sure she'd like to see you ... if you have the time."

"Sure, are you done for the day?"

Martin glanced around his office looking for any loose ends that might need to be tied up. "Erm, yes."

Louisa looked over her shoulder when she heard the men's voices in the hallway. "Well, Chris, this is a nice surprise!"

As far as she knew, Chris Parsons was the only real friend that her husband had. He had been very supportive of Martin when his blood sensitivity first surfaced and was instrumental in getting him the GP position in Portwenn.

He had also supported him when he wanted to try to go back into surgery. Although she was happy that he had chosen to stay in Portwenn, she was glad that Martin had been given the opportunity to make that decision for himself. Chris had been a good friend to him, and for that she was grateful.

"I'm glad to hear you're doing so well, Louisa. A pretty scary week for both of you I would imagine."

"Yes, it was, Chris. But Martin's taken very good care of me, and I'm really feeling about back to normal now, apart from this," she said, wiggling her restricted arm demonstratively. She stepped over next to her husband and wrapped her free arm around his waist.

He looked down at the floor in obvious discomfort with his wife's display of affection. The sudden sound of a wail coming from the baby monitor provided him with an opportunity to excuse himself from the awkward moment. "I'll just—just go—James," he stammered as he turned and walked from the kitchen.

Chris watched his friend disappear around the corner and then smiled, turning his attention back to Louisa.

"Never changes, does he?"

"No, 'fraid not." Louisa gestured towards the table. "Have a seat, Chris."

The chair legs screeched against the slate floor as he pulled it out. "I haven't seen Martin in a while. How's he doing? He looks a bit rough."

"He's been struggling with some personal issues ... not sleeping much, and he's been under a lot of stress."

Chris cocked his head questioningly at Louisa. "Stress ... about what decision the board might come to you mean?"

Louisa looked at him questioningly as she took a seat across from him. "Decision?"

Chris slung his arm across the back of his chair and waved his hand dismissively. "Just work related stuff." He scratched his head. "So ... you were saying?"

Louisa bit her lower lip. "I'm not sure how much I should share with you, Chris. Let's just say that Martin's trying to come to terms with his past."

"Ah. He had it pretty hard as a kid. I always wondered if he wouldn't have to face up to it at some point. In fact, I tried to talk to him about it once, but he insisted that he just didn't dwell on those things. As if ignoring it would make it go away."

Chris had Louisa's attention now. "Has he discussed his childhood with you?" she asked.

"Not in detail, really. Just comments here and there. But I've met his parents. Poor guy couldn't do anything right in their eyes. He was top in our class, and they still couldn't say anything positive about him. He always seemed to be trying so hard to get their approval, but it just wasn't going to happen."

"Oh, where are my manners. Can I get you a cup of tea?" Louisa asked, getting to her feet.

"Just a glass of water, please."

She reached into the cupboard and took out a glass, filling it at the tap. "Martin's pretty reluctant to talk about his childhood ... or his parents for that matter." She set the glass down in front of her husband's friend and returned to her seat.

"I guess that brings us back to ... he never changes," the doctor said with a grin. "Not sure I'd want him to either. Mart's such a good person deep down. Although there aren't many people who'll put forth the effort to get to know him that way. I'm really glad he has you, Louisa. Believe it or not, he's a much happier person since he met you."

Chris sat quietly for a few moments. "Hang in there with him, Louisa. He's worth it."

"I'm not going anywhere, Chris. Not anymore. I'm really quite embarrassed by my behaviour. I was trying to run off to Spain when— Oh, I suppose he told you about that."

Chris gave his head a shake. "No, he didn't mention it."

Louisa traced slow zigzags across the table top with her fingertip as she peered up at him. "I could see he was struggling, and I just didn't know how to help him. If I had actually gone through with it ... taken James and left him ..." Louisa wiped the tears from her cheeks. "I don't think Martin could have handled it. Not the place he's in right now. I was going to do that to him."

Chris nodded his head as he worked his hand around his glass. "The important thing is you didn't actually go to Spain. So, the two of you should leave that in the past and move on. Just don't forget the lessons learned ... right?"

They heard Martin's footsteps on the stairs and the conversation came to a stop.

Martin walked into the kitchen with James in his arms, the pride he felt in his son written on his face.

Chris got up and walked to his friend's side. "Wow, he's really grown since I saw him last. Looks like he's going to take after you, Mart ... big hands already." He took James's fingers between his, stroking his thumb across the back of the boy's hand.

"I never could understand how you got those paws of yours to do the delicate work required of a vascular surgeon."

Martin pulled in his chin. "Mm, yes. Chris, would you like to stay for supper?"

"Thanks, but I think I better get home to my wife. She hasn't seen much of me lately and has started to complain a bit," he said as he headed out of the kitchen. "It was great to see both of you though. Don't be strangers. If you ever find yourself in Truro, look us up."

Martin hurried ahead to get the door. "Ah ... Chris. Thank you for stopping to give me the news. It's a relief to hear it."

"Yeah, it was for me too, mate."

"I really like your friend, Martin," Louisa said after her husband had pushed the door closed.

"Mm, we've known each other a long time."

"Well, he obviously cares about you."

They walked to the kitchen, and Louisa leaned over to put James in his high chair. "What news was it that you were thanking Chris for?" she asked. She turned and took silverware from the drawer, laying it out on the table.

"Erm, I had to take certain measures at the hospital—before your surgery." He reached out to toy with the knife in front of him. "It may have been seen by some as atypical operating theatre etiquette. The governing board looked into what had transpired and decided last night that no actions would be taken against me."

Louisa looked at him quizzically. "Care to elaborate?"

"Not really," Martin said as he studied his shoes.

Louisa folded her arms across her chest and shot him a warning look.

His fingertips tapped on the table as he peered up at her. "I determined that the surgeon who was going to be conducting your procedure wasn't competent. I locked him in a storage cupboard." His fingers flicked the knife slowly back and forth.

Louisa tried to stifle the giggle that was struggling to escape, resulting in a small snort. She clamped her hand over her mouth and turned her back to her husband until she regained her composure, and then walking over to him, she put one arm around his neck and stretched up to kiss him. "Why would a lady need a knight in shining armour when she has a surgeon with a broom cupboard."

"Storage cupboard."

Chapter 13

"He's down for the night," Martin said as he came into the kitchen.

"Thank you, Martin." Louisa turned and leaned back against the counter as she sipped at her cup of tea.

I told you I'd get this when I came down," he said, wagging a finger at the dishes in the drying rack.

Louisa gulped down a mouthful of tea. "I'm not an invalid, Martin. I'm perfectly capable of running some water in the sink and washing off a plate or two."

"And cups. You didn't take your arm from the sling to wash the cups, did you?"

"Oh, Martin, of course not." Louisa huffed out a breath and set her tea on the kitchen table. "I left the silverware for you. It's a little difficult to manage. Hope you don't mind," she said, sliding out a chair and taking a seat.

"No ... no. That's good." Splashing his fingers in the dishwater, he decided it had cooled to the point of needing replacement. He pulled the plug and slipped his suit coat off while he waited for the sink to drain. "What, erm ... did you and Chris talk about earlier?" he asked as he rolled back his shirt sleeves.

Louisa startled, sloshing hot brew down her chin. "Bugger," she mumbled, reaching for a napkin.

Martin whirled around. "What's that?"

"Mm, nothing. I was just trying to remember ... what we talked about." She dabbed at her face before blotting the drips from the front of her jumper.

Silverware clattered into the sink as it began to fill again.

"How was your day?" she asked.

"Tedious. And you?"

"Oh, James and I muddled along without you."

Martin looked over his shoulder. "Is it too difficult for you ... without anyone to help you out with James I mean? I could line someone up."

She gave him a soft smile. "I'm managing just fine, Martin. What I meant is, we missed you. Especially when we'd just had the pleasure of your company over the weekend."

"Really?"

"Yes, really."

"Mm" he grunted before returning his attention to the silverware.

Louisa watched his broad back as he worked. Clouds of steam rose up from his hands and arms as he dropped the forks, spoons, and knives into the rack to dry. She'd never been able to understand how he could tolerate the piping hot water that he insisted on using when he did the washing up.

The draining of the sink and the almost ceremonial folding of the tea towel signalled the completion of the task.

"Want to go relax on the sofa with me?" Louisa asked as he turned to face her.

A pink flush spread up his neck, and he stood motionless. "Erm, I have some reading that I need to get done."

"Good, me too." She got up from the table and moved into the lounge, her husband following after her.

They spent the next half hour with Louisa lying with a novel in hand and her head in his lap as he caught up on the latest medical developments. She glanced up at him surreptitiously now and then, hoping for some sign that his interest in his medical journal might be flagging.

She rolled to her side. Rubbing his knee, she asked, "Martin, do you think you might talk with Dr. Newell about the nightmares you've been having? I think it'd be a good idea."

"It's likely just stress, Louisa."

"But if it's more than that ... don't you think it would be good for Dr. Newell to know about it?"

She rolled on to her back again and looked up at him. "Will you please talk to him ... for me?"

Several seconds passed before he looked down at her. "I will if you want me to."

He was rewarded with a warm smile. "Thank you, Martin."

He hesitated. "You, er ... didn't answer my question earlier. What were you discussing with Chris? Were you—were you talking about me, Louisa?"

Louisa dropped her book on to her stomach and reached up, brushing her fingers against his cheek. "Chris was concerned about you. I think he noticed you'd lost weight."

Air hissed from Martin's nose as his brow furrowed. "What did you tell him?"

"Just that you were trying to come to terms with your past. He did most of the talking."

"Oh, *that* puts my mind at ease. Louisa, Chris is my boss. I don't want you discussing my private life with him."

She swung her legs to the floor and sat herself up. "He's also your friend, Martin. He cares about you, and he was concerned." Leaning forward, she laid her book on the coffee table. "I'm sorry, though. I shouldn't have said anything about it. I should've told him to discuss it with you."

She tugged the *BMJ* from his hands. "Will you go upstairs with me?"

"Are you tired already?"

"Martin, don't be obtuse," she whispered suggestively as she began to undo the buttons on his shirt.

"Louisa, we shouldn't ... your fractured clavicle."

"I think we can work around that, Martin," she said as his tie was pulled from around his neck.

"Louisa, please don't. I just ... I'm not in the right frame of mind."

"Hmm, let's see if I can do something about that then." She slipped a hand under his vest and began to caress his chest.

He pushed her away, creating a barrier with his arm. "Louisa, I said no!"

Tears welled up in her eyes, and he grasped for some way to justify his reaction, or more correctly perhaps, his lack thereof. But how was he to explain what he himself didn't understand?

He softened his tone. "Louisa, not now. And please, don't take it the wrong way. It's just ..." He breathed out a resigned sigh. "Not now."

"All right, Martin. But haven't you been missing me in that way at all? Missing us being intimate?"

His expression was resolute as he looked back at her.

"Forget it then, Martin."

He watched as she disappeared up the stairs, her ponytail swinging angrily behind her. Then closing his eyes, he slumped back against the sofa.

As he drove along the A-39 on Wednesday, Martin was regretting that he had told Louisa he would talk to Dr. Newell about the nightmares which had been plaguing him.

They had been different lately. His earlier nightmares had been clear and focused recalls of childhood memories. Not pleasant memories, just a replay of memories he had always lived with. The recent nightmares had been taunting, giving him glimpses of the whole story. It was the ambiguity about them that made him uncomfortable.

Dr. Newell wasted no time in bringing up the discussion that had transpired on Friday, or the effect it may have had on him later, asking about how he had felt that night.

Martin sat rigidly in his chair, trying to avoid eye contact with the man. "I came down with a virus, so I didn't sleep well," he said with tetchiness in his voice.

"I'm sorry to hear that. Better now I hope?"

"Yes, it had run its course by Monday morning."

"Martin, I suspect from what you've said in the little time we've had together that your relationship with your parents has been difficult. I'd like to explore that a bit more. Your mother was here for a visit recently. It evidently didn't go well. Do you remember a time when you got on better with her?"

"No. She never really had much to do with me. I had nannies for the first years of my life, and then I was sent to boarding school. I didn't really see much of her. Like I said on Friday, she never wanted children, so naturally she spent as little time with me as possible."

"What approach did your parents have to discipline?"

Dr. Newell watched as his patient grasped for an answer before coming to his aid. "Maybe compare the disciplinary methods that your parents used with you to how you intend to discipline your own son."

Martin tried to swallow the lump that had formed in his throat. "Louisa and I love James very much, and any disciplinary measures we take will come from that love for him, not from anger or hatred."

"And how did the discipline that you received differ? Can you remember any specific incidents from your childhood?"

Martin stood up and walked to the window. "I was remembering recently, a time when I had ignored my grandfather's admonitions and picked up a valuable pocket watch so that I could look at it. I was curious when I was young and I couldn't resist. My father caught me with it in my hand. He had a loud voice, and when he yelled at me, I was startled and dropped the watch. It broke. My grandfather forgave me, but my father was furious ... dragged me to the shed by my collar and ... and he used his belt." He spun around, looking at Dr. Newell with fury on his face. "I will *never* lay an angry hand on *my* son!"

The psychiatrist leaned back in his chair, rolling his fountain pen between his fingers. "How do you think your father's approach to discipline affected how you look at yourself?"

Martin stood motionless, staring at the doctor.

"Martin?"

Dr. Newell watched him closely. Seconds passed before the man spoke again. "Martin, are you with me?"

Martin moved back to his chair and dropped stiffly into it. "I'm sorry. I didn't hear the question."

"I was wondering if you think your father's approach to discipline affected how you see yourself. Do you think it had a negative effect on you?"

Martin closed his eyes briefly and tried to shake a strange fogginess from his head. "I, er ... I can be fearful of making mistakes I suppose. The thought of making a mistake causes me a lot of anxiety. I worry about whether I'll be judged fairly ... if I'm going to be seen as being at fault whether I am or not."

"What about your mother? Did she handle any of the discipline?"

Martin sat, his hands clutching his knees. "Yes, but her methods were different."

"Different in what way."

He huffed out a breath and rubbed a hand roughly over the back of his neck. "Having things taken away ... and what people now refer to as time outs."

"The things that were taken away ... tell me about that."

"Favourite toys ... treasures. Gifts that I'd been given."

"Gifts that had personal significance you mean?"

"No. Gifts that I hadn't yet opened. Birthdays ... Christmas."

"And the time outs? She would sit you down on a chair for a period of time? For how long?"

Martin stood up and walked back to the window. "There was a cupboard under the stairs. That's where I spent time outs. The length of time varied. I don't really know how long, exactly. I suppose maybe ..." Martin screwed up his face and huffed out a breath. "Does it really matter? I may not be remembering things accurately."

"I'm just trying to get a clearer picture of how you remember your childhood, Martin. There are really no *right* answers."

Martin tugged at his ear as he thought through the psychiatrist's question. "I know that it was long enough at times that I might have missed a meal ... or it may have grown dark, or the nanny had gone home for the day."

"And what prompted the time outs? What sort of infractions?"

"Sometimes I think I wasn't listening ... paying attention. Or I was getting underfoot. But most frequently ... I wet the bed a lot." Martin rubbed at his palm with his thumb.

Dr. Newell sat for a moment, his jaws clenched as he imagined a small boy, locked up for an offense beyond his control, with no access to a toilet for hours at a time. He nodded his head in understanding as he erected an imaginary veil between his patient and himself, a tactic that proved effective in keeping his professional composure when emotions threatened to get the better of him. "Do you think the punishments fit the crimes, so to speak?" the therapist asked as he rocked back, his chair squeaking in protest.

"I think I could be a troublesome child, and the punishments were probably deserved. I tended to get absorbed in things ... books, projects, exploring outside. Those were the times when I would forget about the rules."

"And do you think your misdeeds justified the punishments that you received?"

Martin furrowed his brow as he stared at the floor. "I'm not sure."

"Martin, I think it might be helpful if you could take yourself out of the picture. Over the next week, I'd like for you to imagine these disciplinary measures being meted out, but I want you to put your son in your place ... imagine him as the one being punished. Think about how fair or unfair the discipline seems to be.

"Then, I want you to imagine yourself as the disciplinarian. Would the same punishment seem fair or unfair to your son?"

Dr. Newell cleared his throat as he pulled himself back up to his desk. "I need to be very clear with you about what you can expect with our upcoming sessions.

"You'll likely be confronted with some very disturbing memories from your past, and those memories can trigger very strong reactions. That's to be expected. I don't want you to feel you need to apologise for those reactions or to be embarrassed by them."

Martin squirmed in his chair. "Are you sure this is all necessary? Maybe we're trying to fix something that doesn't need fixing ... doing more harm than good in the end."

"I do think this is necessary, and I think you know it's necessary as well," the therapist said as he came around to sit on his desktop. "Martin, I'm sure that as a surgeon you've heard patients cry out in pain. I know you wouldn't think less of them for that reaction. You should be as generous with yourself if you experience strong reactions as we work through all of this.

"I also want to caution you that you need to keep this in mind when you get in your car to drive home. If you're feeling shaky, let me know, and we'll find another way to get you back to Portwenn. I gave you an assignment for this week. I want you to wait until you're safely at home before doing this. Maybe find a quiet room in the house where you can be alone."

Dr. Newell got up and moved towards the door. "You did very well today."

Martin shook his head. "It didn't really seem like a lot of progress was made."

"Work through that exercise this week, and we'll talk about it at our next session. The progress is there, but you may not be able to see it over the course of a single session. Give the process a couple of months, then look back at where you started. I'll see you and Louisa in a couple of days."

Martin hurried out to his car. He found himself feeling exposed and vulnerable and in need of the comfort he felt with his wife and son.

Chapter 14

When Louisa heard the jingling of Martin's keys, she picked James up from his high chair and hurried to meet him at the door. He looked tired but happy to see them.

James reached his arms out to his father, babbling his excitement over their reunion. Martin took the baby's hand in his and caressed the back of it with his thumb before brushing his fingers up the boy's cheek.

"How are you?" he asked as his gaze met his wife's.

"I'm good. Missed you though. How was the trip ... the traffic?"

"It was fine." He tipped his head down and pressed his lips to her head, releasing a slow breath and some of his stress along with it. "I'm, ah ... going to go wash up."

"All right, dinner will be ready in a few minutes."

Louisa watched her husband as he walked away from her, his tall frame and broad back hiding the fragile little boy inside. She was relieved that he seemed comfortable with Dr. Newell. Maybe it was his desperation to save their marriage, but he had been as open with the therapist as she had ever seen him.

She feared he may never again be so open with her though. Trust can be so easily lost, and once it is, so difficult, if not impossible, to find again.

Martin sat down on the edge of the bed, kicking off his shoes and peeling off his socks. He stared across the hall into the nursery, remembering that afternoon at his grandfather's house. He tried to picture a seven-year-old James, reaching for his grandfather's pocket watch, mesmerised by its perfect intricacy. The soft ticking being abruptly displaced by the roar of his father's angry voice and the sensation of his heart skipping a beat before racing to catch back up again.

He visualised the watch falling through the air while a young James stood helpless, watching as it hit the floor. He saw the fear on his son's face as his father approached and the shame as his grandfather entered the room.

Martin could not, however, bring himself to finish the task assigned by Dr. Newell. His subconscious would not allow his father's angry hand to hit his son.

He sucked in a deep breath and blinked hard before brushing at a tickle on his cheek. "Gawd," he breathed out as he hurriedly wiped the tears away.

"Martin! Are you almost done up there? Dinner's getting cold!" Louisa called up the stairs.

He cleared his throat. "Yep! I'll be right down!" He went to the bathroom and splashed cold water on his face, trying to erase the disturbing images from his head. Then he trudged back down the stairs to join his wife and son.

Dinner was eaten in relative silence, before Martin and Louisa did the washing up together, their conversation dancing around the subject of Martin's therapy session.

Later that evening, James played contentedly on the floor while his father wrote on patient notes. Martin glanced over at him periodically, his gaze unfocused. Louisa heard him release a soft sigh, before he went over and gathered the boy into his arms.

"I thought we'd take a short walk before bedtime."

She smiled up at him from the sofa. "That sounds nice. Let me grab a jumper."

Martin cleared his throat uncomfortably. "Mm, yes."

"You know, on second thought, I think I'll sit this one out," Louisa said, realising she had falsely assumed an invitation had been extended and hurried to cover her faux pas. "I really should finish this marking. Then I'll run James's bath so it's ready when you get back. That okay with you two?"

"That's fine. We won't be long," Martin replied.

He tucked James inside his suit coat and walked up the hill to the coastal path. Dusk was beginning to fall on the village. It was that lovely time of day when the blue sky is muted with grey, and the daytime songbirds have quieted, exiting the stage to allow the night-time creatures to make their entrance.

Martin found the bench that he and Louisa had shared many times, sitting down with his baby son. It was peaceful with James, listening to the rhythmic sound of the waves lapping at the rocks below.

The boy's warm, moist, breath brushed against his neck. His parents never could have appreciated a moment like this when he was James's age. They couldn't share the same sense of peace and wonder in being close to him ... *their* son.

There must be something different about him ... wrong with him. Something that, if there, would have allowed his parents to feel affection for him. Perhaps a genetic mutation, a missing bit of DNA. This question had haunted him. He hoped that Dr. Newell would finally be able to answer it.

He hugged James closer to him and kissed the top of his fuzzy head before getting to his feet to walk back down the hill to the surgery. He stopped before opening the door and looked down at the perfect little boy in his arms. The child's blonde hair fluttered under his father's whispered words. "I love you very much James Henry, and I couldn't be more proud to be your father."

Martin groaned internally as he was preparing for bed that night, realising that he had neglected to raise the issue of his sleep difficulties with Dr. Newell. Louisa had asked him to do so, and he had forgotten. He'd always prided himself on his ability to retain information and to multi-task. The fact that he let this slip his mind worried him. He should have remembered.

After he crawled in under the blankets, he turned to Louisa. "I, erm ... forgot to mention the nightmares to Dr. Newell today. I'll tell him when we go for our session on Friday."

Louisa fought back her knee-jerk reaction to chastise. "I think that should be fine. Nothing's likely to change between now and then, is it?"

"I wouldn't think so."

She leaned over and kissed him on the cheek. "Goodnight, Martin."

"Mm, yes."

Louisa lay awake, thinking about how she had reacted to her husband moments before. Had she become like her mother, the constantly nagging wife, so quick to criticise? They would both have some things to discuss with Dr. Newell on Friday.

Thursday brought an assortment of patients and maladies to the surgery. Martin was still eating his breakfast when he was interrupted by the sound of banging on the front door. A fisherman had slipped on the deck of his boat, landing on a grappling hook.

He immediately lost the little breakfast he'd had a chance to get down when he peeled away the man's clothes, exposing the bloody wound in his left buttock. He treated the man's injury, jabbed him for tetanus, and sent him away with the fisherman who had brought him to the surgery.

The first patient was followed by a woman with strep throat, a child who had crammed a small bit of crayon in his nose, and an elderly man with the most disgusting case of nail fungus that Martin had ever seen.

By late afternoon, he had been vomited on twice by sick children and had found *himself* spewing into the bin several times while trying to treat an assortment of grisly wounds. It had been an exhausting day.

His last patient was Jim Hanley's boy, Evan. The seven-year-old was presenting with a persistent, rattly cough. Martin pulled off the child's jumper and vest before pressing his stethoscope to his chest.

Glancing down, he noticed bruising on his patient's wrist. When he reached for the boy's arm, he flinched visibly before pulling away. Martin returned his attention to the primary complaint, noting the distinct wheeze on exhalation.

Picking the patient notes up from his desk, the doctor quickly reviewed the child's history before turning to Mrs. Hanley. "Has your son ever been treated for asthma?"

"No. Don't think so. He never stops coughin' though," the woman said. "Just a habit. It's bloody annoyin'. Been tryin' to break 'im of it."

Martin gave her a scowl. "Children don't cough to entertain themselves, Mrs. Hanley. I suspect Evan's asthmatic. And I think at the moment his asthma's being exacerbated by a touch of pneumonia. I'll write you out a prescription. Mrs. Tishell can fill it for you. Make sure you continue to give it to him until it's used up. Don't discontinue it just because his symptoms have cleared."

Mrs. Hanley folded her arms across her chest. "Maybe we could just wait a few days ... see if it clears up on its own, ya know? Don't wanna waste the money on the boy if he don't really need it."

"No! I wouldn't be writing a prescription if I thought it would *clear up on its own!*" Martin hissed out a breath and walked to his desk before scribbling on to his prescription pad. "Take this to Mrs. Tishell," he said. "Tell her to put it on my personal account."

He shoved the sheet of paper towards the woman. "I'm also going to get you set up with a nebulizer. It'll help to reduce the inflammation as well as the constriction in your son's airways. Wait here, please."

Martin walked briskly out to the reception area and waited as his receptionist finished up with a phone call.

"Whatcha need, Doc?" she asked as she laid down the receiver.

"Morwenna, get a nebulizer together for Evan Hanley. I think we have a spare in the storage cupboard. I'll send Mrs. Hanley out, and I want you to show her how to operate the machine."

"Aren't they s'posed ta go to the chemist for those? Mrs. Tishell usually—"

"Just do it, Morwenna!" Martin snapped as he spun on his heel.

The receptionist threw the retreating doctor an annoyed look. "Whatever you say."

Martin ducked through the doorway as he returned to the consulting room. "Mrs. Hanley, please go out and see my receptionist. She'll show you how to use the nebulizer. I'll finish up here with your son."

Mrs. Hanley left the room, and Martin closed the door behind her. He turned his attention back to the child on the couch, picking up his vest and pulling it back over his head. "Evan, I'd like to take a closer look at that wrist of yours."

The boy eyed him warily before hesitantly extending his arm.

The doctor gently palpated the injured wrist and hand, determining that there were no fractures. He looked at the boy's face, his eyes softening. "Can you tell me what happened there?"

Evan sat on the end of the exam couch, his feet swinging nervously back and forth. His gaze met Martin's before he averted his eyes. "I fell. I was running, and I fell."

"Hmm, that doesn't look like the kind of bruising I would expect from a fall. Are you sure that's the way it happened?"

The boy nodded his head, trying to avoid eye contact with the doctor.

"Evan, if you're hurt like this again, I want you to tell one of your teachers at the school. Better yet, go right to Mrs. Ellingham. You can of course call me or come to see me anytime, but it might be more convenient for you to see Mrs. Ellingham. She can let me know if you need my assistance."

Martin leaned down so that he could make eye contact with the child. "All right?"

Evan nodded his head, and Martin gave him a rare Dr. Ellingham smile.

"Okay, down you get then." Martin hoisted the boy on to the floor just as Mrs. Hanley came back into the room.

He handed the woman her son's jumper and walked with them out to the reception area.

As he watched the young boy leave the surgery, a feeling of nausea and dizziness descended on him. He walked briskly back to his consulting room, closing the door behind him. Then he grabbed the bin and vomited for the fourth time that day.

Chapter 15

Martin and Louisa sat looking across the desk at Dr. Newell. The man smiled broadly at them as he made small talk before addressing the serious matter of their precarious union.

"I asked you last week to tell me what you felt were some strengths and weaknesses in your marriage. I'd like to start this session by discussing what each of you thinks you bring to the relationship. Think in terms of how you build the other up. For instance, Louisa, in what ways do you encourage Martin in areas where he excels and where he perhaps struggles a bit more?"

"Hmm, I'm not sure that Martin needs a lot of encouragement in the areas where he excels. He's the finest doctor I've ever known and is very well respected by his peers. He has a reputation as having been one of the best vascular surgeons in the country." She glanced up at her husband, giving him a reserved smile. "I guess when I've had the opportunity to witness him saving lives, I've told him how brilliant I think he is. Extraordinary, really."

"And other areas where he excels?"

"He's very good at repairing clocks. He just finished restoring his grandfather's old clock."

"And how do you encourage him with his hobby?" Turning to Martin, he quickly added, "I'm making an assumption that with a busy medical practice you don't have time for a second career fixing clocks. So, you would consider this a hobby?"

"Mm, yes." Martin pulled in his chin and picked a piece of lint from his trousers.

Dr. Newell looked back at Louisa. "Pardon the interruption. Please, go ahead."

"Well, I don't really know that I can ... or *do* encourage him. He usually works on his clocks in his office, so I don't see him while he's involved with them."

The therapist leaned forward on his desk, folding his hands in front of him. "Keep in mind that there are many ways that you and Martin can encourage one another. It can be as simple as showing an interest in what the other enjoys. Martin, if it's important to Louisa then it should be important to you ... and vice versa, of course."

Louisa picked at a fingernail as she remembered the morning shortly after their wedding when she had popped her head in the door of Martin's consulting room. He had invited her to come in so that he could explain to her about the damaged clock part that he was repairing. Looking back on it, she realised she had let an opportunity to encourage him slip by. She had quietly left the room as he was explaining the mechanics of the clock to her, no doubt sending the message that she didn't care.

Dr. Newell swivelled his chair to the left.

"How do you feel, Martin, when Louisa tells you she thinks you're a brilliant, even extraordinary doctor?"

"I'm not sure." He squirmed uncomfortably under his wife's gaze, focusing his eyes on the bookshelves behind the therapist. "I know that I'm a competent GP and I used to be a competent surgeon. But I never felt pride in being *competent*. It's what I would expect of any doctor or surgeon."

"Is there anything that Louisa does or says that makes you feel special. Like you matter to her in a way that no one else does?"

Martin glanced over at his wife, redirecting his eyes to the floor as a flash of heat travelled up his neck. "When she smiles at me. She has a particular smile that makes me think I matter to her."

"And how do you make Louisa a stronger person? Make her better, more well rounded?"

Martin sat silent for an awkwardly long period of time, looking more and more flustered as the seconds ticked by. He shook his head and mumbled something unintelligible.

The therapist cocked his head. "I'm sorry, Martin, I didn't catch that."

He screwed up his face. "Louisa's perfect the way she is. I don't know *how* I could make her better."

Louisa tipped her head down self-consciously as she struggled to contain a smile.

"Do you know that Martin feels that way about you, Louisa?" Dr. Newell asked.

"Yes, I think I do. But he's never actually said it." Her ponytail flicked as she whipped her head around. "And Martin, sometimes you say such hurtful things that I forget you really think of me that way." She twisted her purse strap in her hand as her brow lowered and her eyes softened. "Or I choose to forget so I can feel angry with you for your unkind words, I'm not sure."

The therapist sat for a few moments, allowing time for Louisa to sit with her last thought. Then he came around and perched himself on the corner of the desktop.

"Martin, why do you think it is that you don't tell Louisa how you feel about her?"

"She *knows*. She just said she knows. Why should I trot out sentimental drivel if she already knows how I feel?" He scowled and slouched down in his chair.

Dr. Newell drummed his fingers on the edge of the desk. "Why do you think people, as Martin so eloquently puts it, trot out sentimental drivel, Louisa? In what way would it strengthen your marriage if Martin were to verbalise his feelings for you?"

"It would reassure me that I haven't misinterpreted your actions, Martin. I wouldn't have to make assumptions, *which* you said last week are the cause of many of our misunderstandings." Her ponytail flicked again.

Martin gave a sideways glance at her fingers as they drummed against the armrests of her chair, clicking out a petulant rif.

She huffed out a breath and brushed the hair from her face. "And I'd know that you haven't changed your view of me over time. And it—it would just be very, very, nice to hear it, Martin. It would make me happy."

Martin looked at her, wide-eyed.

"Can you see the logic in that, Martin?" Dr. Newell asked, lowering his head and staring pointedly at him.

He pulled in his chin. "Yes, it doesn't seem too difficult."

A wisp of a smile crept across the psychiatrist's face. Glancing at his watch, he returned to his chair. "Next week, I'd like to take some time to talk about the ways that each of you helps the other with their weaknesses. We all have them." He tapped his biro on the pad in front of him and shifted his gaze between his patients. "Any further questions or comments from either of you?"

Louisa elbowed her husband. "Martin ..."

"Yes, I know," he hissed before breathing out a resigned sigh. "It's likely just stress, but I've been having some difficulty sleeping—dreams ... nightmares actually. But as I told Louisa, it's likely stress."

"Could be." The therapist tipped his head back and peered down at him. "Are they keeping you from getting a good night's sleep?"

Louisa nodded vigorously. "It's been a very long time since Martin's had a good night's sleep. I'm really beginning to worry about him. He looks so tired and he's been—"

"I'm fine, Louisa," he snapped, throwing an irritated glance her way.

"Martin, let's make sure this is the first item of business at your appointment on Wednesday. It might be nothing more than a disruption in your sleep pattern which a sleep aid would remedy. But I don't want to prescribe anything until I'm sure that's all there is to it."

Dr. Newell stood and stretched his back. "Anything else?"

The couple looked at one another, shaking their heads.

"All right, I'll see you on Wednesday, Martin."

Martin glanced over at his wife as they walked out of the building. He hesitantly slipped his hand into hers before veering suddenly, leading her into a small copse of trees near the office. He gazed at her, swallowing to ease the constriction in his throat. "Louisa, you *are* perfection," he said hoarsely. "You always will be. I'll try to remember to say it more often."

He brushed a wisp of hair from her face before taking her chin in his hand and pressing his lips to hers.

Chapter 16

Louisa watched her husband as he manoeuvered the car through the streets of Truro. "Martin, I was thinking about the time you tried to show me your clock." She reached out and caressed his thigh. "I'm sorry."

His head tipped to the side. "About what?"

"About walking off. Not showing an interest. It was unkind."

"It's fine. It's really not that interesting to someone who doesn't enjoy clocks. I can understand why you might have found it tiresome," Martin said.

"It wasn't that I found it tiresome. I was just upset that ..." She let out a small groan. "It seems so silly now when I look back on it ... verbalise it, but I was annoyed with you for picking at my usage of the word anniversary instead of listening to what I was trying to say."

"I didn't understand why our having been married for two weeks was significant, Louisa. I don't know what you expected me to say. And I thought you'd like to know that, strictly speaking, two weeks is not an anniversary. The word comes from the Latin word *anni* which means year, so—"

"Yes, Martin, I know!" Louisa let out a huff of air as her shoulders fell. "None of the anniversary stuff is important."

Martin turned and gave her a look of incredulity. "You *acted* as though it was important."

She gave her head a shake and took in a breath. "I'm *trying* to say I'm sorry, and I wish I had handled things differently that night. I missed out on a chance to have you share something with me. I threw away something very special, and I'm sorry."

"Mm." Martin always thought himself to be a rather boring person, and he was quite accustomed to having people walk away as he was talking to them. His dull hobby would likely be another thing for her to add to his crap column.

She gave him a coy grin. "I kinda' had an ulterior motive when I came in that night, you know."

"Oh?"

"Martin ... think about it. What do you think I might have been hoping for?"

His eyes flitted nervously before he finally sussed out what she was saying. "Oh, I see."

She reached up and traced her finger around his ear. "I hope you'll try showing me again sometime."

Louisa watched him squirm and waited for the charming flush of pink that she knew would spread up his neck and to his cheeks. She turned to look out her side window, lest he see her satisfied smile.

"Erm, would you like to stop and get something to eat?" he said, clearing his throat. "I know of a couple of restaurants here that pass basic hygiene standards."

"That sounds lovely, Martin. Wherever you like is fine with me."

Martin parked the Lexus in front of a charming little bistro on Lemon Street. The interior was bathed in the early evening sunshine coming through the windows. Brightly coloured tablecloths adorned the tables, and small vases of white lilies sat in the centre of each one, waiting patiently for someone to sit and partake of their fragrance.

They placed their orders and sat for some moments in uncomfortable silence before Martin spoke. "I had a patient in my office yesterday, a young boy. I was examining him for an unrelated medical issue, and I noticed some suspicious bruises.

He wouldn't give me a straight answer when I questioned him about the injury and—"

"You suspect *abuse*? One of *my* kids?"

"Mm." Martin ran his finger around the rim of his glass. "I can't discuss my patients, but I told the boy to let you know if he suffered similar injuries again. That you'd inform me if he needed my assistance. I just wanted you to be aware."

"Thank you, Martin. I'll call you right away if he should come in to see me."

"I'll plan on making some home visits during the summer holiday, just to keep an eye on things."

Louisa pulled his hand away from his glass, holding on to it tightly.

"You *are* a very good and dedicated doctor, Martin. I wish the people in the village had a greater appreciation for all that you do for them."

Martin fumbled with his napkin. "I'd be happy if they followed my instructions now and then."

"Well, yes." Louisa peered up at him. "This is very nice ... just the two of us. Almost like a date, isn't it?"

"Mm, yes. Yes, it is."

They ate a leisurely dinner, losing track of time as Louisa chatted and Martin watched her, nodding occasionally. By the time they left the restaurant and had made it out of the city, the weekend traffic had hit its peak, slowing the trip considerably.

When they arrived back at the surgery, Ruth had already put James to bed. She politely declined an invitation to stay for tea, hurrying out the door to meet up with Al to discuss the details of their budding venture.

As they lay in bed that evening, Martin broached the subject of their childminder situation. They had exhausted Portwenn's supply of nannies in less than one year's time, most scared off by Martin's surly nature or dismissed by him for failure to meet his rigorous standards. The last childminder, though, was lost to the British Army after he surrendered himself for being AWOL. "You know, Louisa, we still need to find a replacement for Michael."

"Oh, Martin," she groaned. "I'm too tired to have this discussion tonight. Can we talk about it in the morning?"

Martin rubbed a palm over his forehead. "Yes, but we can't put it off any longer. The summer holiday will come and go, and we'll be in the same unworkable situation that we were in before. We need to get it sorted. Maybe we should each get some names together, a list of resources before we sit down to discuss it."

"Yes, yes, *yes*. Now, I'm tired. Can we please go to sleep?"

"Mm, yes. Goodnight."

"Goodnight, Martin."

Martin sat at his desk the next morning, reviewing records and sipping at an espresso as he tried not to nod off. "Next patient!" he yelled out.

Adrianne Flinn, the mother of the temp who had filled in during his former receptionist, Pauline's, absence a couple of years ago, walked through the door, limping noticeably.

"What seems to be the problem, Mrs. Flinn?"

"I twisted my ankle, Doc. My foot slipped off a rock when we were walking on the beach ... turned it to the side. It's probably nothin', but it's not gettin' any better, so I thought I better stop in ta see you."

"Take a seat on the couch, and I'll have a look."

Martin snapped on a pair of exam gloves before pulling off the woman's shoe and sock. He gently flexed her foot up and down and side to side. She grimaced and pulled away from him.

"Hmm, you have a significant amount of oedema and bruising in your foot and ankle, but as you seem to be able to bear weight, it could just be a severe sprain. I'm going to order an x-ray just to be sure. Based on the description of how your injury occurred, I'd like to rule out a Jones fracture."

"Jones fracture? What's that, Doc?"

"A fracture of the fifth metatarsal, the bone on the outer edge of your foot. It's in an area with very little blood supply, making it likely that the fracture won't heal on its own. Surgery is usually done, putting in a screw to pull the ends of the bones together so that a proper union is formed."

The woman cast a worried glance at him and he added, "But again, it could be a bad sprain that will heal with time and rest. We'll see what the x-rays show. Until then, stay off that foot and keep it elevated. And you shouldn't be driving with your foot like that," he said. "Do you have someone who can take you to Truro?" He handed the woman her shoe and sock before peeling off his gloves, binning them, and returning to his chair behind his desk.

"My daughter can get me over there."

"Good."

Martin's biro scratched away as he jotted notes on to the card in front of him.

"You remember my Poppy, don't you, Doc?" Adrianne asked as she eased her sock back on over her swollen foot.

He glanced up and scowled at her. "I could care less about your poppies, Mrs. Flinn. You need to stay off that foot. Your flowers will have to fend for themselves until you're fit enough to be up and about again."

Adrianne cocked her head at him. "My *girl*, Poppy."

The doctor pulled down his brow and shook his head. "What about her?"

"She can drive me to Truro. You remember Poppy, don't you? She filled in for Pauline some time back."

"Mm. Blonde, weedy girl? Likes to serve tea?"

"Yes, that's her!" Mrs. Flinn answered, smiling broadly. "She's home for a while. Been lookin' for a job you know, but not havin' much luck."

Martin glanced up quickly from the radiology request he was filling out. "Has she done any childminding?"

"Has she! Just about every weekend when she was a teenager. Loves the little'uns."

Martin handed the woman the request form. "All right, Mrs. Flinn. Take this to hospital with you. Make sure you tell them to forward the x-rays on to me. And keep that foot up ... ice it for ten minutes every one to two hours."

Martin was relieved to have his Saturday morning over and done with. The Ellinghams were sitting down to lunch when Ruth knocked on the door.

Knocking was a courtesy never afforded Martin by Auntie Joan. He thought about the many times he bit his tongue with Joan. He was tempted on occasion to bark at her to knock before entering, but he neither wanted to risk hurting the feelings of the one nurturing soul in his life nor echo his father.

A heaviness settled in his chest whenever he thought of Joan ... the absence of her. He missed her sudden entrances and her greetings. "*Only me!*" singsonged in his head. His wife's voice nudged him from his reverie.

"Martin?"

He turned his head, and her visage brought him back to the present.

"I'm sorry. Did you say something?"

Louisa cocked her head at him. "Aren't you going to say hello?" She furrowed her brow, and her gaze intensified. "Ruth's here."

He turned his head away as he wiped at the tears which stung his eyes before gesturing to his aunt. "Yes, hello. Have a seat."

"I don't mean to interrupt your weekend. I just wanted to see how everyone was getting on over here."

Martin and Louisa exchanged glances as Ruth pulled out a chair, recognising the woman's thinly veiled attempt to obtain information about their therapy sessions.

"We're fine, Ruth," Martin said, refusing to bite on the elderly woman's bait. "We need to be lining up a childminder, so that's the first order of business for the afternoon." He stared at her as he crunched on a raw carrot. "We're open to suggestions."

Ruth dropped her head and peered up at him. "Do you *really* think that I'd have anything to contribute to the matter?"

Martin grunted and raised an eyebrow as he picked up his water glass. "I had Mrs. Flinn in my surgery this morning. She mentioned that her daughter is looking for a job—Penelope."

Louisa's face brightened. "Poppy!"

"Mm, yes. Poppy. She seemed reasonably adequate as a temporary receptionist when she filled in for Pauline several years ago, and her mother says she's done a good deal of childminding." He glanced warily at his wife, adding, "I'm not saying you should call her. I'm just passing on information. You do with it as you like."

"Oh, Martin! She would be *perfect* for James. She's such a sweet girl ... and quite intelligent. Very tidy as well, which you'd appreciate. Did you ask her mother if she might be interested?"

"No, I didn't want you to—erm—no. I thought you might like to give it some thought before contacting her." Martin had stepped over that precarious boundary between showing sufficient interest and taking control before. He didn't want to incur his wife's wrath again.

"I'll call her. I'll call her this afternoon." Louisa gave Martin one of her smiles that made him feel as if he mattered and then leaned forward and gave him a lingering kiss on his cheek.

He dipped his head as he caught his aunt's wry smile.

Chapter 17

Louisa reached Poppy that afternoon. The girl sounded interested in the job as their childminder, but Louisa detected a bit of hesitancy in her voice, no doubt due to her previous experiences with Martin.

She made arrangements with the young woman to meet for lunch on Monday to talk things over, and Louisa was hopeful that she could convince her that her husband's fearsome reputation had been exaggerated.

"Martin, do you think I could join your boys' club for the walk tonight?" Louisa asked as they sat relaxing after supper.

Martin cocked his head. "The boys' club?"

"You and James. The two of you have gone for a walk the past three nights. But if you're wanting to ... you know ... just the two of you, that's fine. I quite like that you have your special time together."

"Mm, I see. I can discuss it with James and get back to you," he said, keeping his eyes fixed on his *BMJ*. When he finished the article he was reading, he laid the magazine aside and got up from the sofa, bending his tall frame to pick up his son. "James, your mother says she'd like to join us tonight. What do you think? Should we let her come along?"

The baby babbled back at the sound of his father's voice, and Martin reached out to take Louisa's hand. "Best get your jumper. It's a chilly evening."

They walked to the top of the hill together, hand in hand. After looking out over the little village for a few moments, Martin gestured to the wooden bench near the path.

"This is nice," Louisa said as she pressed herself up against him.

Martin pulled his arm up around her shoulders and filled his lungs with fresh salt air. The comforting weight of his son on his lap and his wife's warmth nestled up against his side began to loosen his tongue. "Dr. Newell talked with me the other day about my parents ... about their disciplinary methods."

"Oh?" Louisa rested her hand on his arm.

"He asked me to think about memories I have of punishments and to try to picture James in my place."

"James?" She leaned over, placing a kiss on the boy's head.

"Yes, he thought that by removing myself from the situation I might find it easier to be objective when deciding if the punishments were fair or not." His wife's hand tightened around his arm. He quieted as he watched the waves wash into the harbour, pausing briefly to dance with the little fishing boats bobbing on their moorings before retreating back out to the open sea.

Louisa brushed her fingers against his cheek. There had been a couple of occasions over the years they'd known each other, when Martin alluded to his parents' questionable disciplinary methods. Offhand remarks that had been made in such a cavalier manner that she never took the time to probe further. But now she worried.

Martin's hand came up, cupping his son's cheek protectively. "I couldn't finish the assignment he gave me. I couldn't bring myself to picture my father's hand hitting James."

Laying her head on his shoulder, she could feel his body trembling as he struggled to keep his emotions in check.

"Louisa, I don't think I can do something else Dr. Newell wants me to do. I'm supposed to imagine myself being the person administering the discipline—the same punishments I received from my parents. I've tried, but I can't do ..." Martin fought to resist the sobs that were threatening to escape.

He stood up from the bench and took several deliberate strides towards the path before turning to face her.

"I've tried ... *several* times. I get an image of James as a boy, and I think about raising my hand ... pulling off a belt, and I can't do it. I can't even imagine doing what my father did. And what *Mum* did! They were wrong, they were both wrong, Louisa!"

James was unaccustomed to hearing his father's raised voice, and he began to cry, pushing against his chest. But Martin appeared oblivious to his son's distress.

Reaching out, Louisa encouraged her husband to give her the little boy. "Martin, let me take James." Her voice was not registering with him.

Becoming agitated, he started to pace back and forth, the loose gravel on the path under his feet clattering as it was kicked up in front of him. He held tightly to the baby, but his free arm began to gesticulate wildly.

"They were wrong. They were both wrong. Here all my life I thought it was my fault. But, it's *not* my fault. I don't try to do it. It just happens. It just happens, no matter how hard I try not to!"

"Martin, give James to me and come sit back down. You're scaring me." Louisa reached again for her son, but her husband whirled around, placing himself between the child and his mother.

"No. You can't take things away from me anymore. You're mean. You're mean 'cause it hurts when you squeeze so hard, and you're mean 'cause I don't like the cupboard. It's scary in there. Somebody should stick *you* in there ... see how you like it."

Martin kicked at a rock on the path, sending it plummeting over the cliff edge before his rage continued. "And you shouldn't take other people's stuff either, especially when it's special stuff. That's like stealing. And I *know* stealing's wrong, so *you're* wrong, not me!"

Louisa held her hands out in front of her as she stepped towards him, reaching for her crying son. "Martin, *please* give me James. You don't want him to get hurt, do you?" she said, trying to project an air of calm that she didn't feel.

She put a hand on his arm, which only seemed to intensify his agitation.

"Don't touch me!"

"At least come away from the edge of the cliff, Martin."

Martin seemed to be looking through her as she spoke. He began to pace again, his steps more deliberate.

"And *you!* You call me names. Not nice names either. I'm not a waste of time, and I'm not a big girl's blouse. You're just a moron!"

Louisa reached out tentatively as he walked by, her hand brushing against his.

He recoiled. "I said don't touch me!"

He backed towards the rocky cliff which contained the Atlantic waters, and Louisa stepped away from him, realising her nearness was driving him closer to the edge.

"You're too rough! And you yell too loud. It's scary when you yell, and it just makes it worse. I try to do what you want, but you're never happy. I never do stuff good enough, and then you're angry, and you get too rough. It hurts when you get rough!"

"Martin, *please*. Give me, James!" she pleaded. She was terrified for the baby, wrapped tightly inside his father's coat. She knew that he would never intentionally do anything to hurt the boy, but he was not behaving like the Martin that she knew, seemingly unaware of his actions.

"I try, but you get angry anyway, and that's not fair. You get angry, and then you get too rough and it hurts."

Louisa detected a bit of softening in his eyes and took a step towards him. "I know it hurts, Martin. I'm sorry about that. And you're right, it's not fair."

He made eye contact with her. Reaching a hand up, he pulled at his hair, his face anguished. "How come I got such mean parents?"

Louisa inched slowly towards him and stroked his arm. "I don't know, Martin. I don't know."

James had stopped crying and had pulled his head down, curling up in a ball in his father's arm.

"Martin, look at me. Look at me," Louisa said softly. He quieted as he finally focused on her. "We should go home now. It's getting late."

She slowly pulled the baby from his arms before they walked back down the hill.

By the time they reached the surgery, Martin was quiet but gave no indication that anything had been amiss.

Afraid for his safety, Louisa busied him with folding a basket of laundry, and then went upstairs to put James Henry to bed.

The baby seemed none the worse for wear after the unconventional outing. He settled into his cot quickly, and Louisa hurried back downstairs to check on her husband.

The basket of laundry sat, untouched, on the kitchen table, and Martin was nowhere in sight. A sense of panic flashed through her, imagining the worst.

"Martin?" she called. She looked in the consulting room and then ran back upstairs to check their bedroom. *Oh, God. Did he go back up the hill?* The thought sent a cold chill through her, imagining him tumbling over the cliff's edge. She peered down from the window into the dwindling light and could just make out his form on the terrace.

"Are you okay, Martin?" she asked as she stepped out on to the slate moments later. She moved to his side and put her hand on his back.

"I'm fine." He turned his head to avoid her gaze.

As was typical for a Cornish midsummer's night, the air was cool but comfortable. Martin pulled in a deep breath and held it. This had been his place to go whenever he needed to calm himself, and its comforting aura was again working its magic on him.

Her hand slipped into his, and he glanced over at her. "Louisa ... I ... we went for a walk up the path tonight?"

She hesitated and then nodded her head. "Yes."

His fingers twitched at his side as he stared absently out at the harbour. He shook his head and pulled his hand from hers. Rubbing his palm over his face, he drew in another breath of salt air. "I thought so. It's just that ... what did we talk about?"

Louisa cocked her head at him and brushed her fingers against his cheek. "Let's go sit on the step." She took hold of his hand again and gave it a tug. "Come on."

They dropped down on to the slate, and Louisa moved against him, pulling his arm around her. "I'm not sure what went on up at the top of the hill tonight. You were telling me about the exercise that Dr. Newell asked you to do. Next thing I knew, you and James were over on the path. You were very upset and ... Martin, does any of this sound familiar?" she asked when the perplexed expression on his face deepened.

He pressed his hand to his head and grimaced. "No, it doesn't."

Louisa ran her hand up and down his back and leaned forward to catch his gaze. "You don't remember me telling you to give James to me ... that I was worried about you ... and James?"

Martin turned and looked at her as his breaths quickened. "You were worried about James? Did I do something to *hurt* James?"

"No, no. Well ... you were acting very strangely, and you were getting very close to the edge of the cliff. You didn't seem to hear me when I talked to you, and when I tried to take James from you ... well, you wouldn't let me have him."

Martin swallowed hard. "I'm sorry, Louisa. I don't know what happened. I ... God! Do you think I *could* have hurt James?"

"James is fine, Martin. He went right off to sleep."

"Ah. But ..." He turned to face her. "Louisa, I told myself that I would do whatever was necessary to change. Whatever was necessary for us to be together. But if it means anything like this could happen again ... I *can't* take that chance."

"Let's not make any decisions tonight." A gentle breeze came in off the water, sending a shiver through her. "I'm getting cold. Can we go inside?"

"Mm, yes."

"Would you like some tea or cocoa before we go to bed?"

"No, thank you. I'm quite tired actually."

"Hmm, I bet you are. Let's go then, shall we?"

As they lay curled up together in bed a short time later, Martin thought about the episode at the top of the hill. Dr. Newell had warned him that he could have strong reactions when facing these issues from his past, but it deeply distressed him to think that his behaviour had frightened his wife ... that he could have caused harm to his son.

"Louisa, are you still awake?" Martin whispered.

"Yes."

"Are you sure you want to have to deal with this? I'd certainly understand if you don't."

She rolled to face him and cupped her hand against his cheek. "I want this marriage to work as much as you do. And I love you. So yes, I am absolutely positive I want to deal with this."

He reached over to put an arm around her waist. "I'll call Dr. Newell on Monday morning to discuss what happened tonight. I can't bear to think that I could hurt either you or James trying to resolve my own issues."

"That would be good. But at the moment, you need to get some sleep." She rolled towards him and placed a kiss on his cheek. "I love you."

"Yes. I love you too."

Chapter 18

"Martin. Martin wake up." Louisa shook her husband's shoulder, trying to rouse him from his nightmare.

He sat up abruptly and bolted out of bed, running for the bathroom. Moments later, retching sounds could be heard, followed by the trickle of running water.

"Can you tell me about it?" she asked after he had returned to the bed.

The dim light in the room betrayed his stress and frustration as he rubbed at the side of his head. "No, I can't tell you about it, because none of it made any sense!" he snapped.

He rolled away from her and lay silent for several minutes before she heard his voice again. "Just bits and pieces. Flashes of images again. I couldn't move. I started to remember something, and then it just evaporated."

She massaged his back for a few minutes before leaning forward and nuzzling her face into the side of his neck. "I'm going to get some dry clothes, you've been sweating—be right back."

She pulled a vest and boxers from the dresser drawer and returned, sitting down on the edge of the bed next to him. "Here, put these on. Sorry, your pyjamas are all in the wash," she said as he got out of bed and she handed him the dry things.

He kept his gaze fixed on the floor as he pulled off his top and held it out to her waiting hand before kicking off the bottoms.

"Excuse me," she said as she squeezed past him to the bathroom.

"Mm, yes."

She hung the wet pyjamas over the edge of the tub before returning to the bedroom and crawling back into bed, spooning up against him. "Martin, I think Dr. Newell will be able to help you figure this all out. In the meantime, please let me be here for you. Okay?"

He rolled over to face her, cupping her cheek in his hand. "I'm sorry, Louisa. You didn't know this is what you were getting into when you married me. I'm not the man you thought you were marrying, and I'm not the man I wanted to be for you."

"Shh, Martin. You're trying ... doing your best."

He groaned softly. "I don't know what to do about that. I want to make you happy, but—"

"*Martin.* Try to be patient with yourself. I just know in my heart that you'll get past this. It's just not going to happen overnight."

She traced circles in his damp hair and gazed into his eyes. He looked lost. Helpless against the murky memories that had been torturing him. "Try to go back to sleep now," she said, settling in with her head on his shoulder. "Love you, Martin."

"Love you, too. Goodnight."

Ruth stopped in for a chat Monday morning while Louisa was feeding James his breakfast. And she wasn't one to tiptoe around an issue.

"Martin didn't seem particularly communicative when I was here on Saturday, so I thought I'd try my luck with you today. How are your therapy sessions going? All as the two of you expected?"

"Er, cuppa for you, Ruth?"

"Yes, thank you."

Louisa grabbed another tea cup from the shelf and placed it in front of the woman before filling it with hot water. Taking a seat across from her, she gave her a hesitant smile.

"I think it's been an especially hard week for Martin. His doctor gave him a difficult assignment to do, and it's resulted in some rather emotional responses.

"What do you mean, emotional responses?"

Reaching over, Louisa pulled the basket of tea bags from the end of the table, offering it to her before explaining. "He was with James and me during a ... I suppose you'd call it an episode. I found it really frightening, Ruth. He was very upset, and when I tried to get him to calm down, it was as if he didn't hear me, see me even. He was in his own world."

Louisa got up from the table and went to the cupboard, returning with a package of biscuits. "He's going to call Dr. Newell this morning to discuss it with him. I think he's genuinely concerned about whether James is safe around him."

The elderly woman's fingers tapped against her teacup. "Hmm, rightly so. It's called dissociation."

"I'm sorry?"

"What you saw happen with my nephew the other night is called a dissociative episode. In Martin's case, it's a coping mechanism. A defence mechanism, if you will. His mind is using it to minimise, or more correctly, to *tolerate* the stress he's feeling when confronting his memories. He's probably not aware that this is happening, so I would imagine he feels a loss of equilibrium afterwards, a sense that there's a gap in time for him."

"Hmm. He did seem very ... confused I suppose you'd say, after it happened. I've never heard of it before. Is this common?"

"No, not this type of dissociative episode. It's usually the memory of a rather traumatic event that triggers this sort of reaction."

Louisa nodded her head. "It seems like Martin can't escape his painful childhood."

Ruth pulled a chocolate digestive from its sleeve and broke it in half before dunking it in her tea. "What has Martin told you about his memories?"

Louisa reached over to hand James his green frog puppet. "I'm not sure how much of what he told me I should be sharing with you," Louisa said as she set the frog on her son's high chair tray.

"It might be better if you could get Martin to talk to you about these things." Her spoon clinked against her cup as she stirred sugar into her tea. "I just can't risk losing Martin's trust again, Ruth. I suspect he wouldn't mind you knowing these things, but I'd rather let that be his decision to make. I'm sorry."

"No, no." The old woman waved her hand dismissively. "I shouldn't have asked. I'm concerned about my nephew, but you're right, these are things I should be asking Martin." She reached across the table with a frail hand. "Louisa, I'm very glad that he's confiding in you. He needs someone. He *needs* you."

James reached a chubby arm out, his fingers opening and closing as he zeroed in on the package of biscuits. Louisa got up and came back with a piece of Melba toast.

"Did you get your childminder situation sorted yet?" the old woman asked.

"No, I'm meeting Poppy for lunch today. Hopefully, I can convince her that she doesn't need to be afraid of your nephew."

"Well, good luck with *that*." Ruth got to her feet. "I really have to go. I just wanted to check in. Please keep me informed about how Martin's doing."

She moved towards the door and then turned, her hand on the knob. "I hope you'll never doubt your husband's love for you. What he's doing to preserve this marriage is far from easy. But I saw the desperation on his face the day you left for Spain.

He *will* do whatever is necessary to keep from losing you and James."

As Louisa sat at the table, reflecting on the wise woman's words, Martin was trying to muster the resolve to make his call to Dr. Newell.

"Who's next?" he asked as he stood by his receptionist's desk.

"Chippy Miller's comin' in at half ten, but you got a break 'til then. Good time to make yourself a cup of coffee, Doc. Kinda' looks like you could use one."

"Mm," Martin grunted. "Patient notes," he said snapping his fingers.

Morwenna stared at him, wide-eyed and shaking her head. "Your manners are atrocious ya know. You could say please."

"Morwenna!" He snapped his fingers again.

The young woman slapped the sleeves of notes into his hand, giving him a roll of her eyes.

He gave her a grunt and hurried off towards his consulting room. "I have a phone call to make. Make sure I'm not disturbed."

"You want me ta just shut the phone off then, or what am I s'posed ta do if there's an emergency?"

Martin spun around, screwing up his face at her. "If it's an *actual* emergency, then of course, come and get me!"

He ducked through the doorway on his way through to the exam room, slamming the door shut behind him.

Martin stretched his neck and pulled at his collar, hesitating briefly before picking up his phone to dial Dr. Newell's number. "This is Martin Ellingham. I need to speak to Dr. Newell," he clipped.

"Ach!" Martin grimaced as the woman on the other end of the line put him on hold. He grabbed the top set of patient notes and pulled them from their sleeve before reviewing Chippy Miller's recent medical history. "Gammy leg," he grumbled. Why can't these people speak proper English?" He straightened himself in his chair as a male voice resonated in the phone. "Yes, Dr. Newell. Thank you for taking my call ..."

Martin finished his conversation with the psychiatrist fifteen minutes later and rolled his chair back away from his desk, swivelling to turn and gaze out the window. The therapist hadn't given him any assurances that he had seen the last of the unsettling incidents like he'd experienced Friday night. Nor could he assure him that James had been safe that night.

His stomach churned as he replayed the phone conversation in his head. It was discouraging, to say the least, that the psychiatrist was unable to guarantee a resolution to his problems. Not even that therapy would bring an end to the nightmares which had been plaguing him. Psychiatry was clearly not the well delineated science that he had found vascular surgery to be.

He got up and went to the kitchen to get a cup of coffee before Chippy Miller arrived. Louisa had taken James for a walk down to the Platt, so the room was quiet aside from the hum of his espresso machine.

Standing at the kitchen window, he watched a small flock of finches as they darted in and out of the bushes. His mind drifted, as it often did, to the current state of his marriage. Even if his sessions with Dr. Newell *did* prove effective, the man could give him no time frame in which he could expect results. Martin bit at his lower lip. How long would Louisa tolerate life as it was now before packing her bags and leaving Portwenn again?

"Doc?" Morwenna's voice broke through his ruminations. "Chippy Miller's here."

Martin gave his head a shake. "Mm, I'll be right there." He glanced down. A streak of brown stained the sink where his espresso had tipped from his cup. "Bugger!" Martin muttered. After filling the cup with water, he drank it down and headed off under the stairs, pausing in the doorway. "Mr. Miller, come through, please."

Chippy rose stiffly from his chair and followed the doctor into the consulting room.

"What seems to be the problem, Mr. Miller?"

"It's my back, Doc. It's been givin' me trouble since I wrenched it pickin' up a crate off the deck of my boat."

"How long ago was that?"

"Last Thursday, I think. Hard to remember fer sure."

Martin walked behind the man and squatted down slightly while he palpated his back.

"Hmm, you've strained a muscle. What have you been taking for the pain—paracetamol?"

"Yeah, Doc, and I been icin' it, too."

Moving back around his desk, he reached for his prescription pad. "You've done all the right things, but you'll need a muscle relaxant as well as something stronger for the pain. I'll write you a prescription; Mrs. Tishell will have it for you. And keep up with the ice."

"Thanks, Doc."

As Chippy headed for the door Martin stood up and cleared his throat. "Erm, Mr. Miller ... I'd like to thank you for the assistance you gave me down at the pub a while back. I didn't notice who the other men were, but I'd appreciate it if you could pass my thanks along to them as well."

"It was nothin', Doc. You've helped most of us out a time or two. And yer one'a us now, you know."

Chippy turned and left the consulting room, leaving Martin trying to get his head around what the fisherman had said. When had he become one of them?

Chapter 19

Louisa and James arrived at Bert's restaurant, finding Poppy already sitting at a table.

"Poppy Flinn! It's so nice to see you again!" Louisa said, giving her a one-armed hug.

"Hi, Miss Glasson."

"It's Mrs. Ellingham now, Poppy."

The girl pulled up her shoulders as a blush of pink spread across her face. "Sorry, Mrs. Ellingham. It's kind of a habit."

"It's okay, Poppy. I'm still getting used to it, too."

Louisa pulled a restaurant-provided high chair up to the table and took out a packet of antiseptic wipes. "This is James Henry. Can you say hi to Poppy, James?"

James's face lit up, and he gave the girl a broad grin.

"Hi, James. You have a cute smile. How old is he?" she asked.

"Ten months. Hard to believe."

Poppy watched quizzically as the older woman thoroughly wiped the chair and slipped the baby into it.

Glancing up at her curious expression, Louisa gave her an embarrassed smile. "One of my husband's rules when we eat at Bert's." She held up the grimy wipe. "He has a point."

The baby grabbed for the bracelet on his mother's wrist as a string of spittle dribbled from his lower lip.

"Well, should we order our lunch and then talk business?" Louisa suggested.

Bert sidled up next to Poppy and leaned over to tickle James under his chin.

"What can I get you fine ladies today? I can recommend the roast chicken or perhaps a lovely quiche? And, of course, we always have our signature salads if you would prefer something a bit on the lighter side."

"Hmm. The quiche sounds lovely, Bert," Louisa said.

"What about for you, Poppy? Order anything you like; it's my treat."

Poppy ducked her head demurely before scanning the menu. "I think I'll have the chicken, please."

Louisa put her hand on Bert's arm. "Poppy and I are discussing the possibility of her being our new childminder, Bert. I think she's the perfect person for the job."

Bert patted the the young woman vigorously on the back. "Well, I gotta hand it to you there, girl. Don't know that there are many in this village brave enough to face up to our doc every day—be responsible for that little lad of his. Why, the doc goes through childminders like I go through Jammie Dodgers!" Bert chuckled, his jowls shaking.

Louisa groaned inwardly. "Well, to be fair, Bert, we've had a bit of a run of bad luck lately." She looked up and shot the proprietor a warning look.

He gave Louisa a vigorous nod before turning to the prospective childminder. Leaning over, he spoke in an exaggeratedly reassuring tone as he patted her shoulder. "I'm sure there's a perfectly logical explanation for every one of 'em hightailin' it outta there. So, you don't worry that pretty head about it, you hear?" He glanced over at Louisa, giving her a jocular grin as he shook his thumb in the air.

Louisa batted the hair from her eyes. The jowly man straightened himself, adding, "Besides, the doc is almost certainly harmless ... that hippocritical oath that he took ta be a doc and all, eh?"

Clenching her jaw, Louisa forced her mouth into a grotesque smile. "Thank you, Bert. I think we'll discuss this privately now if you don't mind."

"Oh, sure. Didn't mean to discourage you girl. The doc tain't half as scary as people say. He's just all bark and no bite." He dropped his notepad and pencil into his apron pocket and held a finger in the air. "I'll have your food out to you in a jiffy."

"Thank you, Bert." Louisa silently cursed the portly restaurateur as he waddled off. "So Poppy, Martin said you've been looking for a job but not having much luck?"

"Yeah, there don't seem to be very many good jobs right now. I'm stayin' at my mum and dad's until I can find something." She jiggled her foot back and forth nervously.

"Well, my husband was quite happy to hear that you might be interested in being James's childminder. He *is* very protective of his little boy and would never have recommended you to me if he didn't think you would do a good job."

Louisa felt a bit guilty for her slight fabrication. Martin hadn't exactly recommended Poppy, but he wasn't vehemently opposed to her as had been the case with almost every other childminder who had been in the Ellingham employ.

Bert returned with their food, and Louisa headed off any more helpful remarks by quickly asking, "How are you and Jenny doing, Bert? The wedding plans coming along okay?"

"Oh, my Jenny's a doll, an absolute doll, she is. She's handlin' all the nuptial stuff. I just do what she tells me. And I keep—my mouth—shut. I learned that right fast when me and Mary was married. We started out fightin' all the time. Then one day I realised, it was me that was always gonna be wrong. I said to myself—Bert, there's no point arguin' the toss. It's the husband's job to be wrong. Then and there, I started doin' whatever she said. It solved all our problems."

Bert gazed out at the harbour for a few seconds before returning his attention to Louisa. "You know, I bet that's the doc's trouble. Maybe I should stop by... share some'a my hard-learned wisdom with 'im."

Louisa glanced over at Poppy, and then put a hand up in front of her. "No, thank you, Bert. It's very kind of you to offer, but I think Martin and I are doing just fine on our own."

The restaurateur tipped his head to the side and raised his eyebrows at her before scratching his chin. "You jus' never know what life's gonna bring tomorrow, do you?" He stooped over and gave the two women a sly grin. "Lucky for *me*, life brought it in a pretty package," he crooned.

"I'm happy for both of you, Bert." Louisa turned her attention back to to her ultimate objective and the meal in front of her. "Well, we'd better eat before our food gets cold."

"Oh, yeah, yeah. Where are my manners?" Bert said as he adjusted the small vase of flowers on the table. "Well, I'll leave you to it then. Enjoy."

Louisa watched as he walked away before glancing over at the young woman. "So, Poppy, do you think you'd be interested in the job?"

Poppy shifted uncomfortably in her chair and stuffed her hands under her thighs. "I'm not sure. Would ... would Dr. Ellingham be around much, or would it just be James and me?"

Louisa smiled understandingly. "I know that Dr. Ellingham can come across as being rather gruff. But don't let him fool you, he's really quite tender on the inside." She leaned forward and glanced furtively around her before adding, "Just don't let that get out; he works very hard to maintain his surly image."

The two women had finished the meal, and Poppy had yet to give Louisa an answer. She eyed the girl nervously, and then asked, "Poppy, how 'bout we try things out this Friday? Martin and I have an appointment in Truro, and we could use a childminder then. Would you be willing to give it a go?"

Poppy reached her hand out to James, and he latched on to her finger. "Erm, all right."

Louisa breathed a sigh of relief. "*Great.* Could you plan to come to the surgery at two o'clock? That would give me a chance to go over James's routine with you."

"All right, two o'clock!" Poppy's face brightened now that she had made her decision.

"Just come to the back door. That way you won't have to walk through a reception room full of patients." *And avoid any unfortunate encounters with Martin.*

Martin had finished with his last appointment and was filing patient notes when Louisa came into the reception room carrying James Henry. He gave the baby's cheek a quick brush with the backs of his fingers. I just need to sign some prescriptions, and then I'll be done for the day."

"Good. We've missed you." She eyed her husband. "Are you all right?"

"Yes, I'm fine," he responded with an edge to his voice.

"You look very tired, Martin."

He scowled at her before turning and walking off briskly towards his consulting room.

Louisa and James were in the kitchen when Martin entered the room a short while later. She walked over and slipped her arms around his waist.

"Louisa, please," he said, brushing her away.

"Fine, Martin." She turned back to preparing the meal. "Dinner will be ready in about fifteen minutes."

He breathed out a heavy sigh. "I'm going to go wash and change."

Louisa watched as he disappeared under the stairs. Her heart ached for him. She was keenly aware of the stress that he was under, but she couldn't help feeling hurt when he pushed her away.

Martin climbed the steps to their bedroom and sat down on the bed, removing his coat and tie. He rested his elbows on his knees and put his head in his hands as he tried to imagine himself alone on the terrace. There wasn't a corner of the village where he could go to be left completely alone with his thoughts. Trepidation, frustration, anger, grief, and sundry of emotions that he couldn't even identify churned inside him in a confounding stew, so intense that it had made him feel physically ill. He didn't want Louisa to see him falling apart. But the years of suppressed tension had built to an intolerable level, and he felt himself edging ever closer to a complete loss of control.

He finished washing up and now had to go back downstairs to face the wife whose affections he had rebuffed earlier, no doubt leaving her in a less than charitable mood.

Louisa glanced up at him as he re-entered the kitchen, but tried not to make eye contact. She couldn't bear to see the hardened look on his face. They sat and ate quietly, the silence interrupted only by James's occasional babbles.

Martin pushed himself away from the table. "I'll do the dishes tonight," he said to his wife, hanging his suit coat over the back of a chair. "You go and relax."

She managed a weak smile before settling James on the floor in the lounge with his toys and retiring to the sofa.

After making quick work of the dishes, Martin turned to his wife. "I'm going for a walk; I need some fresh air. I'll be back in a while."

He moved so quickly out the door that Louisa's reminder to take his coat was left unheard.

After climbing the hill to the coastal path, he kept walking. His breathing became more rapid as he fought to keep everything from spilling out. He walked faster, trying to distance himself from the village.

The expenditure of physical energy finally brought some relief from the very real pain in his chest and gut. He stopped and looked around, now more aware of his surroundings. He was at Joan's farm. He'd come a long way. Dropping into a chair under the roof of the gazebo, he sat looking out at the sea, now illuminated by the light of the full moon, and realised he was finally alone.

He felt his self-restraint giving way and the emotions began to cascade out in great sobs. A long time passed before the sobs began to wither into whimpers. He drew in long breaths of air, trying to control the attacks of ragged inhalations. When he was a small boy, Auntie Joan would hold him in her arms, shushing his gulps for breath as she softly reassured him. He longed to have her comforting arms around him again. To hear her words of wisdom again.

But she was gone, and he had finally admitted to himself that he had grown up an emotional orphan. He had been blessed with parents who seemed to vacillate between loathing him and being blissfully unaware of his existence.

Somehow, he needed to figure out how to let the baggage of that old life go so that he could start anew with James and Louisa. He began his walk back home, suddenly becoming aware that he had been sitting at the farm far longer than he had realised. The full moon, which had illuminated his route as he made his way towards the farm, was now obscured by clouds. He pulled out his mobile to light the Coast Path as he wound his way back towards the village.

Martin had been gone a very long time, and Louisa was worried. There was now a chilly rain falling, and he wasn't dressed for the weather. She tried to reach him on his mobile, but he didn't answer. She wouldn't allow herself to think about the episode two nights before. It led to too many terrifying images. It was almost midnight when she finally heard the door open.

She rushed to meet him. "Martin! I was so worried. Where have you been?"

"I'm sorry. I went for a walk to clear my head. I must have lost track of the time," he said as a wave of embarrassment washed over him.

Louisa's fear for his safety was quickly replaced by anger. "Martin, it's been *hours!* What were you thinking? Do you have any idea how terrified I was? What if something like the other night had happened? You, off on your own with no one to help. How could you be so *stupid?*

"I didn't know what to do," her harangue continued. "Call Ruth and wake her up in the middle of the night? Call Joe Penhale to get a search party together? Don't you *dare* do that—"

She suddenly noticed her husband's face. His eyes were red and swollen, his hair was wet and his shirt was soaked and clinging to him. He looked like an utterly lost soul.

She took hold of his hand. His fingers were ice-cold. "You're freezing, Martin. Go up and get out of those wet clothes and dry your hair. When you come back down I'll have some hot tea ready for you."

He moved off silently, pulling his tie free as he climbed the stairs. When he reached the bedroom, he stripped off his wet shirt and vest, uncharacteristically abandoning them on the floor. He then waged a brief war with his rain-soaked trousers, managing to tug them down below his knees before dropping on to the bed. His hands fell limply to his sides. He was physically and emotionally spent. An overwhelming fatigue suddenly overcame him, and his eyelids drifted shut before he collapsed backwards on to the bed.

Louisa came up shortly and found him half undressed and sound asleep. She peeled off his shoes, socks, and trousers and then swung his legs up on to the mattress. "Oh, Martin. What am I going to do with you?" she whispered as she gently rubbed his head with a towel, soaking up the worst of the moisture from his hair before slipping a pillow under his head.

After getting a blanket from the linen cupboard in the hallway, she covered him up, smiling as she remembered the last time she had pulled the purple blanket over her sleeping husband. Wine, not fatigue, had claimed him that night.

After going back downstairs to turn out the lights and lock the doors, she crawled in next to him, whispering in his ear before falling asleep, "I love you, Martin."

Chapter 20

When Louisa opened her eyes the next morning, Martin was looking back at her.

"You are so beautiful," he said softly.

She gave him a tender smile. "Thank you, Martin. I like to hear you say that."

"Mm, I'll try to remember ... say it more often." He filed it in his mental list of endearments to be used at a later date.

Louisa hesitated before bringing up the events of the previous evening. "You went to bed wet last night, you know." She tried to smooth the hair that had dried into an unruly, albeit strangely charming, tousled mass.

"Mm, yes. Sorry about that. I guess I fell asleep."

"If I hadn't been so worried about you I might actually have laughed," Louisa said before rolling forward to kiss him. You, half-dressed ... half-on, half-off the bed and sound asleep."

Martin's expression grew serious as he placed his palm against her cheek. "I'm sorry, Louisa ... for worrying you. You were right; it *was* stupid. I just needed to ..." He shook his head. "It's not important. I won't do it again."

"Actually, it *is* important, to me anyway. Will you please tell me where you were last night? What happened?"

Martin rolled over on to his back and pulled an arm up over his head, closing his eyes momentarily while he collected his thoughts.

"I had to get out. To someplace where I could be alone. I talked with Dr. Newell yesterday, and he wasn't as encouraging as I'd hoped he would be."

"You mean you needed some time to think? Or get away and let off steam?"

"Yes. A bit of both I suppose ..."

"Where did you go? You were gone a very long time."

"I was going to go to the top of the hill to sit on the bench. But I just kept walking. I found myself at the farm. I sat in the gazebo and ..."

Louisa watched him intently, his eyes refusing to make contact with hers.

"I, erm ... I thought about Joan."

"I know how much you must miss her, Martin," she said, tracing her finger around his ear. "I'm glad you had the time you did with her when you were a boy ... that you had someone who loved you."

"Mm, yes."

She propped herself up on her elbow. "What did Dr. Newell say to discourage you?"

Martin let out a soft groan. "He couldn't assure me that James would be safe with me if I should have another episode like I had the other night. He said I'm probably not aware of my actions when that happens, and that it would be best if I waited until James has gone to bed if I'm going to talk about these things with you. Louisa, what if you hadn't asked to walk with us that night, and it had just been James and me when ..." He ran a hand across his face.

"Well, you wouldn't have been talking about it if I hadn't been with you, so I don't think it would have happened, do you?"

"Mm, possibly not." He lay quietly for a few moments, staring off towards the window before again turning his gaze towards her. "I asked him when I could expect to see my issues begin to resolve, but he couldn't give me any idea whatsoever. He couldn't tell me how much improvement I could expect to see either. He's hopeful but won't make any promises." He shook his head. "What if I'm never able to be happy ... to make you happy?"

"Martin, you have to try to stay positive. I know the last weeks have been very hard, but you've seen progress already. You realise now that you didn't deserve the treatment you received when you were young."

"I'm not sure that's progress," he said, screwing up his face.

Louisa stroked her fingers along his arm. "Martin, I was wondering ..." She took in a breath. "I was wondering about your childhood punishments. You said some things the other night—"

"Oh, gawd," he groaned.

"It's just that ... Well, I'd like to know what things were like for you when you were growing up."

Martin pressed his fingertips to his eyes and then turned to her. "I don't know what I said. I don't want to know what I said. My parent's disciplinary methods were very harsh. Long periods locked in a little cupboard in the hallway. My father used his belt and didn't stop when he should have. Aside from that ... I'd rather not talk about it." With that, the door slammed shut to any further discussion about his past.

He turned his eyes back to the ceiling. "What did Poppy have to say about childminding?"

"She's definitely interested. I asked her to watch James while we're in Truro on Friday. She'll make a decision about whether she wants to be our permanent childminder based on how that goes. So, Martin, *please* be on your best behaviour."

He tipped his head and his face took on the look of complete innocence he had mastered over their years of botched conversations.

"I mean it, Martin. Don't you dare do anything to scare that girl away. She's really very shy so please ... be nice."

"What do you mean?" he replied with righteous indignation.

"Try not to be so gruff. And don't lecture her or criticise her. And above all, don't yell at her. If there's something you're concerned about or don't like, tell me and *I'll* discuss it with her."

Martin pursed his lips and crossed his arms over his chest, staring up at the ceiling in a pout. Louisa giggled and swung her leg up and over him. She sat, perched astride his lap, and leaned over to kiss his bare chest.

"Oh, Martin. Don't take it that way. You have to admit, diplomacy is not your strong suit. I'm asking you to let me handle it."

She gazed down at the nearly naked man lying beneath her, and she felt a surge of emotions.

"You know, I haven't had the pleasure of waking up to you dressed in nothing but your boxers in a very long time," she said huskily.

Her hand, which had been resting on his shoulder, began to move south, pausing to caress his chest. Her finger traced its way down his belly before stopping to tease the elastic band of his pants. She leaned over and pressed her lips firmly to his.

Martin found himself responding to her ministrations, pressing back against her, his hands being drawn to the curves of her hips and breasts. She felt wonderful; her warmth and softness, her tender touch on his skin. Her beauty took his breath away. He brushed her hair back from her face before his hands dropped to her shoulders. "Oh, Louisa." His words were hushed and velvety as he brought his head up, nuzzling his face into the crook of her neck.

He shut his eyes, focusing his thoughts entirely on her. Erotic images of her above him stoked the physical responses that her movements were kindling. He was lost in her completely when his carnal musing was penetrated by the disturbing images of his nightmares.

He blinked his eyes, frantically trying to erase them, but they had already marred the moment. He longed to make love to her, but his normal male response was now failing him. He pushed her away in frustration.

"I'm sorry. It's not ... happening."

Louisa was startled by the abruptness of her husband's withdrawal. When he pulled his arm over his face and turned away, it suddenly dawned on her why he had been rebuffing her attempts to ignite a fire in him.

Stretching out next to him, she lightly stroked his arm. "Martin, it's all right you know ... with me. I mean, I do miss being intimate with you, but I can wait until you're ready for it again."

He pulled himself from the bed. "I'll get dressed and take care of James."

Louisa watched as he walked away from her, his emotions yet again left unexpressed.

Chapter 21

Martin sat in front of Dr. Newell's desk, rubbing his palms together as he silently implored the man. *Put the bloody notebook away and get on with it! God, he has two eyes on the front of his head and enough grey matter between his ears to know he has a patient waiting!*

The therapist slapped the notebook shut and dropped it into a side drawer on his desk. "Sorry about that. My receptionist jumped the gun a bit sending you back. If I didn't get that written down, I never would have remembered it when I needed it."

Martin gave him a scowl. "Yes."

"I said we should address the issue of your nightmares first thing today, Martin. So, why don't you tell me about what's been happening."

"What do you want to know?"

"Well, for starters, when did they begin?"

"I'm not sure. I would imagine I was around four or five. They could have begun earlier, but it's unlikely that I would remember them. Obviously."

Dr. Newell stared back at him for a moment before clearing his throat.

"I see. I'd like to come back to those early nightmares another time. But for now, let's focus on the nightmares that have troubled you more recently. How long have you been experiencing them?"

"I've had them intermittently all my adult life. They seemed to be associated with periods of high stress. But a year ago they became more frequent, and they've increased in frequency in the last couple of months."

"Why don't you tell me a bit about the stress that you referred to."

Martin shrugged. "When I was a surgeon ... particularly difficult cases, heavy case loads, that sort of thing."

"What about a year ago, when the nightmares became more frequent? What was going on in your life at that time?"

"Nothing out of the ordinary," he replied, furrowing his brow in thought. "I had planned to move back to London shortly before that ... return to surgery. However, after my son was born I decided to stay in Portwenn."

The psychiatrist's chair squeaked as he leaned back and stretched his legs out in front of him. "So, you decided to forgo the resumption of a surgical career to be with your wife and son?"

"Well, I had spent time with James, caring for him. When I originally planned to return to surgery, my aunt Joan was still living. I suppose her presence in the village appeased my guilt in a way."

"Your guilt about leaving?"

"Mm." Martin tugged nervously at his trousers and loosened his tie slightly. "I knew Joan would keep me updated on how Louisa was progressing, as well as the baby after it was born. She would keep an eye on things for me. And to be honest, my presence in the village seemed to upset Louisa—erm, me."

Dr. Newell rolled up to his desk and began to write in his patient's file. "I'm not sure I follow, Martin. In what way did your being in the village upset you?"

His head dropped to the side as he gave a resigned sigh. "She didn't want me around at that point, and it ... it was uncomfortable. I wanted to help, but I kept buggering things up, and my presence seemed to annoy her."

"How about after the baby was born? Did your presence continue to annoy her?"

"Things were tense. I did try. We had a strong difference of opinion about her return to her job. My preference would be for Louisa to be James's primary caregiver. However, she's expressed dissatisfaction with being stuck at home with him."

"I see. Has that issue been resolved?"

Martin shifted in his chair. "She's back at work. We'll have a new childminder for the start of next term, and I'm hopeful this one will be more competent than most that we've had. I just don't want my son to grow up feeling unwan— Well, I want him to be well cared for in every way. I know that Louisa would be the best one for the job. That's what I want for my son."

"What was it like for you to see James left in the hands of less than competent caregivers ... caregivers who showed up solely to change the nappies, feed him, and collect their pay?"

Martin closed his eyes and took in a ragged breath. "It was painful to see him towed around the village like a bag of meat being toted home from the butcher's. I was torn. I have a duty of care to my patients. I took an oath to do my best for them. But that's difficult to do when you're trying to pacify an irritable infant whilst at the same time discussing erectile dysfunction with a patient."

"That sounds extremely stressful to me."

"Mm, yes. Do you think that's what triggered the depression and nightmares ... the stress?"

"Stress could quite possibly be a trigger." Dr. Newell's biro clicked as he tapped it rhythmically against the edge of his desk. "You'd also recently lost your aunt, and you've become a husband in the time since the nightmares increased in frequency. Throw fatherhood in there, and I would say you've been pretty well immersed in stressors for the last year or more."

The psychiatrist's pen scratched notes into the file in front of him before he dropped the implement on to the desk and folded his hands. "Tell me about these nightmares. Do you remember very much about them after you wake up?"

"They've changed lately. The early dreams were replays of old memories, but lately they've been more disturbing."

"Disturbing? In what way?"

"I get glimpses. Flashes of images. Not enough to make sense of it."

The therapist rested his elbows on his desk, steepling his fingers. "Can you be more descriptive about these images?"

Martin rubbed his palm over his head. "No, not really. As I said, I just get glimpses. I wake up and my heart's racing, I'm in a cold sweat, in a panic. There's a sense that I've been cornered by something and there's no way out ... no way to turn that will lead to safety."

Dr. Newell swivelled back and forth in his chair. "I think it might be helpful to explore these images a bit more, see if we can tease out a few more details. Perhaps if we have a better understanding of what these images may represent, we can explain those physical manifestations. Why don't you try closing your eyes ... take a few slow breaths. Try to take yourself back to the dream and see if something comes to you. Do you see any shapes, colours, textures? Or are any of your other senses involved?" The therapist watched as his patient's chest rose and fell and his eyes drifted shut.

Martin's knuckles whitened as he griped the armrests of his chair. "I don't know! It's confusing!" he erupted. "Don't you think I've *tried* to remember more? The harder I try to remember the details, the farther away I seem to push them."

"All right, let's move on. Louisa said last week that she's concerned about your lack of sleep. Are you having difficulty falling asleep?"

"I get anxious about the nightmares. So, I lay awake thinking about it, worrying about it. When I do get to sleep, I wake up in a cold sweat and my heart's racing."

Rolling his chair up to his desk, the psychiatrist leaned towards his patient. "I'd like you to answer some questions, Martin. This is a short written test to see how you're functioning in day-to-day life."

Dr. Newell pulled out a booklet from the stack of papers on his desk.

Martin screwed up his face. "Oh, gawd."

"I see you're familiar with Beck's Depression Inventory."

"Yes. I can save you some time and tell you my score if you like, or we can continue on like a pair of utter morons."

"Let's continue on like utter morons, Martin."

The therapist handed him a questionnaire and a pencil and then stepped out of the office. When he returned, he flipped through the completed inventory before looking back up at his patient. "Well, as you know, your results put you solidly in the moderate to severe depression category, so let's talk about how to proceed from here. Are you open to trying medication?"

"Is that my only option?"

"No. It's not your *only* option. However, if you want my professional opinion, I do feel that medication is your *best* option at this point. I'm going to write a prescription for a sleep aid as well." Dr. Newell scrawled on to his prescription pad and then looked pointedly at his patient. "And I recommend you use it." He rested his elbows on his desk. "Martin, you really must tell Louisa about what we've discussed today. To try to hide the depression from her would be very detrimental to your marriage."

Martin leaned over and held his head in his hands.

"What is it, Martin?"

"Mm ... I just know what my father would be saying to me right now."

Dr. Newell walked around to his patient's side of the desk and perched himself on the corner.

"Speaking of your father, we didn't really discuss the particulars of the assignment I gave you when we spoke on the phone the other day. Did you come to any conclusions about the fairness of your parent's punishments?"

Martin stared at his hands as he slowly rubbed his palms together.

"I didn't actually complete the assignment ... I couldn't. I can't bring myself to imagine my son in my place. Especially if I'm the disciplinarian. I would *never* do those things to James."

"Hmm. And what conclusion did you arrive at? Were your parent's punishments fair?"

"Of course not."

"But you weren't sure last week?"

Martin shrugged. "I always felt it was my fault. That I must have done something to warrant the discipline. But I realise now that their punishments weren't in line with any offense I could have committed."

The psychiatrist leaned back on his hands. "When you think about them, which punishments hurt the most? The beatings from your father or the time outs in the cupboard?"

"The time in the cupboard."

Dr. Newell's head tipped to the side. "You were very quick with that answer. What made that punishment so much worse than the beatings?"

Martin's eyes drifted shut as he gripped the armrests of his chair. "My father was just angry. My mother looked at me with ... with hatred ... contempt. I sat there in the dark ... I kept seeing her face. I spent the time trying to picture her smiling at me instead. Sometimes it worked.

"I guess there were times that she was present when my father was doing the disciplining. That may actually have been worse, now that I think about it—knowing she didn't care enough to intervene. I think she actually took some perverse pleasure in my misery."

"So you knew at a young age that your mother didn't love you?"

"I used to try to get a hug from her." Martin said, shaking his head. "She didn't want me near her. I could see it in her eyes. I was never allowed to touch her; she always had an excuse. She wasn't feeling well. She didn't have time. She didn't want me to get her clothes dirty.

"Even as an adult I knew better than to touch her when I hugged her. Yes, I think I knew how she felt about me. I'd give her awkward hugs, leaving enough room between us to avoid making actual contact."

Martin stared off absently. "She never wanted a child to begin with, and then she ended up with a child like me."

"Tell me about what kind of child you were, Martin. You must have been quite a brilliant boy."

"I was, but I don't think that was a positive to my parents."

"Why do you say that?"

"Because I was very intelligent, I was also very curious. So I asked a lot of questions and found it difficult to not explore, check things out, take things apart to see how they worked. That got me into a lot of trouble."

"But I would imagine you received good marks in school."

"Yes."

"That must have made them quite proud."

"Mm, no. It's what was expected of me. They knew I was capable of being top in my class, so there was no reason for them to be proud."

"Tell me more about what you meant when you said your mother never wanted a child, especially a child like you."

"I was introverted. I'm not sure what precipitated it, but I was teased a lot ... bullied. I also wet the bed frequently. She found it all tiresome."

Dr. Newell returned to his chair and began to add to the notes in his file. Then he rolled himself away from his desk and stretched his legs out in front of him. "Martin, I'm curious ... what is it about your son that makes you feel love for him?"

Martin's eyes crinkled in thought, and then he cocked his head at the man. "I'm not sure. I've always loved him."

"What do you mean by always?"

"From the moment he was born—when I first saw him—held him for the first time."

"What could James do to make you love him more than you do now?"

Martin stared blankly back at the man. "He's a baby. His brain isn't developed enough for him to grasp such a concept."

"I'm sorry, I was a little vague with my question," Dr. Newell said as he scratched at a raised eyebrow. "What I mean is, as he's growing up, what kinds of things could your son do to make you love him more?"

Martin hesitated. "I'm not sure what you're getting at."

"Imagine James as a star athlete, for instance."

"Mm, I don't like sports," Martin said, his head swinging side to side emphatically.

The psychiatrist scratched a little harder at the eyebrow. "Okay, what if James was top in his class? What if he was the boy all the girls swoon over, the kid who everyone wants to befriend? Would that make you love your son more than you do now?"

Martin screwed up his face as air hissed from his nose. "I'm not following your line of questioning. I just told you, I loved James from the moment I saw him, before that actually." Martin tipped his head down and tugged at his ear. "When I first heard his heartbeat."

"So, there's nothing James could do to make you love him more? Not even being top in his class?"

The therapist watched as his patient mulled over the question before a spark of recognition could be seen in his eyes.

"You're trying to get me to understand that James has no control over the love that I feel for him."

"Mm, hm."

"That I had no control over the lack of love my parents had for me."

"Mm, hm."

Martin was overwhelmed by the realisation that there was not something missing in him, there was something missing in his mother and father. He tried to hold back the threatening tears, but he could already feel them on his cheeks. He put a hand up over his face.

"Martin, your parents, for reasons you and I will likely never know, have never been capable of loving another human being," the doctor said softly. "Unfortunately, nature still allows people like that to procreate, and their children suffer horribly for it. You were an innocent bystander in all of this."

Martin was silent, his face still hidden behind his hand as he tried to get control of his emotions.

Dr. Newell rose from his chair. "I'm needing a cup of tea. You think about what we just discussed while I'm gone."

He returned a short time later, setting two cups down on his desk before pulling a chair up next to his patient and taking a seat.

"You seem like a white-no-sugar kind of guy," he said as he slid a cup towards Martin.

"Mm, yes." Martin took a sip of his tea and then said hoarsely, "I've always thought that there must be something wrong with me, something missing in me. Something that exists in other people that makes them worth—" He cleared his throat and wiped a palm across his face. "Something that makes them deserving of being loved. I'm not sure if you can understand how much I appreciate your help today."

"I do understand, Martin. I'm very glad that I could lead you to the correct conclusion. You'll now need to accept the ramifications of this—that you are indeed deserving of being loved."

"I'm not sure that I can ever feel that way."

"You'll have to keep reminding yourself that the notions you had adhered to, prior to today, were incorrect."

The man set his cup back down on the desk. "You have a lot to think about, Martin. I hope that you'll share all of this with Louisa ... talk it over with her so that she can better understand your reactions and behaviours.

"Do remember though that things aren't going to change overnight. You've gained some valuable insight today, but the emotional snarls still need to be untangled. There's a long way to go."

"Mm."

"How are you doing now? Do you feel okay, or are you a bit shaky?"

"No, no. I'm fine."

Dr. Newell walked with Martin towards the door. "Get your prescriptions filled, and be sure you take the sleep aid before you go to bed tonight; get a good night's rest. I'll see you and Louisa on Friday, all right?"

"Yes."

"And, Martin ... you made excellent progress today. Well done."

Chapter 22

Martin felt odd on his drive home from Truro. An unfamiliar buoyancy eased through him as he thought about his revelatory experience in Dr. Newell's office. It was as if a weight which he had carried with him for a lifetime had suddenly been lifted from his shoulders.

Louisa glanced up from the salad she was preparing when she heard the jingle of his keys in the door.

"Hello," she said, quickly returning her focus to the tomato under the knife in her hand. "Was it a good trip?"

Martin's keys clattered into the basket at the end of the table before he stooped to pick his son up from the high chair. "Yes." He sighed and nodded his head. "It was a good trip." After placing a kiss on the boy's forehead, he walked over to his wife and, taking her by surprise, wrapped his arm around her and nuzzled into her neck.

Louisa turned, her arm slipping around him, and he pressed his lips to hers. The kiss lingered and deepened.

"Mmm, that's nice," she cooed into his ear. "Dinner's almost ready ... if you wanted to wash first," she said, caressing his cheek.

"Yes." He touched his head to his son's and slipped him back into the high chair. "I'll be down in a minute." His eyes sparkled as he ducked his head and gave her a shy smile.

The evening passed quietly with no mention of Martin's trip to Truro. James had been tucked into bed, and Louisa sat on the sofa reading when he presented her with a glass of the Zinfandel he had noticed on the kitchen counter.

"A special occasion?" she asked as she held up her glass.

"Not really."

Perhaps it was a vicarious consumption of liquid courage, but watching as his wife sipped at her glass of wine seemed to prepare him to share not only the epiphanic moment that he had experienced, but also what he feared his wife could perceive to be a weakness in him.

"I had an interesting session with Dr. Newell today."

"Oh?" She moved to the middle of the sofa to make room for him.

Taking a seat, he pulled his arm up behind her and she nestled against him before pulling up her feet.

"Well, you're aware of the difficult relationship that I've had with my parents?"

Louisa eyes rolled towards him. "Martin, I *have* met your mother."

"Mm, yes."

She took a sip of her wine and patted his leg. "Go on."

He cleared his throat. "I always thought that there was something wrong with me. Something that prevented them from feeling any affection for me, something missing. That if I tried hard enough they'd like me. Or at least find it easier to tolerate me."

"*Oh, Martin.*" Louisa tipped her head back and peered up at him, teary eyed.

He cleared his throat again and averted his gaze. "If you could avoid being emotional, Louisa, it would make this considerably easier."

"I can't just turn it off, Martin," she replied defensively. She pulled a tissue from the box on the coffee table before wiping her eyes and blowing her nose. "I'll do my best. It's just so sad to think of a little boy knowing that he's not loved. You knew from the beginning?"

Air hissed from Martin's nose, and he fidgeted under her weight against him.

"I can recall a time when their behaviour towards me seemed normal. I don't remember ever feeling like a good thing in their lives though. I assumed, until I went off to boarding school, that parents were all the same. But at school, I'd see my classmates with their parents—the ease they had in talking with them—the way the parents touched their children—gave them hugs—even kisses."

Martin waited as a truck rattled up Roscarrock Hill before continuing on.

"I think that, as a child, the only way that I could reconcile the differences between the sort of relationship that I had with my parents and the sort my peers appeared to have with theirs was to conclude that either I wasn't good enough or, as I grew older, that there was some physiological explanation for it. And I know it sounds ridiculous ... I'm a doctor ... but until today, I was sure that there was something missing in me. Some bit of DNA that failed to replicate properly, perhaps."

"Oh, Martin." Louisa looked up at him and rested her hand against his cheek. "You really thought that there was something wrong with you? Or that if you were a better little boy they would love you?"

"How *else* would it make sense, Louisa? You're seven years old, and your parents seem to loathe you."

"I'm not questioning, Martin. I'm just very sorry."

"Mm, I see."

Louisa drank down the last of her wine and set the glass on the coffee table.

Martin glanced down at her before continuing. "Dr. Newell asked today about the love I feel for James ... when I first loved him, what James could do as he grew up to make me love him even more.

"It helped me to understand that the love I feel for our son comes from inside of me. It's not something James has to earn, or something he'll lose if he's not the sort of person I think he should be ... if he's shy or socially awkward."

He sighed heavily and glanced down at her. "If he turns out ... if he turns out to be like me."

Louisa reached forward and pulled another tissue from the box.

Martin watched her, hissing out another breathe as she blew her nose. He tightened his hold on her. "I'll always love James. My parents never loved me. And I understand now that it wasn't because there was something missing in me, but because there was something missing in them. Nothing I could have done would have changed anything."

Louisa turned and looked at him, shaking her head, unable to think of anything to say that would be worthy of the moment.

Martin pulled his arm from behind her and wiped his sweaty palms on his thighs. "Ruth told me the day you left for Spain that I push you away because I believe you couldn't love someone like me—that I don't think I deserve you."

Louisa's hand instinctively reached out for his. "And do you agree?"

"I think that's probably true. I know I'm not very good at being a husband ... at behaving as a husband should."

"Martin, I fell in love with you the day we met. I suspect I probably didn't give you that impression though, hmm?"

He shrugged his shoulders. "There was a time or two that I thought you were going to slap me, actually."

"You picked up on that, did you?"

"Surprisingly, yes."

"Well, you did seem a bit odd to me at first."

Martin pulled back and looked at her incredulously. "Just at first?"

She smiled up at him and then settled back in under his arm. "Now you just seem ... *unusual.*"

"Ah."

Louise squeezed his hand. "Anyway, at first it was a physical attraction that—"

"A *physical* attraction?"

"Yes, Martin, a physical attraction. But that made me want to get to know you. I'm still drawn to you physically, but it's so much more now. You're a man I can respect. Such a good, honourable, and dignified man. A man whom I can admire. You're a committed doctor ... a brilliant doctor. And I know you try very hard to keep this under wraps, but I'm on to you, Martin. You have a kind and gentle spirit. And for all of this, you deserve whoever you choose to spend your life with. And I'm thankful you chose me."

Martin squeezed her hand and sighed deeply before standing up and going to the kitchen. He returned with the bottle of wine and refilled his wife's now empty glass before setting the bottle on the coffee table.

She gave him a quizzical look as he sat back down beside her.

"I have to admit something to you, Louisa. I'm fine with this because I understand it from a medical perspective, but I don't know how you'll see it. And I hope that you'll still respect me and not see this as a weakness." He slowly rubbed his palms together, keeping his eyes focused in front of him. I'm going to try taking antidepressants. I'm depressed, and I can't seem to shake it on my own."

Louisa put her hand on his thigh. "Martin, that is wonderful news to me. I've watched you struggling, but I was afraid to say anything." She brushed her fingers against his face. "You're such a determined man, and I was afraid that if I said something about it ... well, that you might dig in your heels. Or that you'd feel like you failed somehow."

"I *do* feel like I've failed. But not with that—with our marriage. But, I meant what I said about wanting to learn to be a better husband."

She set her glass down on the coffee table and peered up at him. "When did you say that?"

"Before your operation. You were feeling a bit ... fuzzy. I told you that I'd never been a husband before, and I didn't think I was very good at it, but that I wanted to learn."

"I wish I'd heard you say it."

"You did. I just said it again."

"No. I mean I'm sorry I missed the original version." She stretched up to kiss him on the cheek.

"Mm, I see."

Louisa curled up against him and pulled his arm around her. He gazed down at her for a moment and then pressed his lips to the top of her head.

"Louisa."

"Yes, Martin?"

"Do you remember when we were talking on the terrace, the day after we'd been drinking wine?"

"And you told me you loved me—twice?" She tipped her head back to look at him. "*And* you accused me of having erotomania?"

"Mm, yes. That was the day. I want to explain why I said what I did."

"It might be best if you *didn't* try to explain, Martin. Just leave that one be, maybe?"

"I *want* to explain."

He reached over and picked up her glass. "Here, have some more wine," he said, handing it to her. "I'd just stepped out to get some air. My head had been pounding all day, and there'd been a steady stream of *idiots* coming in to see me under false pretences." He screwed up his face. "Wasting my time with stale clichés and imbecilic wisecracks after I fell asleep on the kitchen floor with that ... parasite-infested canine that used to sneak in here all the time. The selfish, pig-ignorant halfwits can't seem to fathom tha—"

Louisa put her hand over his mouth. "Martin, you've lost the thread."

"Mm, yes." He cleared his throat and shook his head. "Well, when you came up and started talking to me, my head was spinning. When you said you loved me, I just couldn't believe that to be true. I didn't think it was possible for someone to love me. I was grasping for some logical explanation as to why you would say that. I panicked and started in with that De Clerambault's rubbish. I'm sorry."

"Thank you for the apology, Martin. I'm sorry I slapped you," she said, reaching up to caress his long past wounded face.

"It's fine; it was the other cheek."

"That was a joke, Martin!" she said, smiling up at him.

"Yes."

"Very good."

Martin closed his eyes and sat stroking his wife's arm, thinking about the feelings that she had expressed to him minutes earlier. He found himself going through the attributes she had listed, mentally discounting most of them.

Good—How can she possibly see me as a good man when I shout insults at my patients?

Honourable—Well, I am honest—to a fault in fact.

Dignified? From day one I've walked all over that adjective. I ran myself right into a door the first day I met her. Then I made a fool of myself in front of the entire village by getting up on stage and cursing into the microphone. And less than a month ago, I vomited all over Joe Penhale—with a crowd of onlookers to witness it. No, definitely not dignified.

Committed doctor—Okay, I'll give her that one.

Kind and gentle spirit—Well, perhaps in some situations. I am kind and gentle with James. And gentle with Louisa. But kind? How many times have I belittled her job. And why do I do that? I respect what she does with this village's children. And all of my thoughtless remarks to her over the years ... Although, most of the time it was just my social ineptitude rearing its ugly head.

And she said that she admires and respects me. If she respects me, then why does she laugh at me. She had a good laugh with Mark Mylow's sister about my blood problem, then later trivialised the problem by suggesting that maybe I should try homeopathic medicine. And she mocks me. Why would she mock someone she admires and respects? I know she thinks she admires and respects me, but if she thought about the number of times she's felt compelled to apologise for my behaviour, I suspect she might think differently.

And being attracted to me physically? "People are surprisingly eclectic in their sexual inclinations", he recalled Ruth saying. *There's no accounting for taste.*

"Martin, are you listening?"

He glanced down at his wife who was now looking up at him intently. "I'm sorry, what did you say?"

"Never mind, it wasn't important. Are you getting tired? We might be more comfortable cuddling up in bed than we are here on the sofa."

A look of unease passed over his face, and she quickly added, "Just cuddle, nothing else."

"Yes. That'd be fine ... good. Erm, Dr. Newell also wrote a prescription for zolpidem to help me sleep. I'll try it Saturday night. There could be a residual effect, so I don't think it would be wise to take it when I have patients the next day."

"Well, I hope you tolerate it better than you did the lavender oil on your pillow," she said, recalling a previous, and unsuccessful, attempt to alleviate his insomnia.

"It certainly can't smell any worse."

Louisa rolled her eyes at him. "Oh, Martin. I only used a tiny bit."

Chapter 23

The sun rises early during summer in Cornwall and with it, the gulls and the jackdaws. Their heckling calls prodded Martin from his sleep. With a groan, he rolled on to his side before forcing his eyes open.

Light streamed in the window, affecting him like an excessively cheerful person on a bad day. He slapped a hand over his eyes as an ache began in his head.

The happy sounds of his baby son emanated from across the hall, and he knew it would be only minutes before the happy sounds turned into wailing demands for attention and breakfast. Leaving his sleeping wife, he slid the switch on the alarm to the off position and rolled out of the comfort of their bed before crossing the landing to the nursery.

He stood in the doorway watching, unseen by the baby distracted by the sunbeam he was trying to catch in his hand. James was the only human being with whom Martin had ever felt totally at ease. His son never expected him to pretend to be someone he wasn't. He felt accepted when he was with James.

A lump formed in his throat as he watched the little boy he loved so dearly. In time, the child would grow up to discover his many imperfections. He worried that James, too, would find him to be an imposition, a dispensable bit of baggage weighing him down.

He plucked the boy from his cot and held him to his chest, enveloped firmly in his arms. It was a simple gesture that he had longed for from his own parents. He longed for it from Louisa as well, but to ask for it seemed such a selfish and juvenile request. Louisa kept a certain distance. It wasn't that their relationship had been devoid of intimacy, at least not in the strictest sense of the word. But there was a wariness and uncertainty in her touch.

Martin pressed his fingers to his son's lips as they made their way downstairs, an ineffectual attempt to mute his excited babbles.

"Shh, shh, shh, shh, shh. You'll wake your mummy," he whispered in the child's ear.

A surgical video was playing on Martin's laptop, and her son was happily finger painting with what remained of his mashed banana when Louisa came into the kitchen.

"There are my boys!"

James squealed and reached his arms out to his mother, ready to be freed from the confines of his high chair.

"Martin, I think that James and I'll spend some time with Ruth this morning. We haven't seen her in several days."

"Mm, she's been very busy with Al."

"I know. Do you think she's taken on too much with this B&B project?" she asked as she filled the basket for the coffee machine.

"It really doesn't matter what you and I think. Ruth will do what she wants to do, regardless."

"Hmm, I suppose you're right. But maybe you could stop by and talk to her over your lunch break ... remind her not to overdo?" She smiled at him flirtatiously, a wasted gesture as it sailed past him.

Martin slapped his laptop shut and screwed up his face. "You just said that you and James were seeing her this morning. Can't *you* discuss it with her?"

"I just think she'd be more apt to listen to you. You are a doctor ... and her nephew."

"Yes, but I have a full schedule, Louisa."

"But I think Ruth has something planned for you for lunch. A new recipe maybe?"

Martin eyed her suspiciously. "Ruth doesn't cook."

Louisa tossed the tea towel on to the counter. "Oh, Martin! Just go see your aunt and eat whatever she puts in front of you!" Her face softened as her wide-eyed husband sat erect in his chair, staring back at her.

"Yes," he said, ducking his head.

She came around to his side of the table and leaned over to kiss him.

"Thank you, Martin. I appreciate it." She patted a hand on his cheek, feeling a pang of guilt for her well-intentioned deceitfulness. The lunch was a thinly veiled excuse for Ruth to have a heart-to-heart with her nephew.

He tipped his cup back and swallowed the last of his coffee before refilling it and heading off under the stairs.

"Mornin', Doc," Morwenna said as Martin stooped through the doorway to his consulting room.

"Yes."

"Oh, Doc, I was wonderin' ... could I take off a couple hours early today?" the receptionist yelled out as the door began to close. Her volume increased. "Al's goin' to Truro to pick up some supplies for the farm, and he asked me to go along!"

Martin dropped into his chair, rubbing at the throbbing that had begun in his forehead. "Morwenna, if you want to talk to me come into the consulting room!"

"I would but you yell at me to get out when I come in there!"

"Morwenna! Just do it!"

Bangles jangling, she appeared in the doorway. "So, can I, Doc?"

Martin scowled at the garishly dressed girl. "Can you what!"

"All right, no need to shout. I just wanna know if I can take off a couple hours early today. We don't have any patients scheduled after four o'clock."

"Erm, yes. I guess that would be fine."

"Thanks, Doc." The young woman took a step away before turning around. "You doin' okay?"

"Yes, I'm fine. Go back to your desk."

She gave a surreptitious roll of her eyes and then spun on her heel, mumbling to herself, "Thank you for your concern, Morwenna."

With the unanticipated lunch at his aunt's and a late afternoon call that he needed to make to the Hanley farm, Martin now had a hectic day in front of him. The morning passed quickly, and he was about to leave for Ruth's when the ingratiating voice of Mrs. Tishell broke the silence. The village chemist had a long-standing and well-known infatuation with the village GP.

"Oh, Dr. Ellingham, I'm so glad I caught you before you went to lunch. I thought you might be interested in this article from the latest issue of the *M - H - R - A* bulletin, warning of improper packaging of a certain nebulizer adaptor. They've issued a recall of the product. I took the liberty of bringing you a copy. I know you like to stay abreast of these things."

She batted her eyes beguilingly as she slid the article across his desk, leaning down slightly more than necessary. Her fingers teased her cardigan jumper open, drawing his attention to her ever-present cervical collar. After years of wearing the apparatus, for what Martin felt certain to be somatised symptoms, the woman had slipped in the bathtub. The resultant ruptured disc in her neck gave her just cause to sport the appurtenance without fear of recrimination from the doctor.

Martin's eyes snapped back to the patient notes he needed to sign. "Thank you, Mrs. Tishell. Just leave it on my desk."

She hesitated. "Actually, Doctor"—her finger wandered languidly back and forth, tracing lines across the desktop as her tongue slid across her upper lip, her hip swinging out ever so slightly— "it seems like ages since you stopped in my shop, and

I just wanted to say that I've missed you. It's been a long time since we've had a chance to catch up on the latest medical developments. Perhaps—"

"Mrs. Tishell, I have a very busy schedule so if you don't mind ..." Martin gestured towards the door.

"Of course, Dr. Ellingham. You *are* a busy man. I'm so sorry."

The chemist moved through into the reception room, and Martin hurried over to slam the door shut behind her. "Gawd."

He had been oblivious, for several years, to what the rest of the village had found obvious. But then a little more than a year ago, he left a two-month-old James Henry in the woman's care. Unbeknownst to him, Mrs. Tishell had become obsessed with him, driving her to self-medicate. Under a drug-induced psychosis, she absconded with the baby, sending Martin and Louisa on a frantic search before finally tracking her down, waiting for her Romeo to join her in an almost two hundred-year-old pleasure house-turned-holiday cottage.

The woman spent six months in a mental health facility recovering. She had been deemed fit by the General Pharmaceutical Council to resume her duties as the village chemist, but, though almost certainly harmless, she put Martin on the defensive.

As soon as he was sure that the coast was clear, he headed down the hill to Ruth's. He received the typical staid greeting before she led him to the kitchen.

"Have a seat, Martin," she said as she set two bowls of what appeared to be a basic chicken soup on the table. "I had a very nice visit with your wife and son this morning. Al's kept me so busy that I've hardly had the time to get over to see you." She went to the refrigerator and removed a plate of sandwiches.

Martin medically scrutinized her as she walked across the room, noting her gait and general carriage, looking for any sign that she could be overextending herself. She appeared perfectly healthy to his doctor's eyes, but he knew that his visual diagnostic conclusion would never satisfy his wife.

"Ruth, are you sure Al's not asking too much of you? This isn't getting too tiring for you, is it?" he asked.

"Oh, for goodness' sake, Martin. I may be old, but I'm not decrepit."

Martin squirmed in his chair. No matter how he handled the situation, he was going to have a woman annoyed with him.

"*Nooo*, you're not. I'm only saying that you seem to be working some long hours on this project, and I'm concerned for your welfare."

Ruth squinted her eyes at her him. "Well, thank you for your concern, Martin, but there's no need to worry about me. I'm *loving* this."

She paused, taking note of how thin her nephew was getting. "How about you? How's the therapy going?"

Martin focused his attention on his plate, avoiding eye contact with the woman. "Mm, fine. Dr. Newell seems to be quite competent. Thank you for facilitating that by the way."

"You're quite welcome. Erm, Louisa mentioned that you're still not sleeping well. Did you discuss this with your therapist? It could be significant you know."

He glanced up at her before peering under the top slice of bread on his sandwich. "This is just cheese and pickles!" he said, wagging a finger at the modest meal in front of him.

"Some might call it comfort food, Martin. Did they not teach you *any* of the social graces when you were at that boarding school?"

"Yes, but Louisa said you had a new recipe you were trying out. This is just chicken soup and a sandwich."

"Well, if you were expecting Beef Wellington, you came to the wrong place. I'm not a cook. Now, I believe I asked you about your insomnia."

"Mm. Dr. Newell did send me home with a prescription for zolpidem, but after giving it some thought I've decided that, given my position, it would be best to avoid using it. I could get called out in the night, and I need to be able to drive ... to think coherently."

"Hmm. I have to admit, that could be a concern. Just be sure you bring it up with Dr. Newell when you see him tomorrow. He'll want to know about his patient's noncompliance." Ruth hesitated, her soup spoon poised in the air. "Has Dr. Newell been able to jog your memory at all? You and I did discuss the possibility that your blood sensitivity stems from some sort of a traumatic childhood incident."

Martin stared back at her, uncertain of how much information he wanted to disclose. "I've been having nightmares. Just glimpses. Flashes of images mostly."

Picking up her napkin and wiping her mouth, the elderly woman asked, "Martin, do you have memories of your childhood? Disturbing memories?"

"What do you mean by disturbing memories?"

"I suspect if you've had them I wouldn't need to explain. Does that mean you've *not* had any disturbing memories?"

A stream of air hissed from his nose. "I really don't need another person analysing my unhappy childhood, Aunt Ruth."

She gave him a sympathetic smile. "I'm only concerned for *your* welfare, Martin."

He let out a heavy sigh. "Yes, I have had some. You know the kind of parents I had."

"I fear I may not know the half of it. And I'm familiar with that dreadful boarding school that your father sent you to. There were plenty of other schools that were just as well respected and without the reputation yours had for their questionable approach to discipline."

Martin glanced at his watch, wondering how much longer the interrogation might go on. "Dad thought I needed some toughening up."

He picked up his dishes and carried them to the sink. "Ruth, I do remember some things. Glimpses of things. I hope that's all there is to be remembered, but ..."

The old woman looked uncertainly at her nephew. "Do you have some partial memories but can't quite see the whole picture?"

Martin leaned back on the counter. "I'm not sure they're even partial memories. Like I said, they're glimpses, flashes, sometimes sensations."

He had Ruth's attention now. "Sensations? What kind of sensations?"

"Panic, anxiety, fear. I get close to remembering sometimes, but then the image evaporates."

"This must be terribly frustrating for you."

Martin was beginning to feel emotions stirring in him, and he glanced at his watch again. "Well, I better crack on. Thank you for lunch, Ruth."

"You're quite welcome."

She put her hand on her nephew's shoulder. "Martin, I'm here anytime you'd like to talk."

"Mm, thank you."

Martin left his aunt's feeling very uncomfortable about her concern for him. He was much more accustomed to dealing with his problems on his own.

Chapter 24

When he returned to the surgery after lunch, Martin could hear voices in the kitchen. He ducked under the stairs, hoping to spend a few moments with his family before the afternoon patients began to arrive.

James reached his arms out when he saw his father come into view, and Martin lifted him from the high chair. He stroked the backs of his fingers across the boy's cheek, the silkiness of his skin never failing to affect him. Having spent the better part of his life living either alone or in a testosterone charged environment, caressing his wife and son seemed to quench a tactile thirst.

"Did you get a chance to visit Ruth?" Louisa asked as she folded the baby clothes that had just come out of the dryer.

"I did, and she seems to be fine with the workload Al's given her. Enjoying it, actually."

Louisa laid down the baby blanket that was in her hand. "But you did suggest that she should cut back on the amount of time she's working, right?"

"No. I did observe her for any signs that she could be suffering from stress or fatigue, and if you'd like my medical opinion, I don't think there's any cause for concern."

Louisa huffed out a breath. "Oh, *Martin*. Well, I think at the very least you need to keep a close eye on her."

"Yes. You'll be due for a brain scan as well as an x-ray of your clavicle next week," he said, moving the discussion in a different direction. "I thought that I could try to schedule it for Friday. It would save us another trip to Truro."

"Yes, that sounds good, Martin. Does that mean I might be able to get rid of the sling?"

"I would say that the chances of that are good."

"It'll be wonderful to be able to do things with two hands again. Things like this." She came over and embraced him with one arm.

"Mm, yes. But remember, Louisa, I said the chances are good. I don't want you to be disappointed if you need more time to heal."

She stretched up and placed a kiss on his lips. "Don't worry. I won't make you sleep on the terrace if I find out I'm stuck with this stupid thing for another couple of weeks."

"Good. Erm, I'll be driving out to see a patient this afternoon, so I could be running a bit late for dinner."

"Oh. I'll fix something that I can reheat when you get home then."

Martin headed back under the stairs to tend to his afternoon patients.

By the time four o'clock rolled around, the headache that he had started the day with had returned. He knew it was likely a side effect of the antidepressant he was taking. He would mention it to Dr. Newell at his next appointment.

It was a perfect summer day, and Martin drove through the winding country lanes with the car windows rolled down. He inhaled deeply as he drove past a farmer harvesting a field of alfalfa. The sweet smell was reminiscent of his childhood days at the farm.

Auntie Joan and Uncle Phil had a half-dozen or so dairy cows. It was an eventful day when Uncle Phil finally deemed him grown up enough to handle the sharp tines of the hay fork and feed the cows on his own. He was certain that summer, that at the ripe old age of nine years, he had reached manhood. He returned to boarding school with a newfound confidence. A confidence which was quickly squelched during a bullying incident in a quiet hallway, resulting in a painful lump on the back of his head and a caning by the headmaster.

All seemed quiet when Martin arrived at the Hanley farm. Mr. Hanley met him at the door. "What are *you* doin' here?" the man grumbled.

"I've come to remove your sutures, and I'd also like to take a look at your son. Your wife brought him into my surgery a while back."

"Come on in," Mr. Hanley said as he waved him through the door.

"If you could lie down for me ..." Martin gestured towards the sofa.

He knelt down by his patient and, pulling out his forceps and a pair of scissors, proceeded to remove the stitches he had put in to close the gash in the man's forehead. When he finished with the task, he leaned towards Hanley's face, catching the unmistakable door of alcohol on his breath.

Martin got to his feet. "You can sit up now." He hesitated before continuing. "I'd like to discuss your other problem before I leave today."

Mr. Hanley glared back at him. "What problem is that?"

"You have a drink problem, and I think it needs to be addressed, don't you?"

"What are you sayin'? So I enjoy a nip or two now and then. There tain't no crime in'nat!"

Martin screwed up his face at the man. "A nip or two? The last time I was here, you were so intoxicated that you could barely stand. It's how you got that gash on your forehead, remember? And I can smell alcohol on your breath right now."

"I done nothin' wrong. You suggestin' otherwise?"

"I'm *suggesting* that you have a problem controlling your alcohol consumption. I'd like to arrange for you to meet with someone who's trained to treat people with your condition. I can make some calls tomorrow and—"

"Git out! You don't know what yer talkin' about!"

Martin was struggling to keep his annoyance with the man in check and uncertain about how far to push him.

"Mr. Hanley, I can't force you to get treatment, but I would highly recommend that you take me up on my offer to assist you with this. I'm concerned for you as well as for the welfare of your wife and children."

Hanley got to his feet and took several staggered steps towards Martin. He stood, eyeing him menacingly. "Git out! Git outta my 'ouse!"

Martin moved towards the front door but paused momentarily. For once, Mrs. Tishell's incessant sharing of M.H.R.A. bulletins could prove helpful. "I'd like to take a look at your son first. It seems there's been a recall of an adapter on his nebuliser. I'll leave the replacement part here, but I should check him over ... make sure there have been no adverse effects. Is he upstairs?"

Hanley waved his hand towards the outbuildings in the side yard. "He's out there somewhere," he slurred.

"Thank you," the doctor said as he stepped out the door. Mr. Hanley slammed it behind him.

Martin looked in the direction of the barn, but there was no sign of Evan. As he walked around the far side of the building he spotted a small form huddled up against a stone wall.

"Hello, Evan. I stopped by to take a look at you, listen to those lungs of yours."

The little boy didn't answer, but he nodded his head as his gaze remained fixed on the ground in front of him.

Martin reached down to take hold of his wrist, but the child turned away, sheltering his arm. The doctor's heart sank as he knew what he was likely to find when he examined him.

He crouched down. "I'm going to listened to your heart and lungs, just like I did when you came to my surgery."

Evan shook his head and hid his face in his arm.

Martin scratched at an eyebrow before pulling his stethoscope from his bag. "I tell you what, I'll let you listen first."

The little boy pulled his head up, peering warily at the doctor. "Okay."

Pointing to the earpieces on the instrument, Martin explained, "I'll put these into your ears, then I'll unbutton your shirt and put the other end on your chest. You tell me what you hear."

The child's fearful expression eased as he heard his own heart beating out a steady rhythm. "It sounds like, bump, bump, bump."

"Good, that's the way it's supposed to sound. May I have a turn?" Martin asked.

The boy hesitated. "Yeah, but can I listen again after that?"

"How 'bout I listen, then look at that arm? When I'm finished, you can have another turn."

Evan wiped at his face with his shirt sleeve and pulled the stethoscope from his ears before returning it to the doctor.

Martin checked the child's lungs and heart before proceeding to examine the boy as he huddled against the wall.

"Tell me if anything hurts, Evan."

Martin held the child's arm between his hands, palpating gently from the elbow down towards his wrist.

The little boy pulled back and began to cry when Martin's hands neared the injury. He noted nothing else out of the ordinary, aside from a suspicious bruise on his face.

"Evan, I think we need to get some pictures taken of the bones in your arm, just to make sure that everything's okay in there. Where's your mother?"

The child looked at Martin with fear in his eyes. "She went into Wadebridge ... to the supermarket."

The doctor stood up and walked out of earshot of the boy before pulling out his mobile to ring Joe Penhale.

"I need to take the boy to Truro for x-rays, but I can't legally do that without a parent's consent. Mrs. Hanley's in Wadebridge, so I need you to come out here and help me with the father. He's been drinking and isn't in a cooperative mood."

Martin screwed up his face as he listened to the constable's response before answering, "*No*, the boy needs immediate medical care, and it can't wait any longer. Clear it with the boys in Exeter later, Penhale. Just get out here ... now!"

Martin rang off and returned his attention to Evan, retrieving a small splint from his medical bag and affixing it to the boy's arm. He took note of the tremors which had begun in the child, and he leaned over to gather him into his arms.

"How 'bout we wait for PC Penhale in my car, Evan? We can get you warmed up a bit, okay?"

The child glanced at the house and gave Martin a wary nod.

Once back in the Lexus, Martin turned on the heat and opened the bottle of water he had in his cup holder, instructing Evan to swallow the paracetamol he put in his hand.

"Evan, did your father do this to your arm?" Martin asked softly. He pulled his handkerchief from his pocket and wiped the tears and mucous from the boy's face.

The child peered up at him, shaking his head.

Martin's voice became more insistent. "You *must* tell me the truth about what happened to your arm if I'm to help your father."

The boy sat mum, turning his head towards the side window.

"Evan, when you came to see me in my surgery, I asked about your symptoms—if you had a cough, fever, that sort of thing. I needed to know those things so that I could figure out how best to help you to get well again.

"I need to know about your father's symptoms, too, and I need you to help me with that. Did your father injure your arm?"

Evan looked down at his hands before answering timidly, "He doesn't *mean* it. He gets cross when he drinks. I made him cross, so he grabbed my arm."

"Thank you, Evan."

Martin heard the sound of an approaching siren and slipped the stethoscope earpieces into the boy's ears. "Wait right here, Evan. I just need to bring some papers to your father, then I'll drive you to hospital where they have a machine that can take the pictures we need."

"Will it hurt?"

"No. It's just like getting your picture taken with a camera, but the pictures are of your insides instead of the outside. You wait here. I'll be right back."

Jim Hanley was neither a sober nor a happy man when he met the doctor and constable at the door.

"Mr. Hanley, I need your consent to take your son into Truro to get the treatment he needs. He has a fractured arm. PC Penhale has the form. You only need to sign it. I'll take him over there."

"Yer not takin' my son anywhere!"

Martin's patience had been worn threadbare by the abusive alcoholic, and he snarled back, "Your son is going to hospital with or without your consent! I would *highly* recommend that you cooperate and sign the bloody form! If you do, it's just possible that the court will go a little easier on you when you're brought up on charges of child abuse!"

Hanley moved towards Martin. "Child abuse! Who the 'ell do you think you are? Comin' in ta a man's 'ome ... accusin' 'im!" the alcoholic slurred.

"I'm a doctor with a seven-year-old child who's suffering from a broken arm, and he needs *immediate* medical care,"

Martin said through clenched teeth. "I can't provide that care until you sign the *damn — form.*"

Joe stepped forward, holding out the sheet of paper. "Come on, Jim. This would all go a lot easier if you just gave the doc your consent."

Hanley waved a dismissive hand through the air. "He's fine. The boy's jus' a girl's blouse. Can't even take a crack upside the head once in a while." Hanley gave a derisive snort. "Boy runs off blubberin' like a baby, 'e does."

Heat raced up Martin's neck, bringing a flush to his face.

The drunk took several staggered steps forward, pushing the doctor back with jabs to his chest. "You got no right tellin' me what ta do."

With his pulse pounding in his ears, Martin's fists clenched and unclenched at his sides, and he sucked in ragged breaths as Hanley ranted on.

"That boy don't ever listen. The lil' bastard needed some sense slapped into 'im!"

The man's vitriol continued, intensifying Martin's anger until it was no longer a drunken farmer he was facing, but his own father. No longer Jim Hanley's words, but Christopher Ellingham's.

"You had it coming, Martin. If a good rollicking doesn't get through that thick head of yours, what do you expect? Good God, boy! It's a bloody nose! Stop your snivelling and grow a pair."

His father's words tipped Martin's anger into rage and he erupted, lashing out at the belligerent drunk, knocking him to the floor.

Joe Penhale grabbed hold around his chest, but he was no match for the much larger doctor. Martin shook himself free and grabbed Hanley by the front of his shirt, yanking him to his feet. He pulled his fist back, ready to deliver a blow to the drunk's face when the sensation of the constable's hands on his arms began to seep into his consciousness.

Joe's voice returned him to the present. "Stop it, Doc! You need ta calm down ... let me handle it."

Martin squeezed his eyes shut, jerking away from the policeman as he tried to regain his equilibrium. He took in a deep breath, dropped his fist to his side, and walked out the door. Joe Penhale joined him a short time later with the necessary form, now signed by Jim Hanley.

"Doc, you okay?" the constable asked.

"Yeah, just give me a minute." Martin stood facing a porch post, leaning against it with his forehead resting on his hands. He took in several deep breaths before pushing himself erect.

He turned to Joe. "All right, I'll run the boy to Truro." He paused. "I know you'll have to report this Penhale. I'm sorry to put you in the middle of it."

The constable gave Martin a timid smile and grabbed hold of his heavily festooned belt before hiking up his pants. "The way I saw it, Doc ... Mr. Hanley assaulted you when he started pokin' his finger in your chest. It was self-defence. And I don't believe any damage was done, so no report will be necessary."

The doctor blinked back at him. "Mm, thank you Penhale."

After driving Evan to hospital, Martin stayed until the boy had been treated and released to a Children's Services advocate. It was after half nine before he was on the highway and headed back to Portwenn.

Chapter 25

Louisa glanced at her watch again. *Ten-fifteen. Where are you, Martin?* She snapped her book shut and tossed it on to the sofa before going to the kitchen to make a cup of tea.

A dozen what-ifs cycled through her head as she stared out the window into the rapidly dwindling light. *What if he ran out of petrol and is stranded out in a black spot somewhere? What if he's run into trouble with the patient he went to see? Oh, God, maybe he's been in an accident! Oh, stop it Louisa, you're going to drive yourself crazy. But why hasn't he called? Maybe all that's happened lately has been too much. He couldn't take it anymore and just left.*

The tea kettle hissed its readiness, and she turned to lift it from its base before filling her cup with water.

Dropping into a chair at the kitchen table, she sat staring absently as she worked up a self-righteous indignation. *He could have at least called to let me know he was going to be this late. Do my feelings mean nothing to him? Of course not, Louisa. They never have, and they never will. Well, this attitude of his has to change if we're going to stay together. My feelings matter! When he gets home we're going to sit down and have this out, once and for—"*

The lock rattled on the kitchen door, and she jumped up, whirling around, ready to unleash her anger on her unsuspecting husband.

"Martin, where have you been! I expected you home hours ago!"

"Things didn't go as planned out at—"

"And you didn't consider that I might be sitting here at home, having kittens, thinking something terrible might have happened?"

"Louisa, please let me explain before you—"

"I had all these awful thoughts going through my head!"

Martin clamped his lips together as his wife continued to rail against him.

"I kept imagining you attacked by some crazy recluse you'd gone to take care of out on the moor. Lying unconscious in a hospital bed somewhere having been injured in an accident and—"

"Louisa, that's completely illogical. I have identification in my wal—"

"Martin, don't you *dare* tell me what's logical or not logical. It's just what started going through my head, because I had no idea where you were! The considerate thing to do would have been to call to tell me you were going to be late."

He stood, his lips still drawn together in a straight line as his fingers twitched at his sides.

"Well, Martin?" Louisa said, crossing her arms in front of her.

"I *said* I'd be late for dinner, Louisa. And I *did* try calling your mobile on the way over to Truro, but I was in a black spot. The boy was in pain—crying. We got to the hospital. I had this headache. I was trying to keep him calm. I had to get the paperwork done and ..."

He shook his head a few times before collapsing into a chair. Putting his hands over his face, he breathed out a heavy sigh.

Louisa sat down across the table from him and gave an indignant huff. "I'm sorry. I was worried about you." She toyed with her wedding band and peered up at him. "Can I make you something to eat, or have you eaten?"

He pulled his hands away from his face, letting them drop heavily into his lap. "I'm not hungry."

"Martin, is everything okay?"

"Gawd. I completely lost control today, Louisa. The boy I told you about before ..."

She got up and took a seat next to him. "The boy you thought was being abused?"

"Mm. His father's a drunk. I'd been to their place a couple of weeks ago to stitch up the man's head after he lost his balance and crashed into a table. I went there today to remove his sutures and check up on the boy. The man had been drinking again. I tried to persuade him to get treatment. He was being belligerent, and I could see that I wasn't going to get anywhere with him, so I went to check on the boy.

"I found him outside, cowering against a wall. When I examined him, I discovered his arm had been broken. I don't know *how* long he'd been suffering with it, Louisa."

"Oh, Martin," she whispered as she slipped her arm around his shoulders.

"The mother was in Wadebridge, so I had to get Joe Penhale to come out with a parental release form. The father wouldn't sign it. He called his son a bastard and claimed the fracture was the result of justified discipline.

"I don't know what happened, Louisa. I think I shoved him and he fell to the floor. The next thing I knew, Penhale's arms were around me, trying to stop me. The man was standing in front of me and I had him by the shirt. I came so close to punching him in the face."

Louisa's hand caressed his back. "But you didn't? What stopped you?"

Martin blinked hard. "Joe Penhale. If it weren't for Penhale I would have hit the man. I turned and walked out the door. Penhale came out later with the form—signed."

He rested his arms on the table and laid his head down. Louisa stood up and brushed her hand across his head before leaning over to embrace him from behind.

"I'll make you some tea. But Martin, you really need to eat something. You haven't eaten since lunch, have you?"

"I'm not hungry."

Louisa plugged in the tea kettle and came back to the table, taking her husband's hands in hers.

"Martin, I'm proud of you. You stood up for that helpless little boy when no one else did. And you did try with the father."

"I violated the oath I took, Louisa! I just felt this rage explode in me, and I couldn't stop it."

He wiped his hand across his face, discreetly removing the tears that he couldn't contain.

Louisa turned and flipped the switch on the tea kettle. "Come on. Let's go to bed," she whispered in his ear.

Her husband's somnial mumblings and erratic body movements woke Louisa later that night. She spoke softly as she placed her hand on his arm, trying to gently rouse him.

He was clinging to something, a phantasm? The fear he felt, unbearable. He heard his father's voice. "Martin! Let go!" He felt a force grab on to his shirt. He couldn't release his grip on the phantasm, his fingers in fixed clutches. The force pulling at his shirt released its grip only to clamp on to his arm like a vice, tearing him away from the phantasm and throwing him forcefully into the shadows as a horrendous pain coursed through his arm.

"Martin, wake up!" she whispered again. "You're dreaming." She shook him harder as her volume increased. "Martin. Martin, wake up!"

He cried out and bolted upright in bed, his eyes wide as he gasped for breath.

"Martin, it's all right!" She tried to calm him, but he was lunging and reaching out, grabbing at the air. He kicked out against the blankets that had ensnared his feet, finally freeing himself and tumbling to the floor.

Louisa reached for the switch on the lamp. The sudden illumination in the room finally released him from the nightmare, and he leaned back against the bed trying desperately to catch his breath.

Louisa ran around to him and dropped to the floor, embracing him. His breathing began to slow.

"Oh, Martin, it's all right, it's all right." She pulled back and looked at him. The colour had drained from his face, and he was drenched with sweat.

"What was that all about?" Louisa asked.

"A nightmare."

Louisa turned his face to her so that she could make eye contact with him. "I'm going to get a facecloth. I'll be right back. *Don't* move."

She grabbed a cloth from the bathroom, running it under the tap before pulling dry pyjamas from his drawer.

"Martin, you've never been *this* upset by a dream," she said. "Come on, stand up and get out of those wet things." She waited as he peeled down, and then followed him into the bathroom. He tossed his pyjamas over the edge of the bathtub before turning and reaching a hand out for the flannel. "I can *do* it," he snapped, grabbing at it as she attempted to help him.

"What was the nightmare about, Martin?"

He blew out a long breath and dropped his head to his shoulder. "It seemed real. I was hanging on to something ... so tight that my fingers were locked in place. I heard my father's voice. I don't remember him ever sounding so angry. He yelled at me to let go, but I couldn't."

Turning the handle on the tap, he rinsed the cloth and wiped his face. "I couldn't open my hands. Something was pulling at me, at my shirt. I felt it grab on to my arm. It grabbed so tightly that it hurt. Then it yanked me back. I could feel something tearing from my fingers. There was a sound ... a crack."

He reached down and rubbed his arm. "It hurt. I was thrown back on to the floor, into the dark." His head swung back and forth.

Louisa took the cloth from his hand and rinsed it again before wiping his back. "What were you hanging on to?"

"I can't remember."

"Well, why do you think your father was so angry?"

Martin erupted, smacking his fist against his thigh. "Stop asking questions! I don't know!"

After reaching for his pyjamas, he pushed his feet roughly into the bottoms and slid his arms into the sleeves of the top. Taking the wet face cloth from his wife, he gave it a toss, where it joined his pyjamas on the edge of the tub.

He leaned back against the sink, lacing his fingers together behind his neck as air hissed from his nose.

Louisa looked at him sympathetically. "That's all you remember?"

He grimaced and squeezed his forearms against his head.

"Martin, let's go back to bed," she said, taking his hand and leading him back to the bedroom. "You're shivering." She crawled in and pulled the covers up before curling up against him. "Do you think it was just a nightmare, or do you think it was a memory?"

Martin shook his head. "I don't know; it seemed quite real, but ... I don't know."

She wrapped her arms around him and pulled him close.

He pushed away, eyeing her critically. "Louisa, you need to put your arm back in your sling."

"Oh, Martin, I'm fine. It feels perfectly normal now."

"Hmm."

He flipped an arm up over his head. His eyebrows gathered in as a pained expression fell across his face. "Louisa, I'm sorry that I disturb your sleep so much."

"Martin, you need to stop apologising every time you need me for something. I hate to see you go through all of this, but I'm glad that I can be here for you. I wish I'd known that you have the history you do. I could've been more understanding. Maybe even helpful."

"It's not something I would have talked about before. I wasn't sure you'd want to stay with me if you knew. But you were going to leave anyway so ..."

Louisa brushed her hand across his head. "You had nothing to lose?"

"Mm, yes." He gave her a tentative smile. "And so far, you're still here."

"I'm not going anywhere, Martin. I'm not going anywhere."

Martin slept undisturbed through the rest of the night and woke with Louisa in his arms. As was typical, she was still sleeping. He lay, studying her face. She took his breath away.

She began to stir, and he brushed the wisps of hair away from her face. Her eyes opened to his penetrating gaze. "Good morning, Martin."

"Mm."

"How are you doing today? Feeling any better?"

"I ... I feel more rested, yes."

Her hand came to rest on his cheek. "Martin, did you really knock that man to the floor?"

Martin groaned and put his hands over his face. "*Yess.*"

"So did Joe Penhale put the cuffs on you then?"

He whirled around to look at her. "Good God, no!"

Louisa giggled. "That must have taken a great deal of restraint on Joe's part. It would have been the perfect opportunity to brush the dust off of them."

"Very funny, Louisa."

"Oh, Martin, I'm just kidding. Seriously though, he's not going to press charges or anything, is he?"

"No. He said no real harm had been done so ..."

"Mm, good." She smiled apologetically as her thoughts turned to her father, serving time at Her Majesty's pleasure. "We already have one felon in the family; we don't need another."

Chapter 26

This bodes well! Martin will be pleased, Louisa thought when Poppy arrived at the back door of the surgery promptly at two o'clock. The young woman's timeliness gave Louisa ample opportunity to go through James's routine with her, as well as to cover all of the health care instructions that Martin had left for her.

James warmed to Poppy immediately, seeming to recognise her from their lunch together at Bert's. The boy scrambled over, the wood block in his hand clicking against the slate as he crawled towards her.

"Hello, James," she said as the boy reached up to her.

Louisa was pleased. James could be a rather shy child and didn't take to everyone.

She was also pleased to see that her notoriously cranky husband had stayed in the business end of the house, preventing any unhappy encounters with the potential childminder. She was hoping to limit contact with Martin until Poppy had built up some tolerance for his gruff demeanour.

Friday had brought with it cool but sunny weather, a nice day for a drive through the Cornish countryside.

Martin glanced over at his unusually quiet wife as the car wound its way through the narrow lane leading out of the village. "Is, er ... everything all right?"

Louisa gave him a forced smile. "Mm-hmm."

He returned his focus to the road in front of him, fidgeting in the abnormal silence. He replayed the day in his head, attempting to discern what transgression he may have committed to raise his wife's ire this time.

The only thing that came to mind was a small incident before breakfast. He hesitated and then took in a breath. "Louisa, I'm sorry for putting your"—he cleared his throat—"your underthings in the dryer. I was only trying to help. Perhaps you could buy new?"

Louisa turned her head slowly, tipping it down and peering up at him. "I just don't know why you haven't noticed by now, Martin, that I don't dry them that way. Why do you think my ... *underthings* are always decorating the bathroom?"

"Oh, *I've noticed*," he said, a bit more enthusiastically than he intended.

Louisa began to giggle, and he gave her a stern look.

"Am I a source of amusement to you, Louisa?" he asked, his air indignant.

She giggled again. "Maybe just a bit," she admitted, gesturing with her thumb and index finger. "It's quite charming actually, the way you get about my—"

"All right, I see. Is the air cleared now? Will you quit giving me the silent treatment?"

She shook her head. "What do you mean?"

Martin looked at her incredulously. "Louisa, we just passed Winnard's Perch, and you've hardly spoken two words to me since we left home. It's unprecedented ... and extremely nerve wracking!"

Louisa giggled again. "Martin, I'm not quiet because you ruined a bunch of my bras and knickers."

He tugged at his ear as a pink blush spread across his cheeks. "I just have some things on my mind, is all."

"Ah, I see."

Louisa smiled as she watched her husband's chest rise and fall before he relaxed into his seat.

Despite their clearing of the air, a subtle tension persisted through the entire trip to Truro. Now, sitting in front of their psychiatrist's desk, Martin eyed his wife as she fiddled with a button on her cardigan.

She had attracted Dr. Newell's attention as well with her stiff posture and nervous hand movements. He leaned his elbows on his desk and steepled his fingers. "Louisa, you've had some time to process what's been discussed in our sessions thus far. Do you have any thoughts or concerns that you'd like to talk about today?"

She glanced over at her husband and then back at the therapist. "Well, I *have* been thinking a bit about Martin's ... issues. Which, I suppose if I'm honest with myself, maybe haven't ... erm, perhaps my behaviour ... well, I just assumed that our marital struggles were a result of *Martin's* issues."

She tapped her fingers against her crossed legs and then brushed at a wrinkle in her skirt. "It's just that I've been giving some thought to the difficulties that Martin and I have been having, and ... well, though it's true that Martin can be a bit *difficult* at times, maybe I've played a part in this too ... the difficulties I mean." She cocked her head to the side as she stroked her fingers across her throat.

The psychiatrist leaned back in his chair. "That would be quite typical, Louisa. Despite what your husband may say, none of us is perfect. And it's impossible to be in a marital relationship without contributing in some way to the inevitable periods of strife."

She shifted in her chair. "Well, I may have given the impression that Martin is entirely to blame for our problems and that's ... well, that may not be *completely* true."

She ran a hand over her ponytail and shifted her gaze to the floor. "It's just that I've been trying to pay closer attention to my own behaviour lately, and I find myself acting in much the same way that my mother did with my father. She was very critical of him." Louisa crossed her legs, locking her fingers over her knee. "Although, much of her criticism *was* justified. But I don't think it helped matters."

Dr. Newell's biro spun back and forth in his fingertips. "Can you explain what you mean by that?"

She shook her head and brushed a wisp of hair from her eyes. "I don't know. I guess her criticism and nagging didn't seem to have the desired effect, quite the opposite in fact. And she always had to be in control. I think that I can be a bit ... well, a bit that way. I feel like I need to be on the defensive when I'm not in control of a situation."

Martin stared at his wife, a puzzled frown forming on his face.

"Can you give me a specific example of what you're talking about, Louisa?" Dr. Newell asked after noting Martin's reaction.

"Well ... Martin, I *have* to bring up our horrible row on Sports Day. I know you want to pretend it never happened, but I think it's important that we both understand what went on there."

Dr. Newell swivelled back and forth in his chair, noticing Martin's wilting posture and the dour expression on his face. "Why don't you tell me about what happened that day, Louisa."

Louisa's thumbs circled one another as she cast an anxious glance at her tense husband.

"We had an absolutely horrid day several weeks ago. It was Sports Day at my school, and I'd asked Martin to hand out the medals. He *said* he didn't remembered our conversation about it, so he was surprised when I told him that morning that I was expecting him to be at the school at noon. He had a lot of patients scheduled that day and wasn't happy about having to help out. But he did agree to do it.

"He came to the field promptly at noon, but I wasn't quite ready for him, so he had to wait around."

Dr. Newell held up a hand before turning to Martin. "Is this how you remember things, up to this point?"

"I believe so. But Louisa, I didn't say that I hadn't remembered because I was trying to get out of doing it. I honestly didn't remember."

Louisa threw him a dubious look.

"Why don't you continue on, Louisa, and we'll come back to the forgetfulness issue in a little while," the therapist said as he plucked a small ball from a bowl on the corner of his desk.

"Before we got to the medal presentation, I asked Martin to give a speech. An impromptu speech. He told me that he didn't have the time, that he had patients waiting."

Louisa leaned over, resting her elbows on her knees. She pressed her hands to her face and then, huffing out a breath, she straightened herself in her chair.

"I get so wrapped up sometimes in my job that I forget that Martin has responsibilities, too. But I felt that his patients could wait a while. I mean, none of them were emergencies, Martin."

Martin's jaw dropped open. "Louisa, I can't just leave patients waiting, emergencies or not! That would be terribly unprofessional of me. And quite frankly, it was unreasonable for you to ask that of me!"

"Unreasonable! I wasn't asking you to address the bloody Queen, Martin. Just give a short speech to a group of primary school children." She gave another huff before casting a see-what-I-mean glance at the therapist.

"But you're the one who's reminded me practically everyday since ... since ... well, since even before I arrived in Portwenn, that 'Social skills and a bedside manner *are* essential if one is to be a doctor in our village'," Martin said mockingly. "You *do* consider reliability and timeliness social skills, don't you?" He whipped his head to the side.

She huffed out another breath and looked to the therapist.

"Go on, Louisa," he said, giving his head a nod.

"So anyway, I got more and more upset, and Martin got more and more confused about what I expected him to do. He started in with this awful speech about how injuries can occur with running if the instruction isn't good, and how athletics aren't for everyone."

Martin glared at her. "Neither of those statements lack validity, Louisa. Many people have no interest in competitive sport. Why does everyone have to like sports for God's sake?"

"It was the whole point of Sports Day, Martin, and you were completely dismissive about it!"

Martin's mouth opened and closed several times before words came out. "That's a complete distortion! If you didn't want my opinion, then why did you keep pressuring me to give it?"

"I wasn't asking for your opinion! I wanted you to encourage the students to be physically active!"

"Then why didn't you say that instead of going on about sports—as if it's the only way to get physical exercise?"

Louisa put her hands up to the sides of her head as a growl came from her mouth. "Because, *Mar-tin*, it's called *Sports— Day!*"

Martin quieted as he looked at her, perplexed. "Then perhaps you should call it Physical Activity Day."

Dr. Newell got up and perched himself on the desktop.

Louisa's face flushed as she looked up at the man. "Well ... *this* wasn't how I intended for this to go."

"How did you intend for it to go, Louisa?" he asked.

She gave the man a tense smile and pulled in a slow breath. "I *intended* to show how enlightened I had become through my self-reflection," she said, feigning a laugh. "I really had thought this through, Martin. I know I put you in a bad spot, and you're right, I was expecting you to tell the children things that you don't believe to be true. But I don't think it was that I felt like you were being dismissive of Sports Day. I felt like you were being dismissive of *me* ... what I do."

"That wasn't my intention, Louisa. I just can't say things that I don't believe to be true. Especially in regard to health-related issues."

The psychiatrist's gaze flitted back and forth between his patients. "Have you tried to resolve the issues surrounding that day, or have you been avoiding the subject?"

Louisa screwed up her mouth. "We've kind'a tried to forget it. But I know that Martin feels guilty about what ultimately happened, and I can't help but wonder if that could be contributing to his nightmares."

"What do you mean ... ultimately happened?" Dr. Newell asked, cocking his head.

Martin's shoulders slumped as he began to dig his thumb into his palm.

Louisa pulled at the hem of her skirt. "Martin had finally had enough and told me emphatically that he didn't have time. He started walking off, and I chased after him, yelling at the top of my lungs no less. I ran out into the street without looking, right into the path of an oncoming car."

Dr. Newell blew out a breath. "Is that how you hurt your shoulder?"

"Broken clavicle," Louisa said as she wiggled her constrained arm.

"Martin, did you witness the accident?"

"Mm." He tried to blink back tears and gulp down the lump in his throat.

The psychiatrist dropped to the floor and returned to his chair. "That must have been very difficult to see."

Martin stared out the window. "She didn't want me to come with her."

"I'm sorry, come with her where?"

"In the ambulance ... or at the hospital either. I'm her husband. A doctor. And she didn't want me. I felt so guilty. I always will."

Louisa reached out and touched his arm. "Martin, I'm sorry for shutting you out that way. I think part of it was the control thing, and I know that when it comes to James and me, you get a bit ... intense about your medical responsibilities.

"I was angry with you. And at that point, because I was angry, I suppose it was easy for me to put all the blame on you. Then when you came to the hospital and started barking at the doctors and nurses, I was embarrassed."

"I'm sorry, Louisa. But I don't know how you can expect me to behave any differently in a situation like that. I wanted you to have the best care possible. I wasn't asking any more of Samuels and his hospital staff than I always expected from myself, or any of the staff under me for that matter. If you'd been given even the *basic* standard of care you wouldn't have developed the deep vein thrombosis. *I* knew it, and so did that pompous arse doctor you had."

"Martin!" Louisa hissed.

The therapist rocked back in his chair, locking his fingers behind his head. "Louisa, if it's of any comfort to you, your husband's name is well recognised in the medical community, and his behaviour really won't come as a surprise to hospital medical staff. Martin may be a bit blunter in his criticism of people than most of us, but for the most part, he's probably exhibiting typical department head behaviour. I'm afraid one doesn't attain that level of responsibility without having a very commanding authority. People may not like it, but it *is* how the hospital hierarchy tends to work."

It suddenly occurred to Louisa how her behaviour towards Martin must have made him look in the eyes of Dr. Samuels, as well as the nursing staff. *They probably delighted in seeing the big man taken down a notch.*

Dr. Newell looked at Louisa "I'm assuming that there have been other instances where you felt like you were losing control."

She cleared her throat. "Martin and I had a disagreement about the date of our son's christening. He set the date for the christening without consulting me first, and I was upset. That argument ... Well, that's another thing ... sometimes we have these ridiculous one-sided arguments where I get upset and tell Martin what he did wrong—how he *should* have handled things. And he says something like, 'That doesn't seem too complicated'. It's so frustrating! It feels like he's won again!"

Martin shook his head and blinked his eyes in confusion.

Dr. Newell swivelled around to face him. "What are you thinking when these kinds of disagreements arise, Martin?"

Martin's eyes darted between Louisa and the psychiatrist. He knew he was walking on thin ice. "It's not a competition, Louisa. And I'm not sure that I see the problem. If you tell me what I've done wrong and how you'd like me to handle the situation in future, then it really *doesn't* seem too complicated. I'll just do what you want me to do the next time."

"Louisa, do you feel like you never win an argument?" the therapist asked.

She shifted in her chair and crossed her arms in front of her. "Martin's very intelligent, and he's also very knowledgeable about almost everything it seems. Sometimes I feel like I don't stand a chance of defending my position in our rows. He makes complete sense when looking at things logically."

The therapist fiddled with a scrap of paper, folding it and unfolding it. "Martin, do you think every argument can be settled logically?"

He gave the man a blank stare. "Is there any other way to settle an argument? It certainly wouldn't make any sense to settle an argument *illogically*. I'm sorry, but I don't understand where you're going with this."

Dr. Newell leaned forward and tapped the piece of paper on his desk. "I think we're getting into that dangerous thinking versus feeling territory now. Martin, you think things through and come to a logical conclusion—the only one that makes sense to you. For Louisa, logic comes into play, but those messy feelings—emotions rather— get thrown into the mix."

The furrow between Martin's brows deepened, and he blew out a frustrated snort of air.

The therapist could see he was going to have to take a different tack. "Martin, what is it that attracted you to Louisa, apart from her obvious outward appearance."

Martin bristled. "I don't think comments about my wife's appearance are appro—"

Dr. Newell put his hands up in front of him. "Martin, I'm only saying that you have a wife who is quite comely, but I'm sure there's more to her than that. What made you want to pursue a serious relationship with her? What other qualities appealed to you?"

Martin settled back into his chair. "She's the most kind and caring person I've ever known, and I knew she would make a loving and wonderful mother."

Louisa's gaze shifted to him, and she gave him a soft smile.

"So, three of Louisa's most important qualities involve emotions?"

"Mm, but she doesn't need emotions to come to a logical conclusion."

"Martin, Louisa can't turn her emotions on and off any more easily than you can turn your logical mind on and off in social or romantic situations. We are what we are. You both need to remind yourselves of that when you interact in any circumstance."

Louisa turned to look at her husband, unprepared for the tears she saw in his eyes. "Martin?"

She reached for his hand. "Martin, is something wrong?"

He turned away quickly, pressing his fingers to his eyes.

Dr. Newell leaned forward on his desk. "Martin, did I say something to upset you?"

He shook his head and looked down at his hands. "We are what we are—Joan said the same thing, Louisa. The night after the concert ... when you told me you didn't want to see me anymore. She said that it was never going to work between us, that I should let it go. I was sure then that she was wrong. She *was* wrong, wasn't she?"

Louisa reached out and squeezed his fingers. "No, I don't think she was wrong. We *are* what we are. But I do think she was wrong when she said it was never going to work between us. I think that's up to us. I think what Dr. Newell is saying is that we need to respect our differences. Remember to *appreciate* our differences."

Dr. Newell stretched his legs out in front of him and crossed his ankles. "Martin, when you and Louisa have disagreements, try to remember that there will most likely be emotions involved. Remind yourself that Louisa is an emotional individual, and remember that it's a quality that you love about her.

"And Louisa, try to remember that Martin needs you to explain your emotions. He's not going to be able to intuit what you're feeling. You need to put it into words for him. Also, try to remind yourself that your husband is always going to think in very concrete and logical terms. That doesn't mean that he doesn't care about your feelings, but you might need to point them out to him, explain them to him."

The doctor got to his feet and made his way towards the door. "Well, I think we'll wrap it up there for this week. Try to be supportive of one another, and remember to respect your differences."

Martin cleared his throat. "I should mention that I considered the zolpidem and decided against taking it. I can't risk being sedated if I get called out in the night."

"Well, I won't force you to take anything," the psychiatrist said, rubbing a hand across the back of his neck. "And I do understand your position."

Martin gave him a nod. "As for the Prozac, I've been taking it, but I've found the headaches I get to be pretty severe." He gave his wife a sideways glance. "I know it could take a couple of weeks to adjust, though."

Dr. Newell folded his arms across his chest. "Let's see how things are going when we meet on Wednesday. If you haven't seen any improvement by then, we could certainly try a different medication."

"Mm, yes."

"Thank you, Dr. Newell," Louisa said as Martin took her arm and guided her out the door.

Louisa looked over at him as the Lexus wound its way out of the car park. "Martin, you didn't mention to me that you weren't taking the zolpidem, *or* that you were having headaches."

"I didn't realise you wanted to know."

"I think you can just assume I want to know everything about you, Martin," she said as she reached over and caressed his knee.

"Mm, yes."

Chapter 27

Louisa found herself feeling increasingly anxious as they neared Portwenn. Poppy would be a perfect childminder for James, and soon the shy girl would be reminded that with the job would come Martin Ellingham. "Martin, please be very nice to Poppy when we get home."

"Why do you always assume that I'm going to behave badly? I can dish out the same kind of simpering drivel that everyone else does—if I put my mind to it."

"Oh, Martin, don't try to be nice in *that* way. It just doesn't work for you. Just try not to be grumpy. Maybe you could ask her how she's been, tell her it's nice to see her again, that sort of thing."

Martin turned his head to look out the driver's side window, mumbling.

"Martin, are going to make an effort to be nice?"

"*Yes.* But doesn't it seem a bit disingenuous to tell someone it's nice to see them if you really couldn't care less?"

Louisa threw her head back. "Martin Ellingham, you can be the most exasperating man!"

"Well, I can assure you, Louisa, I'm not *trying* to be exasperating." He worked his hands around the steering wheel as his jaw clenched.

"Martin, just talk to her about James. Or ..." She looked at him apologetically before adding softly, "Maybe just don't talk."

Martin sat, saying nothing for several minutes. He pulled at his tie, attempting to loosen the knot before glancing over at her. "Louisa, I *am* trying. I'll do my best with Polly, but—"

Louisa rolled her eyes at her husband's legendary difficulty with names. "It's *Poppy*, Martin. Remember, it's like the flower."

"Mm, yes. Well, I'll do my best with her, but this not knowing if I'm going to pass the next test thrown at me is ... I mean, if I bugger something up are you going to ..." He sighed heavily before turning his head towards the passing landscape again. "I'm trying."

"Oh, Martin," she whispered. Actions speak louder than words, and she had sent a very clear and consistent message over the course of their relationship. If Martin "buggered something up", she either pushed him away or ran away from him.

"Martin, I know that I've been rather dismissive of your feelings over the years. I see that gruff, exasperating exterior and forget that there's a warm, tender, and really very *sensitive* man underneath all that bluster. I've lost your trust, and it'll take time for me to earn it back. But will you give me a chance?"

Martin swallowed and glanced over at her. "You have as many chances as are necessary, Louisa." To be alone again, to live his life without Louisa and James would be unbearable.

He looked at her askance. His mouth opened and closed several times before the words could escape. "Louisa, do ... do you leave me because you know that you could easily find someone else to love you?"

Louisa was left momentarily speechless by his question.

"What I mean is," he continued, "it would be very easy for you to find another man. You're a wonderful mother, you're well-liked by the people in the village, you're bright and quite industrious." The last attribute caused the corners of her mouth to tug up. "And you're very beautiful."

Louisa looked at him, her eyebrows raised. A smile appeared on her face like a wisp of smoke, before a gentle breeze of understanding wafted it away. "You feel replaceable, don't you!

You think I could just throw you away like your parents did! Martin, is that what you think?"

Martin shrugged his shoulders and turned his face away from her, mumbling again.

"Martin, if you have something to say, then say it loud enough so that I can hear it."

He scratched at his ear. "It's just that ... Well, Louisa, what if someone who could really make you happy comes along? I don't want you to feel like you're stuck with me."

She sat quietly for a few moments, looking out her side window before whirling to face him. "Martin, I just don't know what to say to you right now. I don't know if I should feel sad for you, guilty that I might have put that idea into your head, or if I should go spare over that remark. So how 'bout we take them one at a time, hmm? Pull the car over, Martin. We're going to get this sorted right here and now."

Martin was quickly regretting having admitted to his deep-seated anxiety. "Louisa, just forget what I said. It's not worth getting—"

"Pull the bloody car over, Martin. Pull into that car park right there." She wagged a finger at a roadside convenience store, and he made a left turn into the lot.

She turned and stared pointedly at him as he tried to avoid her gaze. "All right—sad. Yes, I feel terribly sad that you can't see all the wonderful qualities that I see in you. That you can't see what an extraordinary man you are."

"Oh, gawd," he moaned under his breath.

"Martin, be quiet. Guilt—" she continued. "Yes, I'm guilty of being the cause of some of your inability to see yourself in a positive light. Your *parents*, of course, take the prize there. But I do remember a time when I made a reference to being stuck at home with you and James. I regretted it the moment I said it, but ... well, the words were already out of my mouth. What can you do, hmm? And I know that I tend to focus on your more ...

unusual qualities, shall we say. What I *don't* do is to point out how those same qualities make life so much more interesting than if you were like everyone else. And how, in addition to being ... *exasperating* at times, you are also incredibly charming in your own awkward way."

Martin stared at her wide-eyed, blinking with each of her accentuated syllables.

"As to whether or not I should go spare over that remark ... I really should. I mean, you *just* got done saying I'm bright. Unless you were referring to my effervescent personality, I can only assume you mean that you find me to be a reasonably *intelligent* person. And if that's the case, Martin, do you *really* think I would have married you if I thought there was someone else on this earth who I could love the way that I love you? *Hmm, Martin?*"

He shook his head. "I knew I shouldn't have said it."

Louisa softened her tone. "No, it was good that you said it. It's something that's been weighing on you, and I'm glad you told me. But Martin, I want to know. Do you feel dispensable? Replaceable? Like some cheap household appliance that gets tossed to the kerb if it malfunctions?"

His head fell back against the headrest and he closed his eyes. When he opened them again, the vulnerability and childlike openness that had been there moments before had turned to a steely resolve.

"We should be getting home to James." He started the engine and pulled back out on to the highway.

The baby was sitting contentedly on Poppy's lap, listening to a story, when Martin and Louisa came in the door.

Martin relaxed a bit as he watched his wife's face light up while reuniting with their son.

"Hello, James! Were you a good boy while we were gone?"

"He's really sweet, Mrs. Ellingham. I had no trouble at all."

Louisa glanced over at Martin, standing just inside the doorway, looking like a mouse in the company of a clowder of cats.

"Hello, Petunia," he said as he hurried past them. "I, erm ... I have some work I need to finish up. I'll be in my office if you need me."

Louisa cringed when she heard the familiar bang/yelp as her husband's head collided with the underside of the stairs in the darkened hallway.

She stuck her head in the door of the consulting room a short time later. "The coast is clear. You can come out now."

"Mm, is she going to take the job?"

Louisa gave him a broad smile. "Yes, she is. I'm so happy about this, Martin. I feel much better about school starting back in now that we have Poppy lined up." She came over and leaned down to kiss his cheek. Thank you for telling me about her ... for making this work."

"You're welcome. Although I'm not sure that I can take any credit for making it work. I don't think hiding in my office counts."

"Well, still, I appreciate it."

"Mm, yes."

Martin bathed James after dinner and put him to bed while Louisa washed the dirty dishes. She joined him in the lounge a short time later carrying two cups of tea.

"Louisa, you don't have approval to have your arm out of that sling yet. Let alone to be carrying weight in that hand," he said as he jumped up and took the beverages from her and set them on the coffee table.

"Oh, Martin, it doesn't hurt so stop your fussing."

"I'm not ... fussing. I'm concerned for your welfare, and I feel responsible for what's ... Well, as a doctor, I know you should wait until you've had your x-rays next week before you start using that arm."

Louisa stretched up and kissed him. Then taking a seat on the sofa, she pulled him down next to her. "Can we finish our conversation now?"

"I'm sorry, what conversation?" he asked as he reached for his *BMJ.*

"Martin, you don't remember our discussion in the car?"

He laid his journal down on the table and leaned back. "Ah, that conversation. Yes."

She pulled his arm up and nestled in under it.

"I need to convince you somehow, that even though I've run off on you several times ... Well, I want to find a way to help you to feel more secure in our relationship, so that you're not constantly waiting for the other shoe to drop."

"Perhaps it'll just take time."

"That's not good enough, is it, Martin? You have to live with this anxiety until time has proven to you that I won't leave you again? That's just not good enough."

"Maybe once I have my issues worked out you'll feel happier, which might in turn make me more confident that you'll stay." Martin raised his eyebrows as he quirked his mouth.

"You know, Martin, I'm already feeling much happier."

His brow dropped as he tipped his head. "But ... all that you've had to deal with ... with me. How can you be *happier?*"

"Martin, I was going to Spain because I couldn't be happy here. Not because I can't be happy *with* you, but because I can't be happy *without* you. And you were shutting me out. Lately, you've been letting me back in. Letting me help. I want to feel like you need me. I don't want to feel unnecessary any more than you want to feel replaceable."

"Louisa, how can you possibly feel *unnecessary?* I've told you that I can't bear to be without you."

"Yes, you have. Maybe it has more to do with needing to feel like I play an active role in helping you. Being included in all that you're struggling with makes me happy because you've allowed me into a solitary place that's off limits to everyone else. That makes me feel like I'm a very special person in your life." She watched him for signs of comprehension. "Does that make sense to you?"

"Mm, yes. I think I understand what you're saying."

Noticing the dark shadows under her husband's eyes, she reached out for his hand, pulling him to his feet.

"You're tired, Dr. Ellingham. And you have patients to see in the morning."

They lay in bed a short time later, Louisa's head resting on her husband's shoulder.

He ran his fingertips slowly up and down her arm. "Louisa, do you remember the day we were talking on the terrace, and I told you to shut up?"

"Mm-hmm."

"If I had let you into ... into my solitary place, as you put it, do you think we'd have ended up in such a mess?"

She sat up. "I don't know, you never told me why you were so rude. What *was* that about?"

Martin breathed out a heavy sigh and pushed himself up beside her. "My mother had just told me she was leaving my father. And, that I had ruined her marriage—her life. When you came up and started talking, I was struggling to keep it together. The longer you talked the harder it was getting. I didn't want to lose the plot in front of you."

Louisa caressed the side of his face, "I'm so sorry, Martin."

He shook his head, "No. No. I immediately regretted speaking to you in that way. I *did* want to talk to you about it later but things ... people, one in particular ..." His lip curled into a sneer as he punched his pillow and dropped back on to the bed.

Louisa's brow lowered. "Wait a minute. What do you mean, your mother left your father? I didn't know they were divorced."

"I'm not sure they ever actually did divorce. She met someone in Portugal and was intending to leave my father. By the time she came back, trying to flog the whole story about his deathbed confession of remorse, they'd gotten back together. I'm sorry I didn't tell you."

"Anything else I missed?" she asked, shaking her head.

"I don't believe so. Just the whole thing with the money— which you know about."

"Did she say why she wanted money? I mean ... your father was a surgeon; I can't imagine she couldn't get by on what he left her."

"He had made some bad investments ... left her with nothing."

"Well that's pretty thick—asking *you* for money after they'd criticised you for your lack of financial nous," she said through clenched teeth. "How much did she want?"

"Three hundred thousand."

"Pounds! Crikey!"

"Mm, yes."

"What did you tell her?"

"I told her no, that I didn't want to have any further contact with her. But Louisa, I'm trying to explain about that day on the terrace."

She rested her hand on his and sighed. "I'm sorry, go ahead."

"Well, there were interruptions, and by the time the opportunity came around to explain myself, it seemed like it would be a bit odd. I just wonder if things might have been different if I'd been able to talk to you about it then ... let you into my ... solitary place."

Louisa lay back down with her head on his chest, "Could be. But we can't change the past can we."

"Mm, no. And we wouldn't have James if things had been any different."

"Well, you never know." Louisa lay listening to his heartbeat, strong and steady.

"The chances of our having intercourse on the exact night that James was conceived would be small," Louisa. And the timing of my, erm ... contribution would—"

"Martin, be quiet," Louisa whispered in his ear.

"Mm."

Chapter 28

Saturday morning patients brought out the worst in Martin, and today was no exception. He came through under the stairs to find his reception room filled with chattering villagers, with fifteen minutes yet before surgery hours were to begin. He blustered over to Morwenna's desk, his yet untouched espresso in his hand.

"Morwenna! What are all these people doing here? You do remember surgery hours start at eight-thirty, don't you?"

"Sorry, Doc. They were waitin' on the steps when I got here. What did you expect me to do, beat 'em off with a stick?"

The doctor growled back. "I expect you to do your job—to tell them to go away and don't come back until scheduled surgery hours and then, and only then, if they have a scheduled appointment, or it's an actual emergency."

He snapped his fingers at her, earning him a roll of her eyes. She reached across her desk and picked up a sleeve of patient notes.

"Who's first?" the doctor asked as he snatched the notes from her hand.

"Eddie Rix." She crossed her arms over her chest and leaned back in her chair. "Or should I tell 'im ta go away until his finger with the fish hook stuck in it gets infected and needs to be amputated? *Then* it would be an actual emergency, wouldn't it?"

Martin threw his head back and stomped off to his consulting room. "Mr. Rix! Come through!"

"Get on the couch," he said as the fisherman came through the door. "What's the problem?"

Eddie held out a bloodied thumb which was adorned with a neon yellow fishing lure, firmly attached with a barbed hook.

"Oh, gawd," Martin moaned as he averted his eyes.

Having previously treated the man for injuries resulting from the Rixes' aberrant bedroom behaviours, he gave the man a visual once over, looking for suspicious contusions, swelling, or burns.

Turning his attention to the presenting problem, he examined the injury and then cleared his throat, a mechanism which he had learned helped to ease the blood-induced roiling in his stomach.

"I need to inject a local anaesthetic into your thumb," he said as he rolled his medical cart over to the exam couch before taking a small vial and a syringe from a drawer. "Then I'll push the hook on through and remove it."

"Inject? You don't gotta use a needle ta do that do you, Doc?" Eddie asked, his face blanching at the thought.

"Of course I do. How else do you think I'm going to get the lidocaine in there?"

The fisherman raised his eyebrows and straightened himself as he watched the doctor draw up the clear liquid. "How 'bout if you just sort'a dump it on there ... let it run in around the hook?"

Martin's scowl deepened. "Don't be ridiculous; give me your thumb," he said, holding a gloved hand out to the man.

Eddie pulled it up against his stomach, protectively, and gave the doctor a smile. "'Ere, Doc. I got an idea. You can do it without the numbin' stuff. I can take it."

"*Noo*, you can't." Martin hesitated, looking at the man askance. "Well, maybe *you* can, but I can't ... won't. Either you give me that thumb and let me inject the lidocaine or the hook stays in there. The thumb will then fester and become gangrenous, at which point you'll return to my surgery and I'll lop it off." He stared unflinchingly at his patient before adding a crisp, "Your choice."

Eddie screwed up his face before thrusting his hand at him. "Just get it over with quick, will ya, Doc?"

Martin ignored the intermittent moans and groans as he anaesthetised his patient's injured appendage and removed the hook. Then he disinfected and bandaged the wound.

"When was your last tetanus booster, Mr. Rix?"

Eddie scowled back at him, "'Ow should I know? I guess when I was a kid."

Martin went to his supply cupboard, took out a small vial, and filled another syringe. "We need to take care of that before you leave."

Eddie's face blanched again. "But, Doc, *another* needle?"

Martin glared at the man. "Tetanus is a deadly disease. If you don't let me give you this injection you could die."

"I'll take my chances," Eddie grumbled.

The fisherman made a move to get down from the exam couch, but before his feet could hit the floor, Martin had jabbed the needle into his arm.

"Ow, Doc! That hurt!"

"Good. Mr. Rix, I don't want you out on your boat until Monday; is that understood?"

"I gotta make a livin', Doc," the fisherman whined.

"It's not going to make a difference one way or the other if that wound becomes infected and you die, is it?"

Eddie gave Martin a dark look as he left the consulting room, his injured hand held in the air.

The doctor had just dispensed with the last of his patients when he heard Bert Large's annoyingly jovial voice drift in from the reception room.

"Hi there, Morwenna. I need ta see the doc. He in?"

"Well, yeah. But he's all done seein' patients today. Unless it's an emergency, you'll need to make an appointment for next week."

"Oh, it is an emergency, girl!"

Morwenna gave the portly man a sceptical look. "I'll go tell 'im you're here. I should warn you though, he's not in the best mood, even for the doc."

Martin looked up from his patient notes when his receptionist stepped through the door. "What is it, Morwenna?" he snapped.

"It's Bert Large. He wants ta see you."

"*No.* Not unless it's an emergency."

"Yeah, I already told him. He says it is."

Martin rubbed his forehead as he tried to ease another headache. "All right, send him in. And bring in his patient notes."

The portly man waddled through the door and plopped into the chair across from the doctor.

"There's a little matter I need your help with, Doc."

"This better be urgent, Bert."

"Oh, it is. I wouldn't be botherin' you, it bein' Saturday and all, but I know you can help me with this one." He reached around to his back pocket and pulled out a small paperback book. "What's a six-letter word for chest pain?"

Martin pursed his lips and slammed his pen down on his desk. "That's *not* a medical emergency."

Bert drew his mouth up like a purse string and donned his most convincing aggrieved expression.

"I never said it was a *medical* emergency. But there *is* an urgency, Doc. You see—"

"Bert! Out!"

Bert put his hand up in front of him. "Don't go gettin' your knickers in a twist now. It's just, I think if I can get this *one* word the others will—"

"Bert, *get—out!*" Martin barked as he snapped his fingers towards the door.

The restaurateur gave him a shake of his head and trudged out of the room.

Louisa was making lunch, and James was picking at the peas and carrots in a bowl on his high chair tray, by the time Martin had finished with patients, making his way under the stairs.

He filled a glass with water and downed two paracetamol tablets.

Louisa looked at him sympathetically. "Another headache?"

"Yeah. That idiot, Bert."

"Oh dear, nothing serious I hope."

Martin released a derisive snort and screwed up his face. "He *said* it was an emergency when in actuality he wanted help with a ... crossword puzzle."

Louisa fought the smile that was trying to creep across her face. "Well, I think when it comes to Bert, it's helpful to remember that he just likes to enjoy life."

"Yeah," Martin sneered. "He's a real go-with-the-flow kind'a guy."

Louisa looked at her husband's taut face. "Martin, why don't you go and have a lie down while I finish getting our lunch together. See if you can shake that headache."

"Mm. You sure you're all right here on your own?" he asked, gesturing to the salad ingredients strewn across the countertop. "I could put things away for you as you finish with them ... if you like."

"Martin, I'm fine. Now, go."

"Mm, yes." He gave one last critical scan over the disarray in front of him and then turned and headed for the stairs.

Louisa huffed out a breath as she shook her head at his disappearing form.

By the time she had finished with lunch preparations and tidied up to conform to Martin's particular standards, he was sleeping soundly on their bed. She reached for his shoulder to wake him but thought better of it.

He had been even more sleep deprived than calorie deprived as of late, so she covered him with a blanket and let him be.

She stood, gazing at him for several minutes. How different he looked when he was sleeping. All the furrowed lines on his face were gone, that ever-present anger which lay just below the surface, temporarily forgotten.

She hoped he could make peace with his past, but first he needed to remember what it was that was haunting his present. She leaned over and kissed his forehead before turning for the stairs.

Martin slept until late afternoon when a growling in his stomach and its accompanying sensation of hunger woke him. Louisa looked up from the book she had been reading to James when she noticed his movement in the kitchen.

"Well, hello sleepy head. How's the headache?"

"Better, I think. Was there anything left from lunch?" he asked as he rooted through the refrigerator.

"Mm, sorry I didn't wake you. I decided to let sleeping dogs lie," she said with an impish smile on her face.

Martin whirled his head around. "What do you mean by that?"

"It's an expression, Martin. It means to leave something ... or some*one* alone because messing with—"

"Yes, I'm familiar with the expression, Louisa. I'm just wondering why you chose that particular idiomatic phrase. Did Bert Large say something to you?"

"You mean at the lunch with Poppy on Monday?"

"No, no, no, no, no. I was wondering if ... Oh, never mind. Do we or do we not have something to eat in here?" he said, his headache returning with a vengeance.

"There's some soup that I could reheat, and some bread. But James and I are getting hungry again, too. Maybe we could go to Bert's?"

A small grimace flickered across Martin's face as he let out a soft groan. "Yes."

The Ellingham family arrived at the restaurant shortly before the dinner rush, so all was relatively quiet. It was a lovely Cornish summer day, just cool enough to make one appreciate the sun's rays, with a barely perceptible breeze blowing, a rarity along the Northwest Coast.

They chose a table with a nice view of the harbour. Bert scurried out to greet them as Louisa took a seat, and Martin wiped down the high chair before settling his son into it.

"Well hello, Doc ... Louiser. To what do I owe the pleasure?"

Martin gave Bert a look of incredulity. "It's a restaurant, Bert. I'd think that would be obvious."

"Oh, sure, sure," Bert replied with a chuckle. "Here are some menus. You peruse at your leisure, and I'll be right back with some waters. Bottled for you, Doc?"

"Yes, please."

Louisa gave her husband an admonishing stare. "Martin, he's just trying to make polite conversation. Can't you just humour him for once?"

Martin's lip curled slightly as he glanced over at the man, now making polite conversation with a couple on the other side of the restaurant.

"He's a plague on all of intelligent humanity."

Louisa glared back at him. "Martin, stop it!" she hissed. "Maybe that lie down was a bad idea. You seem to have gotten up on the wrong side of the bed. Just leave it be now."

She peered up at him over the top of her menu before adding with a small smile, "It would make me happy."

He glanced back at her before quickly returning his eyes to his dinner selection.

She watched him as they ate their lasagne and fish. He seemed especially taciturn.

"A penny for your thoughts?" she said, spooning the last of James's dinner into his mouth.

Martin shrugged. "Mm, just thinking about that dream." He looked off at the sea for some moments. "I had it again today."

Louisa's attention turned quickly from her son to her husband. "While you were having your lie down?"

"Mm. I think it *is* a memory, Louisa. But I can't make sense of it."

"Maybe if you were to discuss it with Dr. Newell on Wednesday it would all come together for you."

"Possibly." His gaze followed a small fishing boat making its way into the harbour. "I think I'll talk to her tonight, see if any of it resonates with her," he said absently.

"Talk to *who*, Martin?"

He blinked as his eyes refocused on her. "Er, Ruth. I'll talk to Ruth tonight."

"I think that's an excellent idea. I know she likes it when you confide in her."

Bert, puffing air, walked up to the table and tapped a finger on James's nose. "What a lovely little family this is. Did you two enjoy your dinner?"

Martin grimaced and Louisa gave him a warning glance before turning a smiling face to the restaurateur. "It was delicious, Bert. Thank you."

"Wonderful. Glad to hear it. Now, can I tempt you with some puds?"

"None for me," replied Martin as he wiped his mouth and folded his napkin neatly before laying it on the table.

"None for me either, Bert. I think we're ready for the bill."

"Suit yourselves." Bert tore the top page from his receipt book.

"Oh, Doc, I should explain about this morning."

"No, you shouldn't." Martin snatched the sheet of paper from his fingers.

"No. I wanna clear the air. I wouldn't want this whole misunderstanding gettin' in the way of our friendship. You see, it really *was* an emergency. I have a bet with my Jenny. You probably didn't know this about me, but I'm quite the whiz when it comes to doing crossword puzzles. Why, I was the Portwenn junior crossword puzzle champion two years in a row. In my youth, of course."

Martin reached into his back pocket and pulled out his wallet. "Congratulations."

"Thanks, Doc. So you see, when Jenny said she could solve that puzzle quicker than me ... well, I gotta defend my title, don't I?"

"Your title from your youth? Do you really think it's likely your title as junior crossword champion still stands after all this time?"

"Yer missin' my point, Doc."

"Well, get to it then, Bert!"

Louisa gave her husband's shin a sharp kick under the table. Bert's voice drowned out Martin's yelp as he continued to explain the necessity for his earlier visit to the surgery.

"Anyhow, we agreed. The last one of us to finish the puzzle has to lose twenty pounds by Christmas." Bert leaned down, and after taking a furtive glance over his shoulder he whispered stridently, "Doc, I just couldn't do it. Twenty pounds? I'd have to do without my puds to lose that much weight!"

Martin handed Bert the money for their dinner, and as he got up to leave, he turned to him. "Abulia."

"What's that, Doc?"

"Abulia. *A-B-U-L-I-A.* It's the word you're looking for."

Bert grinned at him, giving him an enthusiastic head nod and a thumbs-up. "Thanks, Doc. I knew you wouldn't let me down."

"Glad to help," Martin said as he took his wife's arm and walked towards the steps.

She looked warmly at him as they made their way back up Roscarrock Hill. "That was very nice of you—to help Bert. But ... well, maybe you shouldn't have told him. He could stand to lose a few pounds."

He turned, a glint of satisfaction in his eyes. "Mm. It was the wrong word."

Louisa put a hand over her mouth, stifling a giggle.

Chapter 29

As they ascended the hill towards the surgery, a small convoy of fishing boats moved past the harbour walls towards the slipway. Martin came to a stop, cringing as he watched Chippy Miller bend over to hoist a crate full of crabs and lobsters from the deck before throwing it into the dinghy he used to haul everything to shore. He scowled as he mentally predicted an imminent visit from the crab man. *The idiot's going to rupture a disk lifting things the way he does.*

Louisa slipped her hand into his. "Seems a shame to waste a nice evening. Would you like to walk on up and sit for a bit?"

Martin glanced towards the top of the hill, feeling a vague sense of apprehension. His wife smiled up at him, nodding her head encouragingly. He hesitated. "Erm ... if you want to, yes— yes, we could do that." James gave him a wonky grin as he shifted him to his left arm, and he touched his fingers to the boy's head before moving on towards the Coastal Path.

As they neared the top, Martin's apprehension escalated to anxiety, and his pace slowed.

Louisa turned. "Everything all right?" she asked when she saw him lagging behind.

"I'm sorry?"

"I asked if everything's all right. You look a bit pale."

Martin shook his head. "You know, I'm really rather tired. Maybe we'll head back home ... do this another night."

Louisa retraced her steps and reached down to take his free hand in hers. "It *is* beautiful here, isn't it?" she said, looking out across the harbour.

"Mm."

Even Martin had to admit to having an appreciation for the rugged beauty of the Cornish Coast. The grass covered hills which flowed towards the sea, stopping abruptly when they reached the granite cliffs which plunged into the Atlantic waters. The determined flowering plants that set their roots in the oases of soil dotting the rocks, almost as if by some feng shui gardener's design. And the sunsets, famous for painting the landscape in almost other-worldly hues, pastel colours which looked to have been brushed into the wispy cloud strands overhead, and the pink glow that seemed to warm even the chilliest of winter evenings.

He gazed down at his wife. Her eyes were happy, glistening as she took it all in. His hand pulled away from hers and he brushed the backs of his fingers across her cheek. "You look radiant," he said softly.

She gave him a gentle smile. "Thank you, Martin."

"I'm glad you're still here."

"Me too." She stretched up to kiss him and then took his hand as they crossed the terrace to the house.

Louisa settled James in the playpen and then picked her book up from the table and settled in on the sofa.

Martin poured himself a glass of water and a glass of wine for his wife before joining her in the lounge.

They sat quietly for several minutes, Louisa with her novel and Martin with his medical journal. Louisa eventually broke the silence.

"Martin, I erm ... I was wondering why you changed your mind about our walk."

The periodical dropped to Martin's lap, and he huffed out a breath. "As I said, I'm tired tonight." The glossy paper of the magazine crinkled as he roughly flipped a page.

Louisa set her book down and turned towards him, folding her leg under her. "I know that's what you said, but can you tell me truthfully? Was there another reason?"

Martin's eyes drifted shut, creasing at the corners as his jaw clenched and unclenched. "I just wasn't sure if it was a good idea ... after the other night."

"Do you really think that would happen again? I mean, if we didn't discuss your past it shouldn't happen again, right?"

A hiss of air rushed from his nose as he tossed the *BMJ* on to the coffee table. "I'm neither a psychiatrist nor a clairvoyant, Louisa. How do you expect me to be able to answer that question?"

Uncomfortable silence filled the room until Louisa said, "Maybe it's something you could ask at your next therapy session, hmm?" She slid over next to him and reached down to caress his thigh.

He startled and pulled up his hands. "Louisa, could you please not touch me right now? It's not helping."

He looked over at her, his head lowered. "I'm sorry, I didn't mean to snap at you." Rubbing his hands over his head, he groaned. "It's been ... difficult. This resurrecting unpleasant memories has been difficult. All these things that happened, things that I'd been able to forget about are happening all over again. And it's—it's confusing. Painful."

"Oh, Martin," she whispered as she moved closer and leaned against him. "I do understand. When Mum came back last autumn, I'd just gotten to a point where her running out on Dad and me didn't bother so much. But having her around just stirred up all those old resentments and hurt feelings in me. So, I *do* understand."

Martin jerked away and got to his feet. "I said don't touch me! And you *don't* understand. Not if you think I'm referring to resentments. It's like it's happening all over again. It's not just a memory—it's physical. I feel the nausea and the pain in my chest when I have memories of train rides back to London after a summer with Joan and Phil. I feel the sting of my father's belt, my mother's twisting my arm in her frantic attempts to keep me away from her, actually feeling my face warm when I remember the humiliating things that my parents said to me ... about me. *That's* what I mean when I describe this whole hideous process as painful. It's not happening *then*. It's happening *now*."

Louisa sat mouth agape. "Martin, I had no idea. Why didn't you tell me this before?"

He looked back at her consolatory expression and grimaced. "Because I knew you'd look like *that* every time a sordid detail from my childhood surfaced."

Louisa brought her elbows to her knees and put her face in her hands.

Her ragged breaths brought Martin to her side. He sat down next to her and put a tentative hand on her back, attempting several reassuring pats. "I didn't mean for that to come across the way it did. You are very beautiful, even when you look like that. It was just your expression ... I mean, I just can't bear to think that you would pity me."

Louisa brought her head up and wiped her sleeve across her face as she inhaled a wet sniffle.

Martin screwed up his face and pulled his handkerchief from his back pocket, blotting at her tears.

She looked at him and giggled, shaking her head. "Martin, I'm not crying because you said anything wrong about the way I look. I'm crying because you're doing all of this for *me* ... for us. You're going through all of this to keep from losing me. I'm just so moved by that. They're sad tears, angry tears, because you have to endure all of this to right your parents' wrongs. But they're also happy tears, because I couldn't possibly feel more loved than I do at this moment."

"So, you're not upset then?"

Louisa's ponytail swished back and forth as she gave him a shy smile. "I'm emotional, not upset."

He furrowed his brow. "Oh, good."

They sat for a few moments before Martin ducked his head. "I'm sorry," he said. "I *did* get upset."

"That's all right. Sometimes it's good to get upset, get things out in the open. And you're right, Martin. I can't possibly understand what this is like for you. But I can be here for you ... to listen."

He straightened and blinked back at her. "You believe me—about what this is like?"

"Yes, Martin. I don't doubt a word of it. You are the most honest and straightforward man I've ever met. If you came in that door one day and told me that the sky had suddenly turned purple, I'd race out to see it because I'd know that some cataclysmic event or something must have happened to cause it. I trust you completely."

He leaned forward and kissed her. Then he wrapped his arms around her and picked her up as he got to his feet.

"Martin!" she squealed, unprepared for her husband's display of affection.

He set her down quickly and composed himself. "Mm. Sorry—sorry. Did I hurt you?" he asked as he pulled on the hem of her jumper in an attempt to straighten it.

"No, Martin. I'm fine. You just surprised me is all. It was quite nice, actually." She stretched up to kiss him, and his arms slipped around her waist.

James had been growing increasingly disgruntled at being confined to his playpen, and his protestations were increasing.

"I think we're going to have a very unhappy son in a minute if I don't give him a bottle and get him off to bed."

"Mm, I'm sure you're right. I could make a quick trip to Ruth's while you're doing that, if that's all right with you."

"That'd be fine, but maybe don't be gone too long. I really enjoyed what we were doing."

"Mm, yes, so did I."

The light on Ruth's porch was still burning when Martin turned on to Dolphin Street, a sure sign that she had yet to go to bed.

He rapped on the low door of the little cottage, listening for the sound of his aunt's approaching footsteps. Mr. Moysey, Ruth's cantankerous neighbour, walked unsteadily over the cobblestone walkway, grunting a tepid greeting. "Doctor."

Martin turned. "Mr. Moysey."

The latch on the door rattled as it was pulled open.

"Martin, this is a surprise!" Ruth took a step back. "Well don't stand out there in the damp air. You'll catch a summer cold. Has something happened?"

"No, not really. I was wondering if you might have a few minutes."

"Certainly."

He sniffed and wrinkled his nose as he stepped into the house. An acrid odour hung in the air. "What's that smell?"

"That *smell* is my dinner. It was delicious, by the way. Come on in, I'll make some tea."

He followed the old woman around the corner and into the kitchen.

"Well, don't just stand there. Make yourself comfortable," Ruth said as she filled the kettle with water.

Martin pulled out a chair and took a seat. "How was your day?"

"Oh, the usual ... did a bit of writing and looked over several case files I've been asked to review. And I took a trip out to the farm to check on Al's progress."

Ruth plugged the kettle into the wall socket and turned around, leaning back against the counter. She eyed her nephew as he nervously drummed his fingers on the table top. "Well, I know you didn't walk all this way to ask me about my day. Are you going to tell me why you're here, or are we going to play twenty questions?"

"Ah, no. I had a dream a couple of nights ago, and I thought you might be able to help me make some sense of it."

"Well, Martin, I'm not a strong proponent of the Freudian school of thought, and certainly not a big believer in the legitimacy of dream analysis."

"No, it's nothing like that. I'm just wondering if ... Well, if maybe it's not so much a dream as it is a memory. I had the same dream again today while I was having a lie-down. It seemed almost identical to the one I had the other night."

"All right, I'm all ears." Ruth set two teacups down on the table and took a seat, folding her hands in front of her.

Martin cleared his throat. "Well, some of it's foggy. But I think I'm on the floor and I'm hanging on to something. I can't tell if it's a figure or ..." Martin rubbed at his temples as he tried to focus his thoughts. "Whatever it is, I'm gripping it so tightly that my fingers are locked in place. I hear my father's voice. He's yelling at me to let go. He sounds angry ... very angry."

The tea kettle began to hiss, and Ruth got up, lifting it from its base. "Go on, I'm listening," she said as she filled the teacups with boiling water.

Pulling the lid from the container of tea bags on the table, he dropped one into his cup. "Then I feel something pulling at me, pulling on my shirt. But my fingers are locked, and I can't let go of whatever it is that I'm holding on to. And whatever was pulling on my shirt, grabs on to my arm. It grabs so tightly that it hurts. I'm thrown back into the dark. I can hear a cracking sound ... or a snap, and there's pain in my arm. Then, it's just dark. I'm alone in the dark and my arm hurts. And then I wake up."

Ruth sat, her brow furrowed. "Well, I'll certainly give this some thought, but nothing comes to mind right off. I'm sorry, Martin. I was really hoping I might be able to provide you with some answers."

He shook his head. "No need to apologise. I just thought something might sound familiar to you." He slid his teacup back and forth on the table. "Why do you think this has all started?"

"Do you mean the dreams?"

"No, everything. The blood sensitivity, the depression, the nightmares ... everything."

"Martin, I suspect that question may be answered when you remember what it is that you've spent the last forty-odd years trying to forget."

"Mm, yes."

They sipped quietly on their tea for several minutes. When Martin stood to leave, Ruth, stepping out of character for a moment, came over and gave him an awkward hug. "Remember, you have Louisa and me to help you, Martin. Don't try to do this on your own."

"Mm, thank you, Ruth. And thank you for the tea."

Martin hiked back up Roscarrock Hill towards the surgery, disappointed the visit to Ruth's hadn't been more fruitful. But as he neared home his thoughts shifted back to Louisa, to how wonderful she felt in his arms earlier.

When he came in the door, she was coming down the stairs, having just put James to bed.

"How did things go at Ruth's? Was she of any help?"

"No, nothing sounded familiar to her. She's going to think about it though and let me know if anything comes to mind. Is James asleep?"

"Yes, he was tired ... nodded off halfway into his bedtime story."

Louisa followed her husband out to the kitchen. "So, Ruth didn't recognise *anything* from your dream? *Nothing* sounded familiar?"

"I believe I just said that Louisa," Martin answered curtly.

"Yes, sorry. I was just really hoping you'd get some answers. Maybe it *is* just a dream."

"Mm, I don't think so."

She reached up to get a cup off the shelf. "Want some tea before bed?"

"No thank you. I had a cup at Ruth's." Martin went to the sofa, and picking up a book, settled in to read.

"Why do you feel so sure that it's more than a dream?" Louisa asked as she sat down next to him.

"It makes sense to me somehow." He wrapped his arm around his wife's shoulders and pulled her close to him. "Have you ever been talking to someone and you find yourself grasping for a word, a commonly used word that seems to have vaporized in an instant?"

Louisa tipped her head back to look at him. "I think my kids call them senior moments."

"Yes. This dream feels much the same. Like it's there somewhere in my catalogue of events. I just can't pull it out."

She shifted slightly so that she could reach out to stroke his thigh. "Is this okay? Me touching you like this now?"

Martin's eyes closed as he sucked in a breath and swallowed hard. "Mm ... yes. But maybe we should go upstairs."

She leaned over to kiss him as she loosened the knot on his tie and pulled it from his neck before getting up and leading him to the steps.

As he watched her in front of him, Martin found himself looking at her in a way that he hadn't in a very long time. He needed her.

Chapter 30

Martin was roused the next morning by his wife's soft breath against his neck. He gazed at her as the fogginess of sleep cleared his eyes, entranced by the perfection that he saw. What did she see in him? Why, after his protracted period of conscripted celibacy, did a woman as beautiful as Louisa allow him in her bed? If he could inhabit her mind for a few moments, perhaps he could understand what it was that attracted her to him. It's been said that a man falls in love through his eyes, a woman through her ears. *Perhaps that's it.* He sighed.

Before Louisa Glasson walked into his life and tossed all of his expectations for his future to the wind, he had resigned himself to a life of lonely bachelorhood, focusing all of his energy on his work. Now he found himself waking up next to her, with the son they produced together sleeping across the hall.

He raised up on an elbow and studied her form. She no longer used the sling at night, but he didn't need it to remind him of the damage that their rowing had caused. He allowed his gaze to drift down, following the soft curves where the bedclothes hugged her waist and hips. She brushed against him as she moved slightly in her sleep, drawing his eyes to where her hand lay near his. It was a reminder of an ill-fated taxi ride they had once shared, which for a few moments, held so much promise but ended with him watching from the road as the vehicle drove away. He felt a resurgence of the temptation and trepidation that he experienced in that taxi as he tried to find the intestinal fortitude to slide his hand across the car seat to meet hers.

Glancing at his wife's face, he assured himself that she was still sleeping. Then he allowed his palm to glide slowly across the sheet until his skin made contact with hers. Her eyes fluttered slightly before opening and meeting with his. He brushed a strand of hair from her eyes and let the backs of his fingers brush languidly down her cheek.

"Good morning, Mrs. Ellingham."

Louisa gave him a knowing smile. "Good morning. How did you sleep?"

"Quite well. And you?"

"Good. You tired me out last night, you know."

"Mm, yes. I was trying to catch up on my matrimonial obligations. Maybe I should try to pace myself." He leaned over and pressed his lips to hers.

"Don't try *too* hard." Pushing him on to his back, she stretched herself out on top of him, giving his earlobe a playful nip.

Wrapping his arms around her, he lifted his head to place kisses on her neck as his hands gravitated downward to her hips. His fingertips stroked along her thighs before he worked his hands under her nightdress.

She whispered into his ear, "Martin, I want you."

That her husband wanted her as well was becoming increasingly apparent. She sat up on top of him and slipped her nightdress over her head, letting it drop to the floor.

Martin took in a long ragged breath as she bared herself to him. She rolled off him and he quickly shucked his boxers before wrapping his arms around her again.

"Oh, Louisa," he said hoarsely. She once again took his breath away, and he felt a familiar tightness growing in his chest.

His eyelids closed as she enveloped him, his senses focused on her—the sweet taste when his lips touched hers, her alluring scent, borne on the gentle wafts of air as he moved over her, the warmth and softness, the utter femininity of her body as it touched his.

An unfamiliar calmness came over him. He slowed his movements and pressed his lips to hers, the kiss deepening as he allowed his love for her to wash over his emotional walls.

The walls breached, the demons of his nightmares began to work their way into his thoughts as the same confusing bits of memories began to mix with the wonderful images of his Louisa.

His movements stopped suddenly, and he opened his eyes, focusing on her face.

She felt his body stiffen, and she looked up at him. His soft grey-green orbs were staring back at her, the love she saw in them, intense. She cupped her palm against his cheek as he began to move again. A tremor rippled through his lower lip, and she lifted her head to quiet it with her own.

"Mm ... Louisa, lay back down; I need to see you," he whispered, his voice catching in his throat.

She pulled back, and their eyes fixed on one another as the intensity of their lovemaking reached a crescendo.

They lay, wrapped in each other's arms. Martin focused on a crack in the ceiling, thinking about what had transpired moments before.

"Louisa, do you know what just happened?"

Propping herself up on an elbow, she gave him an impish grin. "I'm pretty sure I do. Would you like me to explain it to you, Doctor?"

Martin rolled to his side and ran his thumb across her cheek. "That's all right. I think I might have a textbook in my consulting room that covers the subject."

"I'm sorry, Martin. You were going to say something serious, weren't you?"

"I, erm ... I had those images pop into my head again. But this time I was able to stay in control. I opened my eyes and focused on you, on how much I love you."

Louisa's eyes welled with tears. "That is perhaps, the nicest, most romantic thing anyone has ever said to me."

"I do love you, Louisa."

"I love you too, Martin."

Monday's romantic start to the day turned quickly into an afternoon and evening that Martin would prefer to forget. The usual practice schedule had been suspended so that he could meet with the Children's Services authorities in Wadebridge at four o'clock. A decision would be made, based partly on information that would be provided by Martin and Joe Penhale, as to how best to safeguard the Hanley children.

He had hoped that he would have heard from Jim Hanley before now, but given his own behaviour the last time they met, Martin wasn't surprised that the man hadn't followed up on his offer to help him get treatment for his drink problem. He planned to stop out at the Hanley farm before heading to Wadebridge, a last-ditch effort to persuade him to deal with his addiction.

Martin had one patient after returning from lunch. Eddie Rix was back in to see him about the wound from the fishhook that he had removed two days before. It was now badly infected, and Martin knew why.

"Mr. Rix, were you out on your boat over the weekend?"

Eddie screwed up his face and looked at the floor. "Well, Doc, I had ta be. I can't afford to miss a day out on the water."

"Well, that was just brilliant, wasn't it? Now you're going to miss a solid week of work while we get this infection under control."

He lanced the wound and had started to drain the pus from the abscess that had formed when the expected nausea hit him. Racing to the bin, he threw up the lunch he had just consumed.

He finished draining, cleaning, and bandaging the man's finger and then stared at him pointedly. "Mr. Rix, I'm going to send you off with a prescription for an antibiotic which you can get from Mrs. Tishell. Hopefully, this will be the last time I see you ... for this particular injury."

He held the door for the man, and as Eddie walked out to the reception room he turned to ask, "So if I'm takin' this antibi, can I go out on my boat?"

"No! Of course not!" Martin slammed the door shut. "Why do I bother?" he muttered.

He was writing in the last of his patient notes when Morwenna tapped on his door and stuck her head into the room. "Chris Parsons is on the phone for you, Doc."

"Yes." Martin held the patient notes out to her. "Take these and file them."

She huffed out a breath and snatched them from his hand. "Can you at least say please?"

He grunted back at her, prompting a roll of her eyes and another huff before she turned to leave.

"Morwenna."

"Yeah, Doc?"

"Close the door behind you."

She turned and glared at him before he pulled in his chin and added, "Please."

Giving him a satisfied smile, she returned to the reception room.

Martin reached for the phone, expecting to be informed of a patient complaint about his less than charming bedside manner. However, his friend was calling to ask him to speak at an upcoming joint meeting with the area governing board and a National Health Services investigatory committee charged with managing the reorganization of the nation's ambulance system.

"They want to make some pretty drastic financial cuts as well, Martin. This could have a serious negative impact on the quality of emergency care in your area. I'm hoping that your reputation as a vascular surgeon as well as a GP will sway some of the committee members to reconsider cuts here in Cornwall."

Martin leaned back in his chair, tapping his biro on the armrest. "What are you saying, Chris? We won't lose our ambulance out of Wadebridge, will we?"

"Actually Mart, they want to eliminate our air ambulance. We'd have to share with Plymouth."

"Good God! Where did they dig up these imbeciles! Have they even bothered to look at a map? One air ambulance isn't enough to service all of Cornwall. And it takes at least forty-five minutes, on a good day I might add, for a ground ambulance to get to Truro from here! Haven't they heard of the golden hour?"

"Hey, you're preaching to the choir, mate. So ... can I count on you to be at that meeting?"

Martin let out a long sigh. "Yes, you've got me." He grumbled as he hung up the phone. One of the few advantages of his current position in Portwenn was the relative lack of the bureaucratic monkey business that he'd dealt with as Chief of Vascular Surgery in London.

Glancing at his watch, he realised he needed to get out to Jim Hanley's. He wasn't looking forward to either another encounter with Mr. Hanley or to being confined in a vehicle with Joe Penhale for the afternoon.

The constable's enthusiasm for the outing surpassed Martin's. "Well, this should be fun, eh, Doc? A real adventure. Just the two amigos, exploring the great beyond," he said, gesturing expansively with his arms, landing an inadvertent blow to Martin's chest in the process.

"Penhale! For goodness' sake." Martin huffed. "We're driving to Wadebridge, not trekking into Machu Picchu."

"Right you are there, Doc. Although I hear Japan *is* beautiful this time of year."

Martin furrowed his brow at him before turning his eyes back to the road.

"Did you ever think about doing something like that? Heading out on a great adventure ... to the *great beyond*?" the policeman continued with another expansive gesture.

Martin slapped Joe's hand away and gave him a sneer. "If you're referring to the Promised Land ... Elysium ... Shangri-La, then no."

"Oh, come on, Doc. All of those places sound exciting ... exotic. Don't you think?"

"I'm not in the mood, Penhale."

"Bad day, Doc?"

"Yeah, something like that."

The officer stayed blissfully quiet for the remainder of the drive to the Hanley farm, and the visit with Mr. Hanley went much more smoothly than Martin had feared it would. As far as he could tell, the man had not been drinking.

"I'd like to apologise for my behaviour when I was out here last Thursday, Mr. Hanley. It was very unprofessional of me to strike you the way I did."

"It's okay, Doc. I reckon I had it comin', considerin' what I did ta my boy. Just so you know, I haven't had a drink since then."

"That's good to hear. PC Penhale and I'll be meeting with the people with Children's Services later this afternoon. I'd like to have something positive to report. Are you willing to get professional treatment for your alcoholism?"

"It may not look it, Doctor, but I do love my wife an' kids. I'll do the treatment thing if they promise not ta take 'em away from me."

"They won't make you any promises, Mr. Hanley. But I think that if you can prove to them that you're serious about dealing with this and you can show that you have the problem in hand, they'll allow your children to be returned to you. Do you want me to make some calls and find an appropriate treatment facility?"

"I'd be grateful fer it if you would. Thank you."

"Well, that's a relief," Joe said as they got back in the Lexus to head to Wadebridge. "I was afraid he might smack you or something."

Martin rubbed at his temple and tried to tune out the policeman's incessant chatter.

The meeting with the Protective Services people went as Martin expected. Evan and his younger sister would be allowed to return home once Mr. Hanley had met all the necessary requirements.

Martin was looking forward to getting home to the quiet and solitude he would find with his wife. He had been relatively headache free for the last two days, but the hours of listening to Joe Penhale's constant yammering had taken a toll, and he was now feeling a pounding in his forehead.

They were about halfway between Wadebridge and Portwenn when they spotted several cars pulled to the side of the road.

"I think you better stop, Doc. Could be someone in need of assistance."

"Yes, I'm aware of that," Martin snipped as he pulled the Lexus on to the verge. He noticed a motorcycle off the road and a figure lying some fifteen to twenty feet away from it. He felt a growing trepidation. As a vascular surgeon, he had spent many unpleasant hours in operating theatres trying to piece cyclists back together again.

He grabbed his bag from the backseat and hurried to the person on the ground. It was every bit as bad as he had anticipated. The young male victim was bleeding profusely and showing definitive signs of a traumatic brain injury.

Martin turned to Penhale. "Call for an air ambulance. Tell them to prepare for a haemorrhaging patient with a probable TBI. Then get these gawpers out of here!"

"Right, Doc!"

Martin stayed by his patient until the air ambulance crew arrived. It sickened him to see such a young person having to face a life forever altered by one fateful moment in time.

They watched as the helicopter lifted off and then returned to the Lexus. It was only when he went to pull the driver's side door shut that Martin noticed his blood-soaked sleeves. He had been able to keep his nausea in check while tending to the victim, but he could no longer hold it back. He quickly swung the door open and vomited on to the pavement.

He drove the rest of the way back to the village with the metallic odour of blood hanging in the air and Joe Penhale's voice drumming a steady percussive beat against his already pounding head. By the time he dropped the constable off at the police station, Martin felt as if Ruth's chickens had been pecking at his brain for three and a half hours.

Chapter 31

Martin sat in Dr. Newell's office on Wednesday, a tension building in him as he contemplated the question posed by the man.

"Martin, I asked you to think back to your earliest memory of being abused. Do you have any idea as to how old you may have been?"

"I'm sorry. I don't understand."

The psychiatrist slid the cap over the end of his fountain pen and set it on his desk. "I know that you have memories of being abused, so why do you say you don't understand the question?"

"I have memories of overly harsh discipline. Is that what you're asking about?"

"Okay, let's start with that," the doctor said as he rocked back and forth in his chair. "How old were you when your parents first began using overly harsh discipline?"

"I'm not sure. I can't really remember a time when it wasn't a part of my life." Martin's gaze shifted to the cumulus clouds hanging in the sky outside the window. "My aunt told me once that my father believed a crying baby should be left alone in a room ... solitary confinement is what he called it." He worked a hand over his knee. "I'm not sure that one could say that was overly harsh, however. That was the method my parents happened to believe effective at the time. The thinking's changed on that."

"Did your aunt seem to feel it was reasonable and effective?"

"She didn't share an opinion on it. She said that I cried a lot, so perhaps they felt it necessary."

Dr. Newell rested his elbows on the armrests of his chair, his steepled fingers tapping against his lips. "When you did the exercise I asked you to do, where you imagined James in your place, did the punishments seem abusive?"

Martin stared at the man, his jaw tight.

The psychiatrist wasn't cowed by his patient's intense gaze. He rolled back towards his desk. "Martin, the first and perhaps most important step in dealing with your past is accepting your parents' treatment of you for what it was, abuse.

"Your parents began abusing you at a very young age, and it's extremely traumatic for young children to admit to what's being done to them. They cope with their lot in life by excusing the abuse as punishment that they deserved. This gives them some sense of control over the situation.

"Your father beat you with his belt, because you had disobeyed your grandfather. By telling yourself that you deserved the beating ... that it was justifiable punishment ... you could then decide to obey your grandfather in future, thereby giving you some control over whether or not your father abused you again."

"Isn't that the point of punishment?" Martin snapped, his irritation showing in his fiery eyes.

"Remember the exercise you did with putting James in your place. Your parents crossed the line between punishment and abuse. What you're struggling with now is giving up that sense of control and admitting your parents abused you. That no matter how well behaved you were, you were a child and would commit the inevitable indiscretion on occasion; it's all a part of the learning process. But in your case, the punishments were neither fair nor reasonable."

Martin shook his head and got to his feet. He stood, facing the window, and reached a trembling hand to the back of his neck. "I hear my father's voice in my head. *Grow a backbone, Martin! Don't be such a little girl's blouse!*" He huffed. "I felt ... I suppose I felt ashamed—guilty—like I'd let him down, again. It's ... God, it's—it's emasculating! I don't want to even think about it.

"To say I was—was abused ... I don't want to be that girl's blouse ... be an embarrassment to my wife and son. I want to be the kind of man they want me to be. They're why I'm doing all of this and ... bloody hell, it's having the opposite effect!"

"Martin, suppose you had a patient who required an open aortic aneurysm repair. To the untrained eye, that person may look perfectly normal, functioning adequately in their daily life. Then, as a surgeon, you make that large incision, cut out the affected section of the artery and attach the graft before closing the wound. Think of the process you're going through with me in those terms. We're doing a lot of deconstructing at the moment, and as a consequence of that, you may feel rather vulnerable. But the hope is that you will ultimately be a much stronger and healthier person for it."

Martin's shoulders rose and fell as he took in a deep breath before returning to his chair.

"I'm curious about what you meant when you said that you want to be the man that your wife and son want you to be. Can you describe that man for me?"

The psychiatrist waited as his patient stared absently before squeezing his eyes shut and taking in a deep breath.

"I don't know. I'm not sure," Martin finally answered.

Dr. Newell tossed the paper clip he had been toying with on to his desk. "Okay, how 'bout between now and when I see you next week, you jot down some adjectives describing the kind of man that you think James and Louisa would like for you to be. And then make a separate list of adjectives for the kind of man that *you* would like to be. And it would be perfectly all right if you were completely happy as you are now."

The therapist pulled his hands behind his head, lacing his fingers together. "So, tell me how your week went, are the headaches any better?"

"Yes, some. They haven't been as frequent the last couple of days. Stress seems to trigger them, and they can be rather severe when I do get them."

"What do you think, Doctor? Should we try something else?"

"I think I'd like to give it another week, then revisit the question."

Dr. Newell came around and claimed his perch on the corner of the desk. "All right. How about the nightmares, any better?"

"Not really. There's one in particular that seems very real. I think it might actually be a memory. I don't know."

Dr. Newell listened attentively as Martin related the dream, and then returned to his chair, making notes in his patient's file. He clasped his chin in his hand as he stared contemplatively over Martin's shoulder for a moment before pushing himself back from his desk. "I want you to close your eyes and think for a few minutes about the dream. Don't focus on the obvious. Try to look for anything that you may have forgotten about. Look around. What room are you in? You said that you were down on the floor. What kind of floor is it? Can you see any part of this force that grabs you? Perhaps, shoes or clothing. Is there a smell, a sound? Try to remember things that weren't so obvious initially."

Air hissed from Martin's nose as he screwed up his face.

Dr. Newell got to his feet. "Why don't I step out and get a couple of cups of tea. I'll leave you alone for just a bit. White, no sugar, right?"

"Mm, yes. Thank you."

The therapist shut the door behind him, and Martin closed his eyes, trying to relax and replay the dream in his mind.

What was he holding on to? Nothing came to him. What was the room like? He remembered hearing approaching footsteps which created a hollow, almost resonant sound. When he was thrown back he fell on to a hard surface. Wood floors? Then his father's voice, yelling. He felt something grab his arm. He looked down. A gold ring, embedded with a single square-cut red stone bedecked a finger. It was the ring his father wore. It was his father's fingers grasping on to his arm. Now he could see the man's angry face.

Images and sensations overwhelmed him. His eyes shot open, and the room began to dim before he realised he'd been holding his breath. He inhaled deeply, and the vibrant colours of the paintings on the walls slowly returned.

Dr. Newell re-entered the room, setting two cups down before hoisting himself on to the desk in front of his patient.

"Well, anything new come to you?"

Martin swallowed. "It was my father, I saw his hand. I recognised his ring."

He closed his eyes again before continuing on. "The floors were wood. I think it was my father's study. He threw me back, and as he took a step towards me he put his foot down in something. His foot slipped in whatever was on the floor ... left a smear. I think I had spilt something."

"Was there a colour to what had been spilt?" the doctor asked, resting his elbows on his knees.

"I don't remember. I was responsible. It was my fault. That's why my father was so angry." Martin pressed his fingers to his eyes as a wave of nausea hit him. "My arm broke. When he yanked on my arm, I felt a snap ... and pain. God, he was angry."

His throat tightened as he fought to stay in control, a suffocating heaviness descending on him. "I just wanted to ... I wanted to disappear. It hurt ... and the disgust on his face ..."

Air whistled through Martin's teeth as he sat, jaw clenched.

"He came into my room after I'd gone to bed," he continued. "He told me to be quiet, and then he set my arm."

"He didn't take you to the doctor?"

"My father was a surgeon. He took care of it himself."

Martin closed his eyes again, willing himself to remember more.

The psychiatrist watched his patient closely. "Without anaesthesia?"

"Mm."

Dr. Newell shook his head. "That must have been very painful."

Martin sucked in a ragged breath. "He said to be quiet, not to disturb my mother. It hurt, but I didn't make a sound. I wanted him to know that I could be ... that I wasn't ... that I was stronger than he thought I was. I wanted him to be proud of me. But he didn't seem to notice. He put a splint on my arm and told me to go to sleep. He was still angry."

"And you were left on your own to deal with the pain?" the doctor asked, noting the tremors coursing through his patient's body.

"Mm."

"Martin, do you remember how old you were when this happened?"

"Yes." The room had begun to dim again and, leaning over over, he rested his elbows on his knees, his head in his hands. "I was seven. I was home for the winter holidays."

Dr. Newell got down from the desk and pulled an extra chair over next to him. He took a seat and handed him his cup of tea. "Here, you're shivering. This should warm you up a bit."

Martin sat, trying to hold on to his teacup with shaking hands. "I'm glad he's dead. But he didn't deserve to die so easily."

He looked at his doctor with glazed eyes. "He had a stroke. He deserved a painful death."

The psychiatrist shifted in his chair. "It's understandable that you feel anger for the way your parents treated you, Martin. Adults who were abused as children often turn that anger on themselves. A self-loathing, if you will."

Martin rubbed his palm over his face. "And you think that's what I've done?"

"If you're like the typical abuse victim, yes. Although I have to say, Martin, you aren't like the other abuse victims that I've counselled. But yes, I think that *is* what you've done."

"Louisa said to me once, you're not like the rest of us. I want to be ... for her."

"Well, I for one, am very glad that you're not. I don't think you would have dealt with the abuse as well as you have if you were like the rest of us. And the rest of us would have been short-changed a very fine and talented doctor and surgeon ... husband and father."

Dr. Newell set his cup back down on the desk. "Were any of your relatives aware of the abuse going on in your home?"

"No, I don't think so. I didn't see much of them ... or they me. Aside from my aunt during the summer."

"So, no one did anything? No one intervened on your behalf?"

"Not that I'm aware of. My father was a well-respected surgeon, and my parents were wealthy. I would imagine my father would have hired an expensive attorney, and any efforts would have been thwarted anyway. Things were different at that time."

"Yes, thankfully we have a system in place now that can spare children what you went through."

Martin swallowed hard, thinking of young Evan Hanley.

Dr. Newell eyed his patient. "How are you feeling now? Safe to drive home do you think?"

Martin sighed. "Yes, I'm sure I'll be fine."

"You've made it clear now, that you have the intestinal fortitude to confront these issues from your past. I feel much more confident that our work together can have a very positive impact in the end."

Dr. Newell got up and moved towards the door. "I'll see you and Louisa on Friday then?"

Martin hesitated. "I was wondering if Louisa and I might switch spots next week. I need to be here for a meeting Friday night, and I doubt she's going to want to wait around for me."

Dr. Newell put a hand on his back. "Sure, that's no problem. Whatever works for the two of you."

Dinner was ready when Martin returned home. He watched as his wife pulled a bib over his son's head, leaning over to kiss his cheek.

It filled him with relief and happiness for his son that he would grow up feeling loved and wanted ... a cherished member of a family. But he could no longer deny the void that existed in him ... the absence of a mother and father who loved him.

Chapter 32

"More bread?" Louisa asked as she tried to make eye contact with her husband. He glanced up at her, shaking his head and grunting his preference to give it a miss before returning his attention to his plate.

James picked up his spoon and pounded it loudly on his high chair tray, finally getting Martin's attention.

"Mm, are you all done there?" he asked. Picking up the child's bowl he carried it to the sink, and then ran a flannel under the tap before returning to deal with the sticky mess on his son's face.

"How 'bout we go and have a story, James?"

Louisa worried her lip as she looked across at her husband's half-eaten dinner. She picked up the plate and carried it to the sink. "Could you and James run to Mrs. Tishell's and pick up some nappies, Martin? We're almost out."

He grimaced. "Oh, why don't you do that. You know what she'll be like if I walk in there with James."

"Go to the market then if you'd rather not deal with Mrs. Tishell, but we need nappies."

Martin hemmed and hawed. "How 'bout James and I get his bath out of the way while you run for the nappies."

Louisa cocked her head slightly, perplexed by her husband's sudden bout with agoraphobia. "Oh, for goodness' sake, Martin. I'm just trying to get you two to go out and get some fresh air. Perk you up a bit."

Martin set James down in his playpen and stomped off towards the front door. "Fine, Louisa. I'll go get the nappies and leave *you* to James."

"Martin?" She called to him, but he was out the door and down the steps before she could reach the reception room. As she returned to the kitchen, her old anxieties came rushing back to replace the confidence she had been feeling about their future together.

Finishing the dinner clean-up, she bathed the baby before settling in on the sofa with him. They were just finishing the bedtime story when Martin came in the back door.

"You must have walked all the way to Wadebridge for those nappies. You've been gone forever," Louisa snapped as the baby struggled to free himself of the confines of her lap.

A look of chagrin swept over Martin's face when he realised he had forgotten to pick up what he had been sent out for. "I forgot them."

"*What*? You didn't get the nappies? Everything will be closed by now, Martin."

He grabbed the car keys from the kitchen table. "Not to worry," he said, putting a hand up to quiet the imminent rebuke. "I'll find someplace that's still open." He hurried for the door.

"Martin, it can ... Martin!" she yelled as the door began to swing shut behind him.

Stepping back into the kitchen, he tipped his head to the side and looked at her quizzically. "What?"

"Come back here and sit down."

"You said we need nappies. I better hurry up if I'm going to get to Wadebridge and back before it gets late."

"Martin, we have enough to get by until I can go to Mrs. Tishell's in the morning. I just thought you might like to get out by yourself with James. I didn't mean to ..." She wiped at the tears that had begun to spill down her cheeks.

Martin stood staring at her. "Louisa, I'm very sorry about the nappies. I just started thinking about things and forgot to pick them up."

His chin dropped to his chest as he squeezed his eyes shut. Walking over, he knelt down in front of her before pulling out his handkerchief to wipe her cheeks dry. "I'll get the nappies first thing in the morning."

Louisa looked up at his face and saw the naivety and desperation in his eyes. "Oh, Martin, it's not *about* the nappies. It's just …" She put a hand over her face and began to cry harder. "I was worried about you."

"I didn't mean to make you worry," he said as he shifted himself to the sofa next to her. "It was just … well, a lot happened at my appointment today. Since I try not to think about those things whilst I'm driving I—I think I just got lost in thought and … forgot the nappies."

Louisa took the handkerchief from her husband's hand and blew her nose before brushing her fingers along his jawline. "Why don't I go and tuck James in while you make us something hot to drink. Then we can talk some more." Getting to her feet, she bent down and placed a kiss on his head.

"Mm, yes."

She started for the stairs with James before turning back to him. "Could you make me some hot chocolate?"

Martin opened his mouth to remind her of the harmful effects of refined sugar, but he was brought up short by her steady gaze and gestured shush.

"Yes."

When she came back downstairs she found him waiting on the sofa, a glass of water in his hand and a cup of steaming hot chocolate on the table.

"Thank you, Martin," she said, settling in next to him.

"Mm. Did James go down all right?"

"No problems. He's such a good boy."

They sat awkwardly for some moments, Martin dreading his wife's reaction to what he needed to say and Louisa not wanting to push him.

He cleared his throat. "I er, I had an interesting visit with Dr. Newell today. He helped me to remember a bit more about my dream."

"And ... is it a memory?"

"Yes. I was able to remember some less obvious things that were in the dream. Things that I hadn't considered."

A nervous tightness was developing in his chest. The last thing he wanted was for his wife to look at him with pity ... to feel sorry for him.

"And?"

"It was my father. I remember now seeing his hand ... his ring. I'd spilt something on the floor in his study, and he was angry. He grabbed me by the arm. He was too rough, and when he threw me back my arm fractured."

Martin kept his eyes fixed on the water glass in his hand.

"Oh, Martin." Louisa sat for a moment, staring at the steam coming off her cup. "What did the doctor say? I mean ... well, I assume they had to explain it to the doctor."

He glanced over at her. "No."

"No? Oh, I see. So, what explanation did they give him then?"

"I didn't see a doctor. Well, technically I did. My father came into my room after I'd gone to bed—he set it."

Louisa swallowed several times. She quickly batted away the tears which had escaped.

"Oh God, Martin. That's terrible."

"Mm."

"How could your father do that? And how could your mother listen to her screaming child without intervening?"

"She didn't hear anything. My father said I wasn't to make a fuss ... to disturb my mother, so I stayed quiet. I told Dr. Newell I thought he might be proud of me for not crying ... for taking it like a man, as he was so fond of saying. But he didn't say anything. He put the splint on, told me if anyone asked what had happened I was to say I'd fallen down the stairs. Then he left the room."

Louisa sat quietly for a few moments before speaking. "Martin forgive me, but your father was a bloody arse. I don't know how he could have been so callous and uncaring of his own son. I can't begin to imagine you treating James that way. I'm so sorry tha—"

"Louisa, *don't* feel sorry for me! I can't bear the thought of you looking at me in that way. It was a long time ago, and I was very young. It's in the past."

"Martin, I admire *you*. But I can't help but feel sorry for that little boy. How old were you when this happened?"

"Seven."

"Oh, Martin. What a horrible year it must have been for you. Being sent off to boarding school in September, then to have that happen."

"Louisa ... I'm very happy for James, that he'll grow up with parents who love him."

Martin's words were positive, but she saw a profound sadness in his eyes that made her hurt for him. She and James could love him from this point on, but there would be no giving him back the loving childhood home that had been kept from him so many years ago.

His voice interrupted her thoughts. "I didn't get a chance to tell you yesterday ... Chris called and asked me to speak to an NHS investigatory committee next week. They're reorganising the nation's ambulance system, and the committee's been charged with making cuts. They want to eliminate the air ambulance that flies out of Newquay ... have Cornwall share one helicopter with Plymouth."

"Well that makes no sense. It isn't always available the way it is. How in the world do they expect us to get by if half the time our air ambulance is on the other side of Cornwall? And it'll take longer to get patients to hospital if they have to fly twice as far to reach people."

"That's what Chris is hoping I can get them to understand. Could be a tall order ... they probably already have their minds made up."

"When's the meeting?"

"In a week and a half ... Friday actually. I thought that we could do our couple's session on Wednesday next week. Then I could do my session on Friday. That way you won't have to wait around for me. It's hard to say how long the meeting could drag on. I spoke with Dr. Newell about it today. It's fine with him."

"That's ideal actually. We have the big autumn term kick off celebration on Friday, and I really do have to be there."

Martin breathed a tacit sigh of relief that the issue had been broached and that Louisa hadn't stormed off, accusing him of making another arbitrary decision.

As they lay in bed that night, Martin thought about what Dr. Newell had said about anger. Yes, he did feel anger towards his parents, but grief was the overriding emotion churning in him at that moment. There had always been at least a remote possibility, a hope in his mind that his parents might change over time and come to want him in their lives. But now his father was gone, and he had admitted to himself that his mother had never ... would never love him.

"Louisa?"

"Mm, hmm?"

"Dr. Newell believes it's important that I admit to being ..." He cleared his throat and pulled his arm up over his face. "God, I don't want to say this in front of you."

"What is it, Martin?" she said, sitting up in bed.

He grimaced under her intense gaze. "Could you ... maybe it would help if you turned around. Just lie down with your back to me."

"Martin, you're scaring me. What's the matter?"

"Just ..." He gave her a frustrated scowl and wagged his fingers. "Lie down, I think it'll make this easier."

She gave him a final puzzled glance before humouring him and sliding down on to the mattress.

Martin moved in close, spooning up against her back with his arm over her.

His expanding chest pressed against her before he spoke again. "I'm supposed to admit that my parents were abusive ... that I was abused."

Louisa lay silently, waiting for him to continue.

"Did you hear me?" he asked impatiently.

"Yes, I did," she replied. "But ... I mean, was that an admission?"

"Yes! Of course it was! Were you even listening?"

Louisa rolled over to face him. "I *was* listening ... very closely," she said softly, placing her palm against his cheek. "You said that you're supposed to admit to this. You didn't actually *admit* it though, did you?"

His scowl deepened. "Why are you making this more difficult for me?"

"Martin, I'm not *trying* to make this more difficult. I'm just saying that you need to think about what you actually said."

Martin lay, staring at the ceiling. "I thought I was making a confession," he grumbled.

She leaned over and kissed his forehead. "Why *is* this so hard for you?"

The steady tick of the mantle clock, a sound he usually found soothing, seemed to be tapping out a demand for his answer.

He pressed the heel of his hand to his pounding head. "To admit to being abused would completely validate my father's opinion of me. That I'm weak ... a coward. That's not how I want you to see me."

"Martin, I could never see you that way."

Martin looked at her askance.

"What?" she asked, cocking her head at him.

"You are obviously forgetting our less than pleasant honeymoon."

Louisa pulled her elbow under her, resting her head in her hand. "You mean your stubborn refusal to stay in the lodge until Bert could pick us up in the morning?"

Martin shook his head. "There were health issues to consider! There was, no doubt, harmful particulate matter in that smoke. And no, that's not what I mean."

"Then you mean your refusal to listen to me when I told you we were going the wrong way?"

"No! I was a coward! I couldn't protect you from a stupid errant horse, a flock of chickens ... or an old man! To say my parents' actions were abusive is to say I couldn't handle their punishments. It's embarrassing ... humiliating. And it's not the kind of man I want to be for you. I want you to feel safe when you're with me. I don't want you to feel like you have to protect *me* ... defend *me*."

He huffed out a breath. "That's why this is difficult."

Louisa lay back down with her head on his shoulder. "I see." She reached her hand under his pyjama top and caressed his belly. "Martin, that night at the hospital, after the ambulance ride with Peter Cronk ... do you remember when I went back into the building before getting in the taxi?"

"Yes."

"I saw that doctor, the one who had been one of your pupils."

"Gawd, Adrian Pitts?" Martin groaned.

"Yes. Well, he was in the hallway when we were leaving the building, so I went back to talk to him. I told him you were ten times the man he would ever be. And I meant that. You are ten times the man *any* man will ever be, in my eyes."

"Mm," he grunted, unconvinced, before rolling on to his side and wrapping his arm around her. "Dr. Newell suggested that as a child, I turned the anger I felt towards my parents inward ... directed it towards myself."

"I think he's right," she said as she toyed with his ear. "You don't feel you deserve me. Why else would you feel that way?"

"There are perfectly legitimate reasons for that. I'm gruff, monosyllabic and rude to start with."

Louisa reached up and kissed his cheek. "Don't forget about well-meaning. And that trumps the other three."

"Hmm. I've been making a crap list."

Louisa sat up abruptly. "Martin, please tell me you're joking."

"I don't joke." He rolled over and pulled open the drawer on his bedside table, taking out a folded sheet of paper. "I actually find it useful. It's a reminder of what I need to work on."

Louisa held out her hand, snapping her fingers at him. "Give it to me, Martin. Right now."

Sighing, he handed it to her.

She scanned the list of negative qualities before picking up the pen by her diary. The nib scratched against the paper as she scribbled out half of what her husband had written down.

"Now, *these* are legitimate problems that you could stand to work on. Make another list ... ways to improve in these areas. Then we'll throw this one away," she said, slapping it down on his chest before settling in for the night.

When Martin went into the bathroom the following morning, he found a folded-up piece of paper lying next to the sink. Opening it up, he read, *Reasons Martin Ellingham Deserves Louisa Ellingham.*

Chapter 33

Louisa woke on Friday morning, finding herself alone in bed. "Martin?" she called out sleepily.

Not getting an answer, she got up and pulled on her dressing gown before padding down the stairs in search of her husband. She found him at his desk, scribbling notes on to a piece of paper.

"Martin, what are you doing up?" she whispered stridently.

He startled and hurriedly shoved the sheet of paper into his desk drawer. "Mm, nothing. Nothing."

"It's 6:00 a.m. Couldn't you sleep?"

He sat rigidly with his palms flat on the desktop. "I just had some work to get done, so I thought I'd get an early start."

Stroking his cheek, Louisa leaned over and pressed her lips to his forehead before looking at him askance. "Well, we're both up. Let's have breakfast together for a change."

"I better finish here. I still need to wash and get dressed before my first patient arrives."

"Martin, you need to be eating more. You've been losing weight, you know."

"Yes, it's been pointed out to me." Martin winced at the thought of his mother's derisive comment about his appearance during her last visit.

"All right then, you go up and get yourself dressed. I'll have breakfast ready when you come down," she said as she headed off towards the kitchen.

Martin stood in their bedroom a short time later, working a Windsor knot into his tie and gazing across the landing towards the nursery. As he made his way towards the steps, the soft, happy sounds of his son caused him to pause in the doorway, watching as the boy swung a stuffed rabbit around by one ear. He entered the room and leaned on the rail of the cot, studying the baby, looking for evidence of his own genetic influence in the creation of this fresh new life.

"Good morning, James. Did you sleep well?" Martin picked him up and cuddled him, stealing a breath of sweet baby fragrance from his head. Then he changed the child's nappy, dressed him, and gave him a final inspection to ensure that he was presentable.

Louisa turned around when she heard her husband's heavy footsteps behind her.

"James, how's my boy this morning?" She took the baby from his father and settled him into his high chair, putting a bowl of chopped banana on the tray in front of him.

"Martin, have a seat please." She looked over at him with narrowed eyes. "I don't want you sneaking off on me."

Taking his plate to the hob, she returned it with a generous amount of food. Martin sat staring glumly at it.

"Oh, Martin, you look like you've been led to the gallows. Just eat it ... please," she said, tousling his hair.

"It's fried eggs and kippers, Louisa. It's full of saturated fat, calories, and—"

She pressed her hand to his mouth. "Yes, Martin. Fat and calories are two things you're seriously in need of right now." She tapped her finger firmly on the table. "Sit here until your plate is clean. I can't just sit back and watch you wither away anymore." Detecting her husband's dismissive eye roll, she added a sharp, "I mean it, Martin."

Martin knew when his wife would not give on an issue, and this was one of them.

"Did you remember to ask Poppy to come early?" he asked as he stared disdainfully at the fish on his fork. "You have your scan and x-ray today."

"I did remember. In fact, I asked her to come and have lunch with us."

Martin stared at her, his fork suspended in the air. "Oh. I'll get lunch at the pub then."

"No, you won't, Martin. You'll have lunch with Poppy, James, and me. It'll be a chance for us all to get better acquainted. And you *will* be polite and make a reasonable attempt at conversation."

Martin screwed up his face. "Why don't I leave this to you and James. I can get to know her once you're sure she's settled into the job."

"You'll be fine, Martin. James and I'll do most of the talking, won't we James." Louisa brushed her hand over the baby's head.

Martin sighed. He felt another headache coming on.

The morning passed slowly for Martin, with an assortment of the most mundane maladies known to modern medicine presenting. By lunchtime he was actually looking forward to lunch, Poppy or no Poppy.

Louisa was putting bowls of soup on the table when he came through under the stairs. James was in his high chair, and his face lit up at the sight of his father. Martin picked the boy up, clutching on to him as he stood, awkwardly, waiting for the meal to begin. The childminder sat equally awkwardly at the other end of the table.

"Hello, Pansy," Martin said before turning quickly to put James back into the high chair.

"Hello, Dr. Ellingham." The girl glanced up at Louisa, wrapping her arms around herself as her knees bounced up and down under the table.

"Martin, will you please feed James?" Louisa suggested.

"Mm, yes."

She was beginning to have doubts about the wisdom of her meet-and-greet scheme when Poppy surprised her by addressing Martin.

"Dr. Ellingham, can you tell me where I could go to get some training in first aid. I'm thinkin' mostly CPR, what to do if James would choke on something, that kind'a thing."

Martin looked at the girl, his eyebrows raised.

"Erm, I could do some checking, but I know something could be arranged. And we would, of course, cover any expenses. That's a good idea—the training."

Poppy sat up straighter in her chair, looking as though the Queen had just bestowed on her the highest compliment.

Martin scraped a dribble of applesauce from James's chin. "I could, erm ... show you how CPR is done on a child of James's age. And it would be a good idea for you to also familiarise yourself with the paediatric method of performing the Heimlich manoeuvre. We can go over it after we've finished eating, if you like."

"Good!" Poppy said, smiling broadly at Louisa.

Louisa finished cleaning up after lunch and then went to the doorway of the consulting room to watch as Martin wrapped up his mini-course with the childminder. She had never seen her husband in a teaching capacity. He truly seemed to be in his element as he went over the first aid techniques with the girl. And Poppy seemed to be comfortable with the gruff doctor as her teacher.

The impromptu training session left Martin with just enough time to make arrangements for Jim Hanley's stay at an area drug treatment centre before they needed to leave for Truro.

He dropped Louisa at the entrance to the hospital and drove across the street to park the car in the carpark by Dr. Newell's office. Knowing that his wife's tests would take a little while, he sat down on a bench near the bus stop. His thoughts focused on Wednesday night's conversation with Louisa. Why she took offense with his crap list he couldn't understand. Perhaps he would need to get her help in coming up with the new list she had requested. A glimmer of a smile came to his face as he recalled the letter she had left for him in the bathroom the previous morning.

He stared off at the hospital across the street, thinking about the last time they had been in that building together— the day after he had performed her embolization. They had made good progress since then, and he was learning to be a better husband. That gave him hope. But many of the problems between them were a result of the baggage left from his horrible upbringing, and he wasn't sure that burden was feeling a whole lot lighter. Louisa hadn't asked lately about the nightmares, and he hadn't brought the subject up either, but they were still dogging him. He couldn't shake the feeling that there was some memory lying in wait, ready to surface at any moment.

He was roused from his introspection by a breeze rustling through the trees, and he watched as a parade of leaves danced across the street. Summer would be over soon, and the cold dank winter would return again.

He got up and walked back to the hospital, winding his way through the long corridors leading to the radiology department, trying to ignore the gawps from staff who recognised him as the once brilliant surgeon. Louisa had just finished with her tests when he walked into the waiting area, and they went together to meet with the consultant about the results.

Martin was pleased but not surprised by the good news. Her clavicle had healed, and his repair to her AVM looked good as well.

As they walked between the buildings towards Dr. Newell's office, Louisa reached down and took his hand, pulling him to a stop.

"Problem?" he asked, his eyebrows raised.

"No problem. I just wanted to thank you for taking such good care of me."

Martin swallowed and averted his eyes, but not before Louisa noticed the moisture gathering in them. She stretched up and kissed him.

They continued on to their appointment across the street, and after dispensing with the usual formalities, they now sat in their familiar positions opposite the therapist.

The man rifled through the patient notes in front of him before turning his attention to Louisa.

"I'd like to start our session out today, Louisa, by having you tell me a bit about your parent's marriage. You described your mother last week as having been quite controlling and critical of your father. Do you think that was the key factor in their eventual divorce, or were there other driving factors as well?"

Louisa fidgeted in her seat, straightening her blouse and brushing at the wrinkles in her skirt. "I think it was a factor. I'm not sure if it was the *key* factor. Mum wanted what Mum wanted, and Dad ... well, he was pretty rubbish at being a provider. He tried, but he just wasn't ever going to be what Mum wanted him to be. She found someone else ... in Spain. He could buy her the things she wanted. He was charming ... you know," she said, her hand circling in the air. "I suppose my mum could be described as selfish."

Louisa glanced over at Martin, and he screwed up his face. "Well, *I* could certainly attest to your mother's selfishness ... among other things."

"Martin ..." Louisa said in an admonitory tone.

He pulled in his chin and turned his gaze towards the window.

"So, you think that your mother's selfishness was a factor?"

"Yeah, I think so. And Mum had a tendency to disappear after she and Dad would have a row. I think that made Dad feel insecure in the relationship."

She twirled a strand of hair around her finger. "Dad wasn't innocent in all of it. I mean, he's not the most industrious person, and he got himself into trouble. It started with gambling. He thought he had a sure winner at the horse track. He took some money from the village lifeboat fund, intending to pay it back with his winnings. Of course it didn't work out as he'd hoped. He got found out. Coincidentally, by Martin's aunt Joan."

The therapist rocked back in his chair, "We discussed last week, your concern about being too controlling and critical of Martin ... that you feel it may be a behaviour you learned from your mother. Do you see any of your parents' other habits creeping into your own marriage?"

"I run ... I've left Martin when things aren't going well. I'm aware of what it's done to Martin's sense of security in our marriage and I ..." She wiped at the tears stinging her eyes. "I'm afraid that it won't be possible for me to win back his trust."

Martin reached into his back pocket to pull out his handkerchief. "Louisa, I told you that you have as many chances as you need."

"But you're not happy, Martin. I think you're afraid to let yourself be happy because you don't trust that I'm not going to leave you again ... take that happiness away. And if you can't ever trust me, you can't ever be happy."

Dr. Newell directed his gaze at Martin. "I think you married a very astute woman."

The therapist's fingers beat out a soft riff on the armrest of his chair as he continued on. "Louisa, I want to assure you that your tendency for flight has only been one factor in Martin's difficulties with trust and happiness."

The therapist leaned forward and rested his elbows on his desk. "Martin, did you ever feel happiness as a child?"

Martin rubbed his thumb against his palm, keeping his eyes on his lap. "I think there were times. I think I felt happy at times, when I was at my aunt and uncle's farm." He got up and walked over to the array of diplomas and accreditations hanging on the wall.

"And at what age did that start and end?"

"I was six years old the first time my parents sent me and twelve my last summer there." He walked back across the room to the window.

"Were you no longer enjoying going to the farm, or why did the visits stop?"

"My father *said* that my aunt didn't have the time or energy for me anymore," he said, his tone acrimonious as he folded his hands behind his back.

Dr. Newell came around to take his place on the desk corner. "I take it that wasn't the real reason?"

"I trusted him at the time, so I thought that was the reason. For many years, I thought it was the reason. I found out a couple of years ago that it was actually because my parents had discovered Joan was having an affair. She ended the affair in hopes that my father would change his mind, but ..." Martin sighed, his eyes closed.

"As a child, though, you were led to believe that the one person in your life who loved and cared for you had decided you were too much trouble to have around?"

"Mm." He turned and walked back to take a seat.

The psychiatrist dropped from the desktop and returned to his chair. "Louisa, problems are inevitable in every marriage, and there's no reason to fear them. I'd like to work with you on developing some strategies to use when you feel that compulsion to run away from the problems between you and Martin.

"Over the course of the next five days, I'd like you to write a brief synopsis of each of your flight events. Tell me why you ran ... what purpose it served.

"Then I'd like you to think of a different way that you could have handled each situation, and write down what you think the outcome would be with the new scenario.

"I want you to come up with some alternatives to how you've handle problems in the past, so that when these situations come along in future, you'll be prepared to deal with them in a way that strengthens your marriage, as opposed to causing damage to the relationship ... ways that won't be harmful to Martin's sense of trust and security."

Martin stared intently at the psychiatrist.

"Did you have a question, Martin?" the man asked.

"Yes ... about the assignment you gave me on Wednesday. I've been working on a list." He glanced over at his wife. "I actually started it several years ago. Louisa was unhappy when I told her about it the other night. I'm not sure I understand why."

Dr. Newell looked back and forth between his clients. "Well, you've piqued my interest now. Would one of you like to explain this list to me?"

Louisa shifted nervously before speaking. "Several years ago, I told Martin that there were twenty things about him that were crap, but that if he were a stick of rock he'd be Martin Ellingham through and through. I did mean the last part." She reached out and placed her hand over her husband's. "Martin's the most solid and steadfast person I've known. His principled character is unshakable."

Louisa tipped her head down and peered up at the therapist. "It's the first part I regret. Martin told me the other night that he keeps a crap list, a list of weaknesses ... negatives that he thinks he needs to correct. It upsets me to think that I've reinforced the negative view that he has of himself. That bloody list serves no positive purpose in my opinion."

Dr. Newell pivoted in Martin's direction. "Did this list result in a row?"

Martin whipped his head up. "Of course not. Louisa demanded I give her the list, she scribbled out most of it and handed it back to me. She told me to come up with positive ways to address what she considered to be the truly legitimate problems that remained. That was the end of it."

The therapist smiled at Louisa. "It sounds like you know how to handle your husband. Maybe you can tell me how the list project is coming along when we get together next week."

Louisa looked over at Martin as he was backing out of the parking space a short time later. "How does a romantic dinner out before heading back to Portwenn sound to you?"

"Oh, Louisa," he groaned. "I'm tired. I'd rather just go home."

"Well, we do have something to celebrate," she said, raising her now sling-free arm.

Martin scowled at the windscreen

"It would be my treat. *Although,* I don't have a lot of cash with me. I'd have to pay off my debt when we get home tonight," she said suggestively as she leaned over to kiss him on the cheek.

Martin looked at her out the corner of his eye, and she shot him a coquettish grin. His face warmed, and he pulled in his chin. "Yes," he replied before returning his eyes to the road.

Louisa gave him an impish smile. *Hmm, maybe I do know how to handle my husband.*

Chapter 34

Martin woke Saturday to the sound of rain pattering on the roof. In Cornwall, though, clouds and rain could break into sunshine in moments, which meant that much flexibility was required when making plans. *Hmm,* he thought, *maybe Bert's go-with-the-flow approach to life has some merit after all.*

He lay on his back thinking about the "payment in full" that he had received from Louisa the night before. He gazed at her, deciding that he quite liked this new form of currency. Rolling to his side, he reached into the drawer of his bedside table and pulled out the sheet of paper that she had left for him to find by the bathroom sink. He lay back down to read her words for the fifth time in two days.

My Dear Martin,

You have told me that you don't think you deserve me. I don't know if I can convince you otherwise, but I'm going to try my very best because I can't bear it if you continue to share a life with me while under that delusion.

You have been so terribly cheated, Martin. Cheated out of the love and caring that you should have had from your parents, out of a carefree childhood, out of the joy of having a family to share special occasions with, and a mother and father who would praise your many achievements. No child should ever have to grow up in such an emotionally starved environment, and few who do have the strength of character to grow into successful adults.

But you, Martin, pushed through childhood undeterred. You had a dream for your life—to save the lives of others. What a noble calling. You dedicated yourself to your studies and earned your stripes through hard work and determination.

I know that this chosen career path has taken an emotional toll. You worked so hard to attain the level you did in surgical medicine. I will never understand why fate once again intervened to steal something of which you were so deserving.

And still you persevered. You have committed the last five years of your life to watching over the health of the people in this village, despite the fact that they have often been unappreciative. You are so dedicated to the work that you do, to the people to whom you have a duty of care. You have shown yourself to be honourable, trustworthy, reliable, and even heroic; doing whatever is necessary to safeguard your patients.

My childhood woes don't even begin to compare to what you endured my dear husband, but the failures of my parents have made me insecure and defensive. Martin, you are the man that I need in my life. I couldn't possibly feel more sure of my decision to marry you. James and I can count on you to be there for us whenever we need you, to keep us safe, to provide for our needs, and to always love us. You have proven yourself to be an exemplary father—kind, caring, patient, protective, and loving beyond compare. You will give James the life that you never had. I couldn't want more for our little boy.

And you my dear Martin, are the man that I want to share my bed with. I know you recoil at the sound of his name, and suffice it to say, you know to whom I am referring. So, I will only tell you that when I spent time with him, my thoughts continually turned to you. I would see you in the village, and I wanted to shake him from my arm and run to you. You are the only man who has ever visited me in my dreams, Martin. You stir my senses. I could never desire anyone else.

Life owes you so much, and I feel very fortunate that I can be a small part of the compensation due you, my extraordinary man.

All my love,
Louisa

Martin's stirrings had woken Louisa, and she lay watching him surreptitiously while he read her letter. The sparkle in his eyes and the just perceptible upturn of his mouth revealed his previously unexpressed feelings. She closed her eyes again, picturing the look of contentment on his face.

He slid the drawer shut, and she moved to flop her arm over his chest. Brushing the hair aside from her face, he leaned over to kiss her forehead.

She peered up at him. "Good morning, sleep well?"

"Mm-hmm. And you?"

"Very well, thank you." Moving her head to his shoulder, Louisa inhaled deeply, drawing in his scent. "Have you spoken with Ruth since your appointment on Wednesday? Did you tell her about what you remembered?"

Martin shifted his gaze quickly to the ceiling. "No. I didn't tell her."

She propped herself up on her elbow. "Maybe you should stop by today."

Closing his eyes, he sighed heavily.

"I'm sure she's been worrying about you, Martin."

"Why do you say that? She wasn't worried four decades ago when it was all happening."

Louisa forced back the rebuke that wanted to spill out and attempted a gentler tack. "Don't you think she would have stepped in if she'd known what was going on?"

"She knew something wasn't right, but she did nothing. Why didn't she do something?"

"Maybe you should ask her," she said, stroking her fingers across his chest. "Ask her how much she knew—Joan knew."

"Mm, I'm not sure that would be a good idea. If she didn't know about it before, how's she going to react when I accuse her brother of child abuse? No one believed me then; why would they believe me now?"

Martin turned his gaze towards his wife. "Aside from you and James, Ruth's the only family I have. I don't want to lose her over this."

Louisa wrapped her arm more securely around him. "I really don't think she'll be angry with you, but I can certainly understand your concerns. Want me to come along when you tell her?"

He hesitated before pulling her in tightly. "If you don't mind, yes ... I do."

"I can call her while you're seeing patients ... see if she wants to come for lunch."

"Mm, yes. That would be good."

Martin walked through to the reception room after finishing breakfast, and Morwenna handed him a stack of patient notes. It looked to be a pretty typical schedule for a Saturday morning, made up almost entirely of routine jabs for childhood diseases and a case or two of intestinal upset and cold symptoms.

Having worked quickly through the majority of his appointments, Martin's mind was now free to wander. His thoughts drifted to the memories he had of his father. He couldn't think of a single positive memory that the man had left him with when he died. Louisa was right; he was a bloody arse.

"Doc?" Morwenna's voice interrupted his musing. "Doc, do you want me ta send Mr. Townsend in yet?"

"Ah, yes ... yes. Bring in a new patient form and any notes you can pull up on him as well. I didn't see anything in this stack," Martin said, handing her the pile of cards.

Nigel Townsend had recently moved to Portwenn, replacing the now retired Mr. Coley as the custodian at the primary school.

"I'm assuming you're here to register as a patient at this practice, Mr. Townsend?" Martin asked, as the man sat wheezing in the chair across the desk.

"I am, Doc. But I been feelin' poorly and havin' some difficulty breathin', too."

Martin took a medical history, and the paperwork for the man's registration was filled out before he wagged a finger at the exam couch. "On the table."

He picked up his stethoscope and got up from behind his desk.

"You have an interesting history of complaints, Mr. Townsend," he said as he approached the man. "Unbutton your shirt, please."

Martin plugged the ends of the scope into his ears and placed the other end on Nigel's chest. "Take a deep breath for me." His brow furrowed as he worked his way up the patient's respiratory tract. "And again."

Hooking his foot around his wheeled stool, he pulled it over to the couch. "Please take a seat here, Mr. Townsend."

He took a small mirror, the sort one would see in a dentist's office, from his medical cart and his torch from his breast pocket. "Open your mouth." He slipped the mirror between the man's open jaws. "Tip your head back." He shined the beam from his pocket torch down Nigel's throat, crouching down as he moved his head around to study the image in the mirror. His patient began to gag and the doctor withdrew his instrument. "I'm sorry about that, Mr. Townsend. I needed to see past your vocal cords."

He snapped off his exam gloves, tossing them into the bin. "You have a significant narrowing of your airway. How long have you been experiencing the breathing difficulties?"

"It's been gettin' worse for the last year or so. What do you mean, Doc? Narrowing of what?"

"You have a subglottic stenosis. Which means that scar tissue has formed in your trachea, or windpipe if you prefer— just below your vocal cords. It's caused a narrowing that is now restricting air flow, making it difficult to breathe. From your other symptoms, I suspect you may have an autoimmune disease called granulomatosis with polyangiitis, or GPA. I'll make an appointment for you with both an ENT and a rheumatologist. They'll run some tests ... urinalysis and blood work. The results will help them to make a definitive diagnosis. The ENT can remove the scar tissue, and you should see an immediate improvement in your ability to breathe."

Nigel sat with a hand to his throat, his eyes darting.

"Mr. Townsend, I'm quite confident of my diagnosis, but they'll be able to tell you conclusively once you get to Truro. If you do indeed have GPA, I think we've caught it early enough to stop the progression of the disease. It'll be treated with a course of oral steroids, usually prednisone. This can be fatal if left untreated for too long, so I strongly recommend you follow through with the people in Truro. I'll make sure someone sees you within the next week."

Martin was finishing with Nigel Townsend's patient notes when Louisa stuck her head in the consulting room door a short time later.

"Ruth wants us to meet her at the farm. I've packed a lunch and we'll eat together out there. She and Al want us to see the changes that have been made. Will you be done soon?"

Martin glanced up at her. "Yes, give me five minutes."

The Ellinghams sat with Al Large at the old wooden farm table in the kitchen a while later, finishing up with lunch. Ruth glanced over at her young assistant. "What are your plans for the afternoon, Al?"

"I need to fix that squeak in the hinges on the front door, then I was thinkin' I'd put a coat of paint on the window boxes before I hang 'em back up. They're gettin' a bit seedy lookin', don't you think?"

"Hmm, perhaps you're right. But check with me about the colour first. I don't want to come back out here to find you've chosen a lovely shade of pink," she said, giving him a crooked smile.

"I'll see what we have in the barn ... bring in some samples." Al rose from his chair. "Thank you for lunch, Louiser."

"You're welcome, Al."

Ruth waited until the young man had closed the door behind him before turning her attention to her nephew.

"How did your visit with Dr. Newell go on Wednesday, Martin?"

He glanced over at Louisa, and she gave him an encouraging nod.

"It was ... productive. He helped me to remember some things. It ... it *was* a memory, it seems."

Ruth stopped trying to chase down the piece of lettuce on her plate and looked up at him.

"Well, go on ... do tell."

Martin worried the remains of his sandwich, sending crumbs dropping to the table top. "I had spilt something on the floor in Dad's study. He was, quite understandably, upset with me."

The elderly woman glanced up at him before returning her attention to the tomato she had been attempting to spear. "Go on."

Martin tipped his head to the side and shrugged his shoulders in feigned nonchalance. "He pulled me back out of the way. He was a bit too rough, and it fractured my arm."

Ruth sat with her fork in mid-air, staring at him.

"Are you saying that Christopher broke your arm?" She pulled in her chin. "That *my* brother broke his own son's arm?"

Martin glanced over at Louisa as a flood of adrenaline began to course through his body, raising his heart rate and causing a sheen of sweat to break out on his upper lip. *She doesn't believe me.* The same sensations he experienced as a child washed over him again. The sense of hopelessness he felt when trying to tell someone about what had been happening to him, only to be chastised for spreading tales.

He stood quickly, knocking his chair over behind him. As he hurried towards the door, he ran into Al, carrying an armload of paint cans. The cans scattered, the lid on one of them popping off as it hit the floor. Paint spilled from the can, spattering Martin's trousers as a red puddle spread out in front of him. He stared down at the mess, momentarily frozen in place.

Seeing the distress in her husband's eyes, Louisa jumped from her chair to go to him. Ruth placed her hand on the younger woman's arm. "Let him be for a minute dear," she said softly.

Martin struggled to catch his breath before turning to race out the door.

Ruth got to her feet. "I'll go. Just wait here." She followed, catching up to him in the field near the house. He was sitting on the ground, his fingers clasped over his head.

The old woman put a frail hand on his shoulder causing him to jerk away.

"Care to talk about it?" she asked as she joined him on the grass.

He turned his head slowly towards her, taking in a ragged breath. "Did you know about it, Aunt Ruth?"

Ruth cocked her head at her nephew. "The dream? That it was a memory? No, I didn't."

"No. The—the—what my parents did. How they were with me."

"I'm not sure what you mean, Martin."

Martin's face reddened as tears stung his eyes, and he snapped, "You know bloody well what I mean, Ruth!"

The elderly woman stared back at him, unfazed by his temper. "If you're going to ask me a question Martin, then ask it."

"The abuse!" he spat out. "I said it, Ruth. I said the word. Now tell me, did you know about it?"

"Martin, I knew that your father was an idiot. And I knew that he used disciplinary measures that I thought were inappropriate. But I did *not* know of what you are rightly calling abuse. If either Joan or I had known about it, we would have stepped in."

She sighed. "I do have to admit to you though that I think we both secretly harboured suspicions, and we should have looked into it. My saying I'm sorry for that won't change the past, but do know Martin, I *am* deeply sorry that I didn't trust my instincts and pursue the matter. I think Joan and I were afraid that it would only hurt you more if we couldn't prove anything."

Martin sat, staring out at the distant sea. "I had spilt paint. That's why he was upset with me."

Ruth stretched her legs out in front of her. "I realise I wasn't around much while you were growing up, but I don't remember you having a broken arm. When did this happen?"

"When I was home for Christmas. I had just turned seven. Dad reduced the fracture ... in my bedroom that night."

"What ... with no anaesthesia?"

"Mm."

"Oh, good Lord, Martin!"

Ruth paused momentarily before putting her hand on her nephew's solid paw. "You know, Martin ... inside, when you told me about what had happened ... I hope you don't think that I was questioning your honesty. It's just that I didn't know that my brother was capable of being that cruel. I'm sorry if I made you feel otherwise." Ruth patted his hand. "I will always believe you. Remember that."

Martin sat on the sofa that night, working on the assignment given him by Dr. Newell. He listened to the nightly duet being sung by his wife and son upstairs, Louisa singing the melody and James joining in with a harmony of baby gurgles and delighted giggles.

The sounds coming from the nursery quieted, and footsteps could be heard on the stairs. He quickly slipped his homework into his binder and set it under his *BMJ* on the table in front of him. Louisa went to the kitchen before joining him on the sofa, a cup of hot chocolate in her hand. She nestled in next to him and pulled her feet up against the front edge of the table.

"Did you finish your assignment already?" she asked.

"Mm, yes. It really wasn't very hard."

A period of uncomfortable silence passed before she asked, "Martin, is everything okay with you?"

He looked over at her, his eyebrows lowered. "I'm fine."

She worked her hand under his arm before letting it come to rest on his thigh. "Today at the farm, you seemed very upset about the paint that was spilt on the floor."

Martin groaned silently, knowing that this could turn into a stressful discussion for which he lacked either the desire or the energy. "I saw the paint on the floor, on my trousers. I think I had spilt paint in my father's study, and that's what made him angry."

Louisa gave him one of her penetrating stares and he knew she suspected there was more to it than he was letting on. "I don't know *why* it upset me, Louisa."

"Did Ruth have any ideas?"

"I'm not sure she saw through me the way you did. As far as I could tell, she thought I was upset by her reaction to what I told her about my father, not by the spilt paint."

"Did it upset you? I mean, she didn't seem very happy about it, so I could see where you ..."

"Yes, I *thought* she was questioning my truthfulness, but she did believe me," he said, his annoyance with his wife's questions bubbling just under the surface.

"Did you ask her if she and Joan were aware of what was going on?"

"Yes, we discussed it. They had their suspicions, but they had no real proof of anything."

"It really is a shame, Martin. Your life could have been so different if you had grown up in Joan's care." She leaned back against his shoulder.

"Mm. But I might not have ... well, I might not have come to Portwenn. I might not have met you."

Louisa tipped her head back and smiled up at him. "You would have already known me because we would have grown up in the same village."

"Well, strictly speaking, I would have grown up at the farm, not in the village. And with the age difference between us, I highly doubt I would have had any interest in you."

"Okay, I see your point. But still ... What do you think you'd be like now if you *had* grown up with Joan?"

Martin rubbed a palm across his face. "I'd probably be just as irritated with this conversation."

"Sorry, you're tired. Ready for bed?"

"Mm. It's been a long day." He got to his feet and started up the stairs, his wife following close behind.

She eyed him as he moved along in front of her before pulling him to a stop at the top of the steps.

"You may not have had an interest in *me*," she said, "but I bet I would've had an interest in *you*." She reached around and patted his bum.

"Mm." He tugged at a reddening ear and hurried off towards the bathroom.

Chapter 35

Life in the Ellingham household returned to the more chaotic school term schedule on Monday morning. Poppy arrived promptly at 8 a.m., giving Louisa ample opportunity to go over last-minute instructions for James's care.

"Now, if you have any questions or concerns, Martin will be down the hall. I'm going to run upstairs to say goodbye to him, and then I'll be back to say goodbye to the two of you," she said brushing her palm over her son's head as he sat in the childminder's arms.

Louisa found her husband in the bathroom, scraping the last of the shaving foam from his face. She reached up and caressed his cheek before wrapping her arms around his neck. "Come down here where I can reach you," she said as she gave him a gentle tug. She pressed her face to his and sighed softly. "You smell nice," she whispered in his ear.

"So do you. Are you wearing perfume?"

She pulled back and looked at him warily. The last time he had asked that question, the conversation had turned into a humiliating explanation about hormones associated with the onset of the menstrual cycle and her telling him she didn't want to see him anymore.

But now his expression of bashful euphoria, more typical of an adolescent boy about to kiss his first girl, brought a smile to her face.

"Yes, I am, and let's leave it at that, shall we?"

"Mm."

"Poppy's here," she said softly. "I've gone over some instructions with her. I told her she could come and talk to you if she has any questions or concerns."

"I'll likely be with patients, Louisa. She'll need to check in with Morwenna first, unless it's an emergency of course."

"I'll remind her of that." She stretched up and pressed her lips to his before heading towards the landing. "I'll miss you today," she said over her shoulder.

"Me too."

She had just reached the top of the steps when she heard Martin's voice, soft and velvety.

"Louisa."

She turned. "Yes, Martin?"

He stood in the bathroom doorway, his toothbrush in his hand and toothpaste foam around his mouth. He glanced down at the floor before looking up and making eye contact with her. "Good luck today, and ... I love you."

Louisa walked back and embraced him. "Thank you, Martin. I love you, too."

The first week of term went smoothly, both at work and at home. Poppy's presence had made a world of difference for Martin as well as for Louisa.

Martin had gotten on well with Michael, their previous childminder. He was always very punctual and kept the house impeccably tidy, but some of his eccentric ways had made Louisa uncomfortable. And Martin had grown weary of the constant distraction that Morwenna seemed to be for him. Poppy was timely, competent, and did her job while keeping to the domestic area of the surgery.

Wednesday brought the next couples session with Dr. Newell, and Louisa found herself the centre of the therapist's attention.

"Louisa, on Friday I asked you to do some reflecting on the times that you've left Martin. How did that go?"

"Well, I've written some things down," she said, handing Dr. Newell a piece of paper. "Just my chicken scratches. Not like my husband's neatly typed spreadsheets." She gave Martin a quick glance.

Dr. Newell scanned over what she had written on the paper before handing it back across the desk.

"Have you discussed any of this with Martin?"

"No, it's just my own thoughts." She bit her lip as her fingers worried the strap on her purse.

The therapist rested his elbows on the armrests of his chair, folding his hands in front of him. "Why don't we start at the beginning then. When did this pattern of running away begin?"

"Well, I s'pose the first time I left Martin, I didn't actually *leave* him. I sort of pushed him out ... of a taxi we were taking back to Portwenn."

Martin tugged the list from her hand. "I don't think that particular occasion qualifies as running. Why don't you move on to the next one on your list," he urged, his eyes pleading with her.

Dr. Newell held his hand up in front of him. "Louisa, please continue."

Louisa gave her husband a sympathetic look and returned her attention to the therapist. "One of my students had suffered a ruptured spleen, and I went in the ambulance with Martin when they took him to hospital.

"Martin had been ... quite heroic. I was already attracted to him, but after watching him do what he had to do to save Peter's life, despite the effect the blood had on him ... well, when he kissed me," Martin's head whipped to the side, "I grabbed him and kissed him back. It was such an intensely romantic moment, and then he pointed out my bad breath ... a consequence of being up all night drinking coffee."

Martin's shoulders slumped, his head dropping to the side, and he screwed up his face as his wife continued with her humiliating narrative.

"I was embarrassed. And then angry. I had the driver stop, and I told Martin to get out."

"And did that result in the outcome you were hoping for?"

Louisa looked back at Dr. Newell, abashed. "Well, Martin avoided me for the next week. We ran into each other one day and that conversation ... well, it didn't go well."

"I was trying to explain myself, Louisa," Martin said. "And for the record, you did the grabbing and kissing. Although ... I did kiss you back."

"Fine ... I kissed you, you kissed me."

"I just thought you should get your details straight," Martin said, pulling in his chin before he turned his gaze towards the ceiling.

"Okay, I stand corrected. But, Martin, you turned our later conversation into *another* medical lecture!" Her ponytail swung to the side. "I was angry and started berating him about his inexcusable behaviour."

The psychiatrist turned towards Martin. "If Louisa had given you time to formulate your thoughts and explain yourself, do you think she would have been able to understand your actions?"

"I don't know. I didn't understand what I'd done to upset her. I do now, but I didn't at the time." Martin sat stiffly with his hands folded in his lap. "She caught me unawares. I tend to revert to medicine if I don't know how to deal with a social situation."

"Louisa, if you could go back and redo that scene in the taxi, is there anything you'd do differently?" Dr. Newell asked.

"I suppose the way I handled things cut off communication between us. I thought about it. If I had it to do all over again, I guess I might still throw him out of the taxi, but I'd give him a chance to explain himself later."

"And in what way would riding away from him help the immediate situation?"

Louisa's fists closed tightly around her purse strap. "It'd get me away from what was painful at the moment," she said through taut lips.

"And is that what you wanted ... ultimately? To be apart from Martin?"

Martin turned to her, watching her anxiously.

"No! Just the opposite. I think it upset me so much because I wanted you to want me, Martin. I thought you weren't interested in me. I wasn't angry with you; I was hurt."

Dr. Newell leaned back in his chair and pulled his ankle up over his knee. "And the next time you left was when?"

"That was after our wedding, or the wedding that we called off. I moved to London."

Martin slumped lower as he picked at a fingernail.

"Did Martin try to persuade you to stay?"

Louisa crossed her legs and jiggled her foot. "I didn't tell him I was leaving. I just needed to get away."

"Get away? From the village or Martin?"

"Both I suppose. But Martin mostly. I didn't want to have to face him all the time ... living in the same tiny village."

"Was moving back your idea or Martin's?"

"It was my idea. Martin had no way to contact me. He didn't know about the pregnancy. Not 'til I showed up at his door."

Louisa's fingers toyed nervously with the top buttons on her blouse. "You know, I think we can stop. I understand that I'd rather run than try to work things out. And I understand that it doesn't work out well, especially for Martin."

The therapist's chair creaked as he shifted and pulled himself up to his desk. "Louisa, you're married to a naturally taciturn man. To get Martin to talk, to open up to you must be a bit of a challenge."

She gave an anxious laugh. "To put it mildly. He's been making a real effort lately though. I've definitely seen improvement."

Martin glanced down uncomfortably as she reached over and rested her hand on his knee.

Dr. Newell rolled his biro in his palms. "Louisa, men tend to need a bit more time than women do to respond to a question. We prefer to think through our answers carefully before we speak. Some of us require more time than others.

"The next time you and Martin have a row, I want you to try to identify the real issue. Then, I want you to address it, as briefly as possible. Men don't want as many details as women do. Give Martin a day to think things over. Allow him time to sort out his thoughts and allow yourself a cool down period.

"I find it very difficult to think about what I'm actually feeling or to sort out my thoughts without a bit of space to think in. You of course don't want to let problems brew, but try not to rush to a resolution either."

Dr. Newell came around and sat on the front of his desk. "I'd like to discuss the event at the school ... when you had your accident. I think it was a good example of the communication difficulties that the two of you struggle with."

Martin looked off towards the window, groaning softly.

"I realise this is a tender subject for both of you, but I think it would be helpful to look at why you ended up where you did.

"I want to make you aware, Louisa, that Martin, in all likelihood, really did not remember you asking him to help out with the Sports Day event. I suspect, given his *usual* focus and intellect, that the depression played a role in that. It does affect memory, so be aware of that and try not to take it personally if he has some occasional lapses.

"Now, as to what can be learned from the breakdown in communication that day ... Louisa, if you could replay that scenario, what would you do differently?"

"Well, I suppose if I'd reminded him the day before, it would have given him time to reschedule his patients."

"Would you have had any other options?"

"I guess I could've had Pippa Woodley hand them out. But I *am* the head teacher. I would think my husband would want to help."

"Martin, what went through your head when Louisa reminded you of Sports Day?"

"I had a full schedule. I was thinking about how I was going to fit everything in," he said, shifting in his chair and tugging at his suit coat.

"Did you consider telling Louisa that it just wasn't going to be possible for you to help her out with this?"

Martin sat, his brow furrowed as his right eye twitched.

"Did you consider telling Louisa that it just wasn't going to be possible for you to help her out with this?" the doctor asked again.

"I'd agreed to it. Whether or not I remembered agreeing to it was irrelevant," he said with more than a hint of tetchiness.

"I'm sure that Louisa would have understood if you had explained the situa—"

"If I say I'll do something, then I *do* it."

"But what about your patients? You had also made a commitment to *them*, hadn't you?"

Louisa watched nervously as her husband's hands gripped the armrests of his chair, his knuckles whitening.

"I was confused! I didn't remember it, and it confused me!" he erupted. "That doesn't happen to me. I thought something was wrong with me ... physically. But we'd discussed this, and I couldn't remember discussing ..."

Martin stood up abruptly and strode towards the window, his hands balled into fists. "I was worried! I was embarrassed! My godawful mother was sitting right there at our kitchen table, salivating as she watched me squirm."

He rubbed his hand across the back of his neck and quieted. "I just wanted the whole embarrassing conversation to be over."

Louisa sat silently for several moments before glancing up at him. "I'm sorry. I didn't know all that was going on with you."

Martin breathed out a heavy sigh and returned to his seat.

Louisa continued. "They say you should choose your battles. And lately, I've been insisting on things from Martin that, in hindsight, weren't important. That weren't fair."

"Can you give me an example?" Dr. Newell said, leaning back on his hands.

"There was a weekly playgroup session that our childminder was unable to take our son to. I think it's very important for James to have this sort of social interaction, and I didn't want him to miss a week. Martin balked at the idea of taking him. It's not exactly his cup of tea, as you can imagine. I explained to him that I didn't want James to grow up to be shy and introverted."

Dr. Newell winced at Louisa's words.

"I'm sure Martin doesn't want him to grow up to be shy and introverted either," she said. "And I know it was an awkward experience for him, but Martin does need to push himself outside his comfort zone ... participate more socially." Louisa crossed her legs and clasped her fingers around her knee as she flicked her ponytail to the side. "But I suppose Millie's Playgroup probably wasn't necessary for either Martin or James that week."

"Martin, what went through your mind when Louisa said she didn't want James to grow up to be shy and introverted?"

Martin's gaze fixed on the floor. "I think she was saying that she didn't want him to grow up to be like me." He rubbed his thumb into his palm. "I do worry about that Louisa. Very much. I worry about whether my being around James is good for him. I worry about whether I could start behaving like my father. That thought terrifies me. These are the things that keep me up at night."

Louisa reached for her husband's hand but he moved it away.

Dr. Newell returned to his chair. "Martin, let's pick that subject up again on Friday. I think it's worth exploring," he said as he jotted notes into the patient file before focusing his gaze on Louisa.

"It's important that you both understand that each of us comes into this world either on the introverted or extroverted side of the temperament scale. One is not superior to the other, and it's not something that needs *fixing*, so to speak.

"Love and accept James for who he is. If he's anything like you, Martin, he will be sensitive. He'll likely pick up on any feelings of dissatisfaction that either of you may have with who he is. Give him opportunities and experiences, but respect his uniqueness. Don't try to force him into a mould."

Martin said very little as they left Dr. Newell's office a short time later. Once they were on the A-30, Louisa reached out and put her hand on his leg.

"Martin, I'm sorry that I worded my comment about not wanting James to be shy in such a negative manner. I should have said that I wanted him to be comfortable in social situations. James *is* shy, that's in his makeup. But there are things that we can do to help him to have more confidence when he's around other people. That's what I should have said. I'm sorry."

Martin shook his head. "It's fine. I do see your point."

She tapped her finger against his thigh. "Erm, I was wondering ... how are you doing with your amended crap list?"

Martin grimaced and breathed out a heavy sigh. "I could use some help with that."

Picking up his hand, she pulled it to her cheek. "I think I might be available tonight."

Martin glanced over and gave her a small smile.

Chapter 36

"Got your list?" Louisa asked as she settled back against the headboard that night, pulling the blankets up over her legs.

Martin grunted. "Mm." He rolled over and pulled open the drawer on his bedside table, removing the piece of paper and passing it back to her before sliding the drawer shut again.

"Okay, let's address the social ineptitude," she said as she reviewed her husband's whittled down crap list.

"First of all, I don't think you're as inept as you think you are."

"No, I'm quite confident of my social ineptness, Louisa."

"But you *are* able to carry on a conversation with Ruth ... and Chris Parsons. You two get on quite well, don't you?"

"Yes. But Ruth and Chris are both doctors. I'm quite comfortable with conversations relating to medicine, remember?" Martin said as he adjusted the pillow under his head.

Louisa rolled her eyes at him. "Maybe you just need to get to know people a little better. You don't really know how to relate to people of, erm ... of more average intelligence. What about Joe Penhale?"

"I think you're being rather generous in your assessment of Penhale's cognitive ability."

"Oh, *Martin*," she said, slapping her hand down on his chest. "Maybe if you learned a bit more about Joe you could find something that you have in common ... give you something to talk about. Do you know where he grew up, what he enjoys doing when he's not working?"

Martin screwed up his face. "I have it on good authority that he's on duty twenty-four—seven, which would leave him no time at all for any sort of outside interests."

"All right, perhaps Joe wasn't the best example. Al—Al Large, how about him? You could make an effort to get to know him," she said, her head bobbing vigorously. "You two seem to get on."

"Mm, possibly."

"Okay, so write that down. Make an effort to get to know Al Large," she said, handing him a piece of paper and a pen while she reviewed the list again.

"Rude. Okay, most of the time you're not being rude, just brutally honest. We can work with that, can't we?" Her head bobbed again.

"I can't be dishonest, Louisa."

"No, and I don't want you to be. But sometimes, maybe it's better to just not say anything at all. For instance, if you tell a patient they're an idiot, what purpose does that serve?"

"It alerts them to the fact that their reasoning or behaviour runs counter to logic and common sense, a scourge which seems to be found in epic proportions in this village, by the way."

She shot him a black look. "Are you even going to try here?"

"I am trying, Louisa! How do I know when I should find something to say and when I should keep my mouth shut?"

"Martin, if you're going to say something that could offend someone, it's probably best to stay quiet. But if staying quiet would make the other person uncomfortable, then it would be best to try to find something to talk about. This is all going to take practise," she said, caressing his arm. "I'll help you. Maybe we could practise with Ruth, too."

"Oh, gawd," Martin moaned.

Louisa sighed. "All right, next one. Unromantic. What could you do to make some positive changes in that area?"

"Louisa, you'd be the first to say—and you *were* by the way—that I'm hardly Mr. Hearts and Flowers."

"Mm-hmm. There's a clue for you in that sentence."

She watched as inspiration flashed in his eyes.

"Flowers. Yes, I could bring you flowers."

"Very good, Martin. Now, what about the "hearts" part?"

His brow deepened again as he wracked his brain for anything related to hearts. Forcing out the mental images from anatomy and cardiology textbooks, he visualised Valentine's Day cards and heart-shaped boxes of candy. "Chocolates?" he asked hesitantly.

"No, Martin. Although, that would be nice too. What about sharing what's in your heart with me?"

"Ah, I see. All that mawkish—"

"Martin!" Louisa took a deep breath. "It's not mawkish ... or rubbish if it's something you genuinely feel. And I would *like* to hear you say it if you feel it. Hmm?"

"Yes."

Louisa leaned over and kissed him on the cheek. "I tell you what, let's just tackle those three for now. You don't have to take care of everything at once, right?"

"Mm. May I go to sleep now?"

"I think we're done," she said, rearranging her pillow. "I'm sorry Martin, this must make you feel like one of your clocks. Broken parts being tossed aside and new ones forced to fit in."

He rolled over and put his arm around her. "Is that what I am ... broken? How could I have worked my way up to Chief of Vascular Surgery and still be so ignorant of the most basic communication skills, Louisa?"

"I'm not sure I have an answer for you. Dr. Newell might be a better one to ask. But Martin, please don't worry about this too much. It'll come; you just need practise."

"Mm."

"And you're not broken. You just need a few adjustments."

"Well, be careful. My mainspring could break, and that can be quite dangerous," he said eyeing her mischievously.

She cocked her head at him. "Your mainspring?"

"It's a coiled-up strip of metal inside a clock. When you wind a clock, you're tightening that metal coil. There's a great deal of energy stored in the coil, and if it breaks, a lot of damage can be done to the clock repairer's fingers."

"Hmm," Louisa purred. "Wouldn't want all that energy to be released at once then. That what you're saying?"

"Something like that. Goodnight, Louisa. Love you."

"I love you, too, Martin."

Martin left early on Friday for his appointment and meeting in Truro. He wanted to stop to see Louisa before heading out of town. When he arrived at the school he found his wife in the gymnasium.

"What are *you* doing here?" she asked when she looked up from the decorations she was setting up on the tables.

"I just wanted to stop by before I left. I, erm ... I wanted to tell you good luck tonight."

"Thank you, Martin. That's very sweet of you. I hope all goes well for you and Chris tonight, too. It would be nearly impossible for the people of Cornwall to support the air ambulance entirely through fundraising."

"Yes, it would. I better be going, or I'm going to be late for my four o'clock appointment." Martin fidgeted, toying with a roll of tape lying on the table next to him. "I also wanted to say ..." He hesitated, glancing around quickly. "I wanted to say I love you."

The colour rose in his face, and Louisa reached up to brush a kiss against his cheek. "I'll do that properly when you get home tonight."

Tipping his head to the side, he tugged at an ear. "Mm, yes. I'll look forward to it," he said before turning towards the door.

Martin's awkwardness with her modest display of affection brought a smile to Louisa's face as she watched his tall frame disappear around the corner. Martin would always be Martin—gruff, monosyllabic, well-meaning, but rude to be sure. But also shy and sensitive. And of course, always her "stick of rock".

They had finally been facing their relationship challenges together and had made amazing progress. But the challenges they had faced up to now would pale in comparison to those that were to come.

Special preview of "Fractured"—Book Two In The Battling Demons Series

The rain had stopped, but the wind had turned colder as Martin walked from his psychiatrist's building to the hospital next door. He found Chris in his office going over statistics and operating costs for the Cornwall ambulance system.

"Mart! Good to see you."

Martin laid his binder down on Chris's desk and took a seat. "Mm, yes. How have you been keeping?"

"Quite well," Chris replied as he put down the pen in his hand and scrutinised his friend. "You've lost a bit of weight, mate ... all okay?"

"I've just been a bit preoccupied with some personal issues," Martin said, shrugging his shoulders. "Not much appetite ... you know."

Chris cocked his head at him. "No, I don't know. Is there trouble over there in Paradise?"

Martin gave a derisive snort. "No. I've, ah ... been seeing a therapist. Just trying to work through some things from my past."

"About your parents?" Chris asked as he tried to conceal his surprise at his friend's openness.

"Mm."

"How's it going?"

Martin rubbed at a fingernail. "It's been ... difficult. Some memories have resurfaced that I'd rather not think about. But I need to deal with things if I want Louisa to stay with me."

"Well, I admire you. You know, Mart, you really did get stuck with some crap parents."

"I'm aware of that."

Martin cleared his throat and got up from his chair. "How do you think we'll fare with this NHS committee tonight?"

"I just really can't say. Money's tight, and they have to make cuts somewhere. I just hope it doesn't have to be at the expense of the citizens of Cornwall. I need you to make a pretty convincing argument that the air ambulance is absolutely vital to the coastal communities, Martin. That any cuts right now could put lives at risk."

"I'll do my best."

Chris got up and walked towards the door. "Let's go see if they have anything decent to eat in the canteen."

The committee meeting started promptly at half six. Martin glanced around the room, noting the usual assortment of pencil pushing bureaucrats and puffed-up time wasters.

He had presented his arguments, stressing his point the best he could. But he was getting the feeling that the committee members did not appreciate the patient transport problems that were unique to Cornwall, the isolated moors and coastal areas in particular.

The meeting dragged on, and Martin was getting anxious to get on the road and home to his family. After all the other presenters had pleaded their cases Chris led everyone out to the hall, where a Royal Cornwall spokesperson was waiting to begin a tour of the hospital, focusing on the services they provided and concluding with an assemblage in the Emergency Department.

They were just beginning to move the group down the corridor when Chris pulled Martin aside. "Why don't you slip out and head on home, mate. It'll be late by the time you get back, even if you leave now.

"Are you sure? You may need someone to back you up later."

"Nope, I'll be fine. This thing could go on for a while. You've done what I needed you to do."

"Good luck," Martin said as his friend turned to catch up to the group.

Martin groaned when he looked at the clock in the Lexus. *Eight-twenty already. No time with James and Louisa tonight.*

Traffic was light, and he made good time. James would be sound asleep in bed by now, and Louisa, once the activity at the school had wrapped up, would come home and curl up under a blanket on the sofa with whatever book she happened to be reading at the moment. The corners of his mouth tugged up as he remembered her promise of the proper kiss that would be awaiting him when he got home.

He was coming up on Wadebridge and would be back in Portwenn in another ten minutes. As he approached the bridge over the River Camel, headlights from a vehicle coming around the curve on the other side of the span shone in his face, blinding him momentarily. As his eyes readjusted to the darkness, the outline of a large oncoming transport lorry loomed in front of him. He hit the brake and tried to veer, but the guardrail prevented him from avoiding a collision.

The fear that he may be leaving his wife a widow and his son fatherless swept through him in an instant, before a tremendous jolt of energy coursed through his body.

Don't miss out!

Click the button below and you can sign up to receive emails whenever Kris Morris publishes a new book. There's no charge and no obligation.

Sign Me Up!

https://books2read.com/r/B-A-PAJD-QBSK

BOOKS 2 READ

Connecting independent readers to independent writers.

Also by Kris Morris

Battling Demons
Battling Demons
Fractured
Fragile
Headway
Insights
A Cornwall Christmas

About the Author

Kris Morris was born and raised in a small Iowa town. She spent her childhood barely tolerating school, hand rearing orphaned animals, and squirrel taming. At Iowa State University she studied elementary education. But after discovering a loathing for traditional pedagogy and a love for a certain tall, handsome, Upstate New Yorker, she abandoned the academic life to marry, raise two sons, and become an unconventional piano teacher. When she's not writing, Kris builds boats and marimbas with her husband, who she has captivated for thirty years with her delightful personality, quick wit, and culinary masterpieces. They now reside in Iowa and have replaced their sons with ducks.

Read more at www.ktmorris.com.

Made in United States
North Haven, CT
24 January 2022

15229814R00176